RUSSIAN STRATAGEM

Joe Daniel

This book is a work of fiction. Names, characters, businesses, places, events, locales, and incidents either are the products of the author's imagination or used in a fictitious manner. Any resemblance to actual persons, living or dead, or actual events is purely coincidental.

Every effort has been made to obtain the necessary permissions with reference to copyright material, both illustrative and quoted. We apologise for any omissions in this respect and will be pleased to make the appropriate acknowledgements immediately to this novel's *e*-listing or subsequently in any future editions when this paperback is published or finally also marketed as an audio book.

Cover illustration and general design were created using Amazon Kindle Publishing's guidance and software supported by Microsoft Word.

No part of this publication may be reproduced, distributed, or transmitted in *any* form or by *any* means, including photocopying, recording, or other electronic or mechanical methods, without the prior written permission of the publisher, except in the case of brief quotations embodied in critical reviews and certain other literary journals

Joe Daniel has asserted his right under the Copyright, Designs and Patents Act 1988 to be identified as the author of this work.

Copyright © 2022 Joe Daniel
All rights reserved.
ISBN: 9798834234159

Imprint: Independently published

An unequivocal 'thank you' once again to my long suffering Editor, Stephen Knight, who has read and re-read the manuscript not only to correct spelling and grammatical errors but also importantly to review the story's flow for readers

Dedication

For all of us buried under the weight of simply living, working, and surviving in today's unequal world.

Where you are born more than ever determines whether the dream of a better life is ever realistically within reach while politicians continue to garner power and wealth with scant regard for their populace's better future

READER'S QUICK REFERENCE LISTING TO THE CHARACTERS NAMES & ROLES IN ORDER OF APPEARANCE

Dagmāra Grāvkalējs – Latvian Interior Minister
Grzegorz Politczek – Lieutenant-General, Poland's Head of ABW, Special Forces, & Counter-Intelligence with Ministerial Rank
Jan Chmura – Colonel, ABW Special Forces, & Counter-Intelligence
Kuba Pawlukowicz - Colonel, ABW Special Forces, & Counter-Intelligence
Witoria Hanko – Lieutenant Colonel, ABW Head of Cyber Security & Geopolitical Counter Intelligence section
Alexandra Król – wife of Major Król, former MI6 Capitan ex SAS
Radek Król – Major GROM Polish Special Forces, accredited SEAL, & ABW counter intelligence
Pawel Adamski – Major, ABW, aide-de-camp to Lieutenant-General Politczek
Ruslan Laskutin – Colonel General, Head of Russian Federation GRU Forces
Boris Ivanov – Major, GRU & aide-de-camp to Colonel General Laskutin
Igor Yedemsky – Colonel, GRU & Counter-Intelligence
Weronika Cieslik – Major, Polish Army Air Corps
Piotr Lewandoski – Kapitan, Polish Army Air Corps
Kemal Erdoğan – Colonel Turkish Army
Bartek Nowak – Master-Sergeant (Master-Chief) GROM Polish Special Forces
Stefan Zysk – Major, Polish Army Medical Corps, Doctor & Surgeon
Gabriella Russo – Maggiore (Major), Italian Army Medical Corps, Doctor & Surgeon
Anwar Hassan – Syrian refugee, former civil servant, & designate United Nations administrator across various refugee camps
Amal Ibrahim – refugee, young widow, internally displaced mother from Aleppo with young children
Kacper Jankowski – Polish Navy Lieutenant in GROM Special Forces
Konstantin Makarov – Cappitan Russian GRU
Kadyn Suleiman – mid ranking officer in Syria's General Intelligence Directorate
Piotr Okolski – Kapitan, ABW undercover administration
Eryk Shevchenko – ABW asset in Belarus
Gul *'Seagull'* **Wazeer** – Major, Afghan National Army Special Forces
Abdul Habibullah – Deputy Minister, Ministry of Internal Affairs
Jean-Philippe Bernard – Capitaine, French Air Force

Bruno Müller – Hauptmann, German Air Force
Abdul Ahmadi – Afghan translator on Polish Special Forces missions & active soldier
Abas Mohammad – Sergeant Afghan Special Forces & participant on GROM missions
Asal Nasrin – daughter of deceased Polish Special Forces soldier
Abdul Rahman al-Logari – Afghan suicide bomber, ISIS terrorist
Gosia Bronski - graduate of the Institute of Oriental Studies at Krakow's Jagiellonian University
Maja Stanek - graduate of the Institute of Oriental Studies at Krakow's Jagiellonian University
Tomek Jureki – GROM Team 6
Piotr Vrubel – GROM Team 6
Kuba Michnik – GROM Team 6
Wotjek Tarnowski – GROM Team 6
Stepan Nalyvaichenko – Colonel Ukrainian Army Special Forces
Pawel *(Boruch)* – GROM Team 6 with specialist IT skills
Rafal Dudek – GROM Team 6
Kirill Vasilyev - FSB Director Special Programmes for the President
Vladimir Bogdanov - FSB Director Special Programmes for the President
Aleksey Makshakov – Russian spy in Ukrainian Ministry of Defence aka codename 'Kursk'
Gennady Sidorov – FSB Major, based in the Kyiv Embassy & 'Kursk's handler

[**GROM** - the Polish military equivalent of special forces units like the United States' Delta force, Green Berets, and SEALS, the United Kingdom's SAS, and Israel's Sajjeret Matkal]

Table of Contents

Chapter 1 1
Chapter 2 16
Chapter 3 33
Chapter 4 57
Chapter 5 66
Chapter 6 79
Chapter 7 97
Chapter 8 107
Chapter 9 130
Chapter 10 162
Chapter 11 187
Chapter 12 208
Chapter 13 225
Chapter 14 248
Chapter 15 270

Chapter 1

It was early spring in Riga. The Latvian capital was shrouded in a heavy mist before the warming rays of sunshine would burn away that early morning fog. The Interior Ministers of the Baltic States (Estonia, Latvia, and Lithuania) were joined by their opposite numbers from Germany, Hungary, Poland, Romania, and Slovakia. A routine six monthly meeting of politicians whose countries, apart from Germany, formed NATO's eastern flank to a seemingly aggressive and expansionist Russia.

Dagmāra Grāvkalējs, the Latvian Interior Minister, was in the Chair and hosting this highly classified and regular conference. The last item on an agenda was the forthcoming August Presidential Election in Belarus where Alexander Lukashenko was seeking a 6th term in office having come to power in 1994. There was a general consensus that Vladimir Vladimirovich Putin, President of Russia, would be watching events closely similarly to those present. Viktor Yanukovych's removal from office in February 2014 as President of Ukraine through a popular uprising if not in effect a coup d'état had left Russia deeply concerned. The prospect of Belarus forging closer ties with the European Union and especially NATO only heightened such nervousness in Russian political circles if a pro-Western candidate was ever elected.

The assembled Ministers all held the view that regime change in Belarus would neither be accepted nor tolerated. Russia would not stand by and do nothing.

Poland's Interior Minister voiced that concern – 'Madam Chairperson and colleagues, whilst our respective intelligence services have all indicated that there is a popular swell of opinion amongst Belarussian voters for change. There has not been a free and fair election since Lukashenko first came to power in 1994. His authoritarian regime has responded brutally and violently to any opposition utilising its police force, the Belarussian KGB, and the notorious Alpha Group within its KGB. Human rights violations and political repression have been and continue to be common place in Belarus. This has been self-evident to us all in Central and Eastern Europe since the dissolution of the Soviet Union. The United States continues to see itself as a benign hegemony and flag bearer for democracy across the world with regime change at its core - simply to provide another Western leaning country. Yet our concern now must be the security of all our borders with Belarus. From Poland's perspective, this is over 400 kilometres long, much of it through heavily forested areas. Yet, with the continuing conflict in Eastern Ukraine *(in particular within the Donetsk and Luhansk Regions)*, my country and all of us as members of NATO, can no longer ignore our common borders with also Ukraine in addition to Belarus. In our case, we have 535 kilometres of common border with our Ukrainian friends but geopolitics is, as we all have learnt over the last four years in respect of our

American allies has been more like the ever-changing Saharan sand dunes'.

A murmur of agreement around the room was evident as the Estonian Minister then began to speak.

'Our Foreign Intelligence Service has confirmed that the United States Central Intelligence Agency has not been active within Belarus leading up to this August's 2020 Presidential Election. It seems the Americans are more concerned about its influence in Asia-Pacific with China's seemingly rapid rise as a major economic and world power. Washington politics are also frozen with a November Presidential election against the backcloth of the worsening COVID pandemic. Today's problems with Russia stem from all our leaders failure at the Bucharest NATO Meeting back in April 2008 to stop the United States steamrolling this addition into the press release *'NATO welcomes Ukraine's and Georgia's Euro-Atlantic aspirations for membership in NATO. We agreed today that these countries will become members of NATO'*.

There was no dissent from those attending as the Estonian Interior Minister's factual comments.

Grzegorz Politczek put down the Top Secret folder containing the circulated minutes of the Riga Interior Ministers meeting only some 48 hours earlier. A worried frown crossed his face as he walked away from the conference table to gaze deep in thought across Warsaw from his 8th floor office in ABW's Rakowiecka Street Headquarters.

The door to the Lieutenant-General's office swung open as Colonels Chmura and Pawlukowicz entered, saluted the half turning Grzegorz, and joined Lieutenant-Colonel Hanko who was already sat at the table drinking an espresso. Witoria Hanko pushed the Top Secret folder towards them as Major Adamski, the General's Aide de Camp, placed cups of fresh coffee in front of them. A nod of Grzegorz's head indicated that Pawel Adamski should now sit.

'At 17:00 hours this afternoon, I am requested to join the Prime Minister's meeting with the Interior Minister, the Minister of Defence, and our Minister responsible for Special Forces. I will have to deliver ABW's thoughts on how the impending Belarus Presidential election will affect the geopolitics of its neighbours and particularly Russia. In addition, its probable impact on Poland and of course NATO so Colonel Hanko, please commence the briefing'.

Witoria Hanko was the highly regarded Head of ABW's Cyber Security Department that is now merged under her leadership with ABW's Geopolitical Counter-Intelligence Section. She was now only thirty one years old. Yet, within ABW, she was quite rightly credited for her high-level intelligence recommendations some two years earlier.

'Gentlemen, deeper integration between Belarus and Russia has been a long term Russian Foreign Policy goal since as long ago as when the so called 'Union State' was formally created in 1999. Nevertheless, from Russia's perspective it has lacked substance as a federal state within a Russian orbit or being an integrated economy under an overarching combined economy similar to the European Union. Nevertheless, whatever the spats over the last two decades, military drills have been back to normal since September 2017. The strategic importance of Belarus has continued to rise for Russia – a country that it has always seen as part and parcel of Mother Russia. NATO's enlargement eastwards through former Soviet Warsaw Pact countries becoming democracies and looking westwards; the United States military activities since the 2001 September 11th attacks; and deployment of NATO missile defence systems have only served to heighten Russian unease. If we factor in NATO's 2008 Press Release regarding Ukraine's future membership, it is no wonder Russia is being made to feel encircled and if not a pariah state, then humiliated as a global power.

This discussion cannot ignore the United States Foreign Policy for virtually the last two hundred years known as the 'Monroe Doctrine'. In simple terms, the Americans will not tolerate any country interfering in its policing of the Western Hemisphere and its inalienable right to involve itself in Latin American affairs. I will refrain at this juncture from commenting on the acceptability or otherwise of the United States Central Intelligence Agency's covert and clandestine activities under the 'Monroe Umbrella'!

Yet our United States friends seem unable or unwilling to understand Russia's concerns when history's 1962 Cuban Missile crisis is a direct corollary of how it feels today as the United States did back in October 1962.

In 2012, the Russian ground force presence in the western parts of the country was scant and militarily this part of Russia was clearly insufficiently protected. Since then, modernization and reorganization processes have swept across the Western Military District *(Western-ZVO)* whereby today its military has never been more capable with strong offensive capabilities in addition to purely a defensive stance. Russia's willingness to use force in order to achieve foreign policy objectives eg in Georgia, Ukraine, and Syria, have raised concerns within NATO as to the real goals of the military modernization particularly in the Western Military District. Russia has been involved in two wars - Georgia and Eastern Ukraine. They had one thing in common to deny NATO, or the West in general, a presence in countries Russia still considers to be in its privileged sphere of influence. The Western Military District forces are constantly being augmented with new or modernized equipment and organizational reforms. Drills and large scale exercises have maintained a constant state of preparedness to address various scenarios and contingencies. By way of example, out of the four airborne divisions, three are garrisoned in the Western Military District. These forces have high readiness levels. They are the best trained and best equipped forces in the entire ground component of the Russian armed forces. Their role, however, is not limited to airborne operations behind a line of contact. In Ukraine, they can now be utilized in infantry roles since the addition of tank battalions to each division. This enables these troops to be placed directly on the front line underlining the strategic presence of airborne forces *(Vozdushno-Desantnye Voyska: VDV)* as a standalone battlegroup. Such forces could tip the balance in Russia's favour on the battlefield and is part of today's military reality. Nevertheless, Russia has real concerns about a conflict in the European theatre including a direct military clash with NATO countries. It has readied itself to meet that challenge head-on if necessary.

It is thus the opinion of the Department that Lukashenko will be re-elected notwithstanding the actual result from the ballot box. Any protests by activists will be brutally put down with physical beatings, imprisonment, and probably also, with live rounds being used, numerous deaths. The population will within a matter of weeks be completely cowed into submission as State controlled Media will spin whatever is happening on the streets. Access to Social Media via the internet will be curtailed. Trials and sentences will hark back to Stalinist times – there will be no prisoners!

As to how this will immediately affect Poland, we will need to be ready to process and accept asylum seekers in their hundreds if not thousands attempting to escape the Belarusian Authorities clamp down.

We should expect Lukashenko and Putin to bring that long ago perceived Union much closer from economic links to far more integration of their respective military forces. This will move far beyond simple drills to battlefield readiness of battle groups. Ukraine remains an issue for both Belarus and Russia that may require the use of arms. Certainly, there is no appetite within the Russian Hierarchy ever to allow Ukraine to become a NATO member – a well-publicised 'red line' for Moscow. Nevertheless, the absence of an Article 5 NATO commitment, ie an attack on one is an attack on them all, means the West support will be limited to arms and advisors – hardly a deterrent.

Ukraine's population does not seem to have any desire to be anything other than a sovereign state. This would make invasion by Belarus and Russia unlikely and high risk. From President Putin's perspective, enough Russian soldiers have returned in body bags from the 'Frozen War' around Donetsk and Luhansk. For the West, Ukraine remains a 'failed state' with endemic corruption and a deteriorating economy with much of its heavy industry together with its infrastructure in the Donbass Region ruined. Oligarchs still hold the levers of power while nearly fourteen thousand people have so far died during this conflict with close to one and a half million being internally displaced people.

The Russians, apart from their own experience, have seen how the United States efforts at regime change have led to cataclysmic disasters for civilian populations. Syria is of course a prime example. The Central Intelligence Agency's covert operation 'Sycamore Timber' to arm rebels against the totalitarian Assad Regime in 2011 resulted in a surfeit of arms flowing into an already unstable and volatile region that is the Middle East. One is left with the open question as to how much of this clandestine operation assisted in the growth of the Islamic State of Iraq and the Levant (ISIL / Daesh-the militant Islamist Sunni group) across Eastern Syria and Western Iraq. This so-called caliphate required an international coalition from mid-2014, led by the United States, to destroy by December last year what the United Nations had even declared a Terrorist Organisation.

Syria is relevant in terms of where we are today and how we look at the forthcoming Belarussian Presidential election. It is rather like a large meteorite hitting a lake – we are facing the 'Law of unintended consequences'. By that, what we perceive as force of circumstance bringing two irascible brothers together in the form of Lukashenko and Putin cannot bode well'.

'Thank you Colonel, Colonels your thoughts'.

Jan Chmura looked at his empty cup and with a nodding gesture towards Major Adamski, fresh coffee was soon being poured. 'General, this reminds me of GROM room clearance exercise training in Gdansk. You have no idea where the 'threats' are lying within that or any room. Hence, my best guess is Belarus will erupt into civil disobedience if the 'intel' is right and as it is quelled, Lukashenko and Putin will double down strengthening their historic family ties across many areas. They have no real friends in the West which only adds to the impetus to strongly support each other. The European Union will undoubtedly place sanctions on Lukashenko and his immediate team. However, with Russia accounting for close to fifty per cent of Belarus's exports, the EU's sanctions will simply be nothing more than an ineffective political gesture.'

'I tend to agree with Jan, General. Whilst it is impossible to second guess precisely the reactions to any threat of Lukashenko losing power, any meaningful attempt within Belarus political circles or its populace to move closer towards the West and the European Union will be violently, savagely, and coldly extinguished. Ukraine will become as a result even more unstable if that is possible. In addition, lest we forget, we have an unpredictable US President attempting a second term as this COVID virus is forcing countries into knee jerk reactions including locking down economies. The United States Department of State is now considerably weaker under this Presidency and with the focus on the China trade dispute/trade war, little attention is being paid to Russia's angst about NATO expansion or the concerted attempts to move Ukraine politically westward.'

'Thanks Kuba'.

Grzegorz Politczek stood up and walked towards that place again in front of floor to ceiling glass curtain walling where he could once again gaze across Warsaw and fall into deep thought. After what seemed like minutes but was in fact a few seconds, the General turned towards the conference table.

'Thank you all, and well done again Witoria. It seems that ABW's input to this afternoon's meeting with the Prime Minister will simply be that Lukashenko and Putin will become by circumstance very much closer and Ukraine's instability will be undoubtedly greatly heightened. In terms of prevention against 'the unknown consequences', this has to start with improving our border security along the 950 odd kilometres. Simultaneously through diplomatic efforts along with our European colleagues at the highest levels and back channels, we must convince our American friends to take a more alert and measured approach to the increasing Russian threat under President Putin.'

Alexandra Król was watching her husband as he sat astride his recently delivered Stiga Garden Tractor. It was the first grass cut of the season as his face showed all the excitement and pleasure of a young boy with a new toy. His father and mother in law, Elisa and Tomek, were sat on the couple's newly built veranda enjoying refreshing tumblers of her fruit kompote. It was only mid-April but it was a warm sunny and early spring day in Niepolomice. Alexandra's and Radek's new home had been completed the previous summer and was nestled in a mixture of forest and parkland next to Elisa's and Tomek's home. There was no internal fencing between the properties effectively creating a family compound. Nevertheless, the external boundary fencing around the compound had been much improved with substantial planting of nature's razor wire, prunus spinosa bushes otherwise known as blackthorn or sloe.

Tomek's love affair with St Bernards continued with two pups having been added so now four of these large beasts patrolled the perimeter. However, most of the time they were slumped around their master or guarding the youngest and newest addition to the Król family, Alexandra's and Radek's eight month old daughter – Maja.

The house landline phone began to chortle. Alexandra disappeared into the house taking the now empty kompote jug to be refilled whilst in the kitchen. The incessant ringing stopped and as Alexandra reappeared with a full jug of kompote, her relaxed demeanour had changed. She walked and waved to Radek to stop his grass cutting but he was in a world of his own listening to music through his ear defenders. It was only with his wife standing in front of the Stiga tractor that he was jolted out of his dream like trance. 'Grzegorz called on the house phone to speak to you. I told him you would call him back once I could separate you from your new toy!' 'Very funny darling' as Radek turned off the machine and stepped off giving her a passing kiss as he headed indoors.

Major Adamski was as ever at his desk by 08:00 in order to review the emails in the General's 'in-box' before his arrival. Amongst the incoming tsunami requesting the General's attendance at various meetings and inevitable changing of dates / timings as COVID continued to impact Government, there was one from Oberst Bruno Böhler of the BND, the common abbreviation of Bundesnachrichtendienst – Germany's Federal Intelligence Service.

'Our Federal Police have over Q1 2020 arrested within ten kilometres or less of our Eastern and Northern borders 5 Syrians, 3 Iraqis, and 1 Afghani. What is unusual is that arrests of illegal asylum seekers and refugees are usually happening in the west and south in greater numbers not only from Syria and Iraq but also Sudan, Libya, and other North African / sub-Saharan countries. Basically, the illegal migration is following the well-known trafficking routes across the Mediterranean. Interrogation did not reveal how any of the individuals found themselves in Northern and Eastern Germany, except each one had unusually more than €1000 in new high denomination notes.

Against this background, BND's President has asked that I bring this anomaly to your attention as such individuals would have, most probably, had to transit Poland to cross onto Germany soil. With the issue of Schengen Border Security and Migration Policy under scrutiny, we would welcome your assistance in establishing whether or not there are now new and additional smuggling routes into the European Union's heartland from the East'.

Thirty six hours after speaking with the General, Radek Król entered Grzegorz Politczek's 8th floor office.

In full dress uniform with chest full ribbons reflecting his battle honours serving Poland and the West, Radek saluted. A broad smile crossed the Lieutenant-General's rugged face - 'Sit down soldier and relax'.

Pouring them both a coffee, Grzegorz began the mission briefing. 'Probably much to your frustration, since your highly successful 2017/2018 mission, the Government and ABW has resisted placing you in harm's way. Not that you are not expendable rather the politics of such a highly decorated Polish Officer being killed in-country or worse captured, has meant when not training in Gdansk, you have been forced to fly a desk at our Krakow office. Hardly exciting stuff for an adrenalin junkie used to being in the thick of battle but another tour in Afghanistan was frankly too high risk and for what. You may not be aware of the positive impact you have on ABW's morale when news that you would be here today gradually leaked. Nevertheless, I now find myself in a position where Poland has to ask you to be once more the sharp end of democracy's spear'.

Pulling out a cigarette from his newly opened pack of Marlboro's, Grzegorz lit it with a flick of his zippo lighter reflecting as always on the inscribed motto 'The Only Easy Day was Yesterday' - so true he thought to himself. 'Radek I find that not only are you the most experienced operative for this task but also the only fluent 'arabic' speaker within ABW. I realise Alexandra, or your family, will not be very pleased with me or the Government for the mission you are about to undertake. However, they should know the decision was not taken lightly with both the Prime Minister and President having to authorise your return to active overseas duty'.

'What's the mission General'?

'The Syrian Civil War began in 2011. Today, according to the United Nations, about 6.8 million Syrians are refugees and asylum-seekers, and another 6.7 million people are displaced within Syria. This means more than half of the country's population has been forcibly displaced by the conflict with some 11 million people needing humanitarian assistance. Turkey is a reluctant host to 4 million refugees with 3.6 million being Syrians. European Union Migration Policy remains torn between international obligations focusing on migrant security and then set off against its responsibility to maintain the security of its citizens. This highlights migration can be considered an economic, cultural, and even a clear terrorist risk. A number of European Union countries have also voiced openly deep concerns about unwarranted Islamization because of illegal entry and poor integration policies. So we have inconsistency within Europe from closed borders to non-acceptance of quotas. Greece and Italy still bear the brunt of refugees seeking asylum with smugglers still profiting from such human trafficking. Three billion euros annually have been paid to assist Turkey since 2016. The European Border and Coast Guard Agency (Frontex) based here is directing its efforts along the North African coast to force smugglers to cease and desist. Nevertheless Radek it is a political plaster over an intractable problem caused by war, poverty, and failing states. With this in mind, our German Counter-Intelligence colleagues suspect that new illegal migration routes may be being established across Poland and maybe even the Baltic States with the capture of predominantly illegals from Syria.

We are sending a Polish Military Medical team under the Polish Red Cross and banner of the United Nations Refugee Relief into northern Idlib. You together with Master Sergeant Bartek Nowak and a GROM team will provide 'white helmet' protection for the doctors, nurses, and support staff of some forty people. You will face a desperate sea of humanity trapped between the continuing war in southern Idlib and a closed Turkish border. Our commitment to the United Nations Humanitarian Relief programme is for six months with extraction not later than December 18th this year so you will all be back for Christmas Eve.

As you move around these tented camps supporting the Medical Unit, overcrowding and lack of infrastructure will mean often you will face unhygienic conditions leading to a high incidence of infectious diseases and epidemics on top of COVID. Such cross-infection is likely to be your most dangerous enemy even with the Medics laying down draconian protective procedures. Amongst this mayhem, I need you to be intelligence gathering as to whom or what is promoting new ways to enter the Schengen Area – particularly with regard to the Baltic States and ourselves.

The mission is being pulled together by Jan Chmura so he will be your line of command so have a brief word with him on your way out of Headquarters. Wheels up, is likely to be early to mid-May – stay safe Radek'. With that the men shook hands with Radek replacing his military cap and a click of heels as he saluted and left for Colonel Chmura's office along the corridor.

Chapter 2

Colonel-General Ruslan Laskutin left the Grand Kremlin Palace after his audience with his President, Vladimir Vladimirovich Putin, a day before the annual May 9th Victory Parade. His chauffeur eased the black Aurus Senat out of Staraya Square following the Colonel-General's motorcycle escort of four outriders all riding IZH heavy escort machines. The convoy weaved easily through the constant traffic jam back towards 'the Aquarium' – the nickname given to GRU's headquarter complex at Khodynka. Major Boris Ivanov sat quietly in the front passenger seat ensuring that no incoming calls disturbed the Colonel-General who led the Country's military counter espionage, cyber, and intelligence arm - Glavnoye Razvedovatel'noye Upravlenie (GRU).

Moments before turning into the Khodynka airfield, Ruslan Laskutin picked up the car phone between the rear seats and barked an order to Colonel Igor Yedemsky – 'Assemble 'Rokossovsky' in the Gorky Park conference suite for 13:00 – organise sandwiches and coffee'. 'Rokossovsky' was the internal code for the GRU officers heading up the various arms of its intelligence machine to assemble as a matter of immediate urgency.

[Konstantin Xaverevich Rokossovsky was one of the most highly regarded Red Army Marshals of the Great Patriotic War with his ashes being buried in the Kremlin Wall Necropolis on Red Square. Yet his refusal to sign a false statement, when arrested in Stalin's pre-war Great Purge of the military, and also to stand firm, on his battle plan for a major soviet offensive, directly with Stalin made his name synonymous with being a true patriot. Hence its choice as a codename within GRU for an emergency meeting at the highest military level was not surprising]

Whilst Major Ivanov instinct was to turn round and ask what the fuss was about, his head remained unmoved looking only forward under his military cap. His wife would not thank him for achieving a posting to the Murmansk Military District for the rest of his career or worse a secret base in the heart of the Siberian wilderness.

The Colonel-General addressed his senior officers. 'Most of you will now be aware that the President requested my presence at short notice this morning at the Kremlin.

President Lukashenko had assured him yesterday afternoon in a video conference call that his re-election would be a foregone conclusion. According to the Belarussian President, the establishment (nomenklatura) being the *de facto* elite, hold or control both private and public powers across media, finance, trade, industry, the state and institutions. All these bodies are controlled directly by Lukashenko, his administration, and the Belarussian Security Council which is also under his personal control. As a pillar of the regime, the security and law enforcement bodies exercise control over the *nomenklatura* and the business elite, as well as over the citizens, the opposition and those activities perceived as anti-regime. In his mind, the decades of internal security spending that has taken precedence over external security underlines the importance Lukashenko attaches to securing the loyalty of those within the security sector.

Gentlemen, one of our responsibilities today will be to ensure that in our planning there is no putsch within that security apparatus.

As our President reminds us, our entanglement with Ukraine and in a protracted military operation in the Donbass for the last six years increases the importance of Belarus in our strategic military planning as we seek a halt to NATO expansionism. It is not rocket science in military planning to recognise actions against Ukraine, Poland or the Baltic states could be launched from Belarusian territory – hence the great importance of Belarus strategically for Russia.

Our Government continues to work towards ever more closer integration with Belarus political, military and economic dimensions under the 1998 Union State formula. Nevertheless, to date, Lukashenko's only political concession to us has been within the common military and defence space in exchange for freedom to manage the internal situation and retain his domination of Belarus's political system.

It is clear from our embedded agents within Belarus across all levels of society that there is a groundswell of opposition to re-electing Lukashenko. The main issues appear in the main to be the country's economic stagnation and his rather stupid public response to the COVID pandemic. In addition, there is also an understanding that after 26 years in power it is time to let someone else carry the burdens of state.

Hence this is opportunity to support Lukashenko's re-election through a 'rigged ballot' and simultaneously see our Government's strategic aims substantially advance.

Many of you round this table know most if not all the officers currently holding leadership positions in the security sector of the Republic of Belarus. Their skills were like yours acquired in Soviet and Russian specialist universities often with you all attending the very same courses. This provides us with the great advantages of interoperability as we begin the common protection of our borders from NATO and the European Union, leading to intelligence and counter-intelligence cooperation and the protection of the joint grouping of the two countries' armed forces. Some of you will already be aware that the Western Military District in St Petersburg has for some considerable time wanted to have serious military bases within Belarus. This will be part of the price to be paid for Russia's support keeping Lukashenko in power for now.

I shall leave Colonel Yedemsky to formulate with you all a clear plan whereby we can maximise the advancement of Russia's medium term strategic objectives. In anticipation of course of the highly probable explosive reaction of the Belarussian populace to the 'rigged' result of this forthcoming August Presidential Election – the re-election of Lukashenko for a further 5 year term so Igor be ready to present the plan no later than 18:00 today'.

There was a shuffling of chairs as the officers stood to attention, placed on their military caps, clicked heels, and saluted the departing Colonel-General.

At 17:40 hours Colonel Yedemsky laid on the Colonel-General's desk a document coded 'Rokossovsky Protocol 8th May 2020' & left the building.

The protocol laid out the action plan for GRU's involvement over the coming months up to and after the Belarus Presidential Election.

Ruslan flipped open the 'EYES ONLY:TOP SECRET' folder addressed to the President of Russia, Minister of Defence, Chief of the General Staff, Heads of the Foreign Intelligence Service (SVR), Federal Security Service (FSB), and Federal Protective Service (FSO)

The following will now be initiated in support of President Lukashenko's re-election in August 2020-

SIXTH DIRECTORATE-Cyber Operations Unit 26165

Denial-of-service attacks to prevent key political opponents, anti-government activists and opposition from accessing computer networks and devices including severe disruption of the internet;

Hacking and theft of critical data from the Opposition and the individuals Candidate *(Sviatlana Tsikhanouskaya)* and her team enabling pro-active threat removal;

Cyber espionage resulting in the theft of information that compromises his opponents whereby Belarus's national security and stability can be protected;

Disinformation campaigns targeted to weaken disrupt and ultimately destroy the Belarussian opposition;

Identifying those activists and opposition members who should be placed immediately under arrest and remain incommunicado in conjunction with the Belarussian KGB and our in-situ assets

EIGHTH DIRECTORATE – GRU Spetsnaz Special Forces

If one takes into account the fact that the Belarusian armed forces are a part of the joint Belarusian-Russian grouping, the Belarusian military intelligence service is, in effect, a part of Russian military intelligence.

On Election Day, 9th August, in the early hours, they will assist in the blocking of all roads and entry points into the main cities including Minsk.

GRU Regiments are undertaking planned manoeuvres in the Smolensk area next month. These activities are the normal bi-annual battlefield training exercises. This year the training will incorporate 'public order and riot control' so we can, if required, assist the Belarussian Riot and Para military Police quell any disorder on the streets.

This public order training will include breaking up large crowds, chasing down smaller groups of protesters, and seizure of specific activists. If as 'intel' strongly suggests there will be a groundswell of opposition prepared to fight against security forces and police in various cities and towns, Belarussian Law enforcement will need to do more than use batons, rubber bullets, and water cannon. Grenades with lead balls, tear gas, and stun grenades together with live ammunition will be necessary to suppress any such protests. There will be unavoidably critical injuries and deaths that will also serve to intimidate any protesters from taking to the streets.

Access into Belarus will most likely be along the E30 motorway in terms of quickly putting supporting 'boots on the ground'. Our forces will be dressed identically to the Belarussian Riot police but without name tags.

WESTERN MILITARY DISTRICT

The 104th and 217th Airborne Regiments are based in Pskov alongside other Airborne Divisions including the nearby Airborne Division HQ in Cherokha. A contingency plan should be formulated whereby the price of Russia's support will be making, amongst other things, Belarus an effective extension of Russia's Western Military District. This should move beyond the previous joint training exercises of Zapad 2017 and planned for Zapad 2021 to both a permanent base probably in the Hrodno Region near the Lithuanian and Polish border. In addition, a frequent rotation of Russian forces will ensure a permanent *de facto* military presence.

The Colonel-General allowed himself a half-smile of satisfaction. After tomorrow's May 9th Red Square Military Parade celebrating victory in the Great Patriotic War, there will be ample opportunity to gain unanimous approval later that afternoon to these supportive proposals for Lukashenko's re-election.

[Each copy was of course suitably identified with an individual marker so any copying would easily expose the source of any unauthorised circulation and a potential internal threat]

Colonel Chmura's briefing had placed into context why the Polish Government had moved to support humanitarian relief efforts in the Idlib Region. The Secretary–General of the United Nations had reminded the World in March 2020 that the Syrian conflict had entered its tenth year and peace still remained far too elusive. The brutal conflict had exacted an unconscionable human cost and caused a humanitarian crisis of monumental proportions. Millions of civilians continued to face protection risks, over half the population has been forced to flee their homes with millions living in precarious conditions as refugees, and 11 million continued to require life-saving humanitarian assistance. Nine years of horrific atrocities, including war crimes and human rights abuses, on a massive and systematic scale, had lowered international norms to new depths of cruelty and suffering.

It was this clarion call *(together with the March 5th Additional Protocol to the Memorandum on Stabilization of the Situation in the Idlib De-Escalation Area agreed between Russia and Turkey)* that made the Government act. Although there were concerns for the safety of Polish personnel, hostilities were to the south of Idlib and the greatest danger was posed by disease within the make-shift and tented camps with limited if any sanitation and the absence of fresh uncontaminated water rather than COVID, bombs, or bullets.

Following discussions with the United Nations Humanitarian and Refugee Agency, the decision was taken to deploy a

NATO mobile combat field hospital north of Idlib in an area surrounded by numerous temporary and unorganised refugee camps. Whilst delivery and erection would be carried out by Poland's logistical engineering corps, the provision of medical support staff would be shared between Medici senza Frontiere Italia and the Polish Army Medical corps. The field hospital will be capable with its enhanced configuration of offering the possibility of operating on 16 patients by 2 surgical teams every 24 hours. Nevertheless, the hospital's primary focus will initially be attempting to forestall a wave of communicable diseases. A generation of children are unvaccinated. Such lack of basic healthcare could have disastrous consequences. Diseases, like polio and measles, could soon reappear with also overcrowding, malnutrition, and poor sanitation leading inevitably to outbreaks of cholera and giardiasis diarrheal.

Colonel Chmura had reconsidered that with the medical staff, the size of the field hospital, the storage of medicines and water to be protected plus the on-site accommodation within the field hospital, two GROM teams rather than one would be required.

What had sounded like a relatively easy mission in Lieutenant-General Politczek's office back in April took on a rather different feel after listening to Jan Chmura. There was a difference fighting a visible enemy as opposed to one that was unseen that could easily kill the fittest soldier. Walking towards one of the three Boeing Globemaster C-17s stood on the Gdansk tarmac, all fully loaded with everything to make the combat field hospital operational apart from of course medical personnel, Radek's thoughts were broken by Master-Sergeant Bartek Nowak. 'Major, our GROM teams are boarded. We are scheduled to be in the air in ten heading for Incirlik air base. The flight will take us over 3 hours flying time and then we face a road journey to Darat Izza of about 4 hours'. 'Are all the Engineering Team boarded Master-Sergeant? 'Yes sir'. 'Then let's get our mercy mission airborne'.

Radek had some sympathy for the Turkish Government who had created a demilitarised and safe zone. By advancing militarily some 20 to 30 kilometres, it had stabilised an area by removing insurgents and terrorists. With Turkey hosting over 3.5 million Syrian refugees within its borders, resources were extremely stretched to the extent that allowing further increases would only exacerbate tensions already running high with local Turks.

Radek felt his shoulder being roughly shaken. It was the C-17 Flight Sergeant. 'We land in 20 minutes Major. Major Weronika Cieslik would be pleased to welcome you onto the flight deck'. Radek was still trying to become fully awake and questioning why the driver required his presence. Begrudgingly he began to stand up and then followed the airman. When Radek entered the flight deck, Weronika Cieslik left her cockpit controls. Seeing the briefest flash of concern on Radek's face, 'Major Król, we are still on auto-pilot and my colleague, Kapitan Piotr Lewandowski, has the tiller'. Radek was in fatigues with only his surname, Król, on the flap of his left upper pocket. 'How can I be of assistance Major Cieslik?' 'You will I hope forgive my and my crew's curiosity but it is not every day we have had the privilege of flying one of our Armed Forces most decorated officers. We wanted to be able to say we had indeed met you and you were a real person not a fictional story to gain recruits'. A broad smile crossed Radek's face coupled with a rather sheepish grin. 'Please don't believe all the Mess and bar room banter within our Armed Forces we are all doing our part'. 'So a Mercy Mission hardly seems to need one of our best soldiers?' 'Whether you are correct or not, selection was not on the basis of soldiering but rather on my ability to speak and understand arabic!' This made all those present relax and burst into laughter.

After Radek left the flight deck, Major Cieslik stepping back into the cockpit turned to Kapitan Lewandowski 'For a soldier who holds the Virtuti Militari Knights Cross and bar and probably many more gongs, what an unassuming and humble man.'

The Turkish Military had organised a convoy of trucks to carry all the contents of the C-17s together with modular NATO chilled containers for medicines and vaccine storage that would integrate into the Field Hospital format. Two air-conditioned coaches carried the Polish Engineers and Radek's men.

After everyone had been billeted for the night, the assorted company of Polish engineers and soldiers made for the Turkish Military's mess hall at the camp. They were all hungry and all armies march better on a full stomach.

Colonel Kemal Erdoğan, designated NATO liaison for this joint humanitarian mission between Poland, Medici senza Frontiere Italia, and the United Nations High Commissioner for Refugees, began to brief Radek as to what to expect over tapas-like Turkish appetizers (Meze). Notwithstanding that most Turks are at least nominally Muslim, 'Raki', known as

'Lion's Milk', was served. This Turkish national drink is made of twice-distilled grapes and aniseed resulting in a 45% proof strong spirit and food is traditionally served well into the night in part to help dampen the effect. The taste reminded Radek of his time year's back when he was seconded to the French Foreign Legion in Mali. Somehow there was always a bottle of Paul Ricard's pastis for an evening around the desert campfire. In Turkish culture, Raki is often drunk for more than soothing the mind or heart, especially in the military where missions can take them into unfamiliar territory.

'I am guessing tomorrow is going to be a leap into the unknown for you and your team'. 'You could say that Colonel – it is for all of us our first humanitarian mission'. 'Please call me Kemal and enjoy the meze as you sip your Raki.' As the evening wore on, Kemal opened up about what the Field Hospital would be facing.

'There are hundreds camps of varying sizes within the immediate vicinity of Idlib - housing about a million internally displaced refugees. Civilians forced to leave their homes, in some cases multiple times, and cities so as to avoid being caught in the deadly crossfire between Bashir al-Assad's army - assisted by the Russian Military and Air Force, and the remaining Syrian Opposition fighters. It was hardly a choice – leave or die. Your field hospital will be 2 kilometres or so away from the nearest larger camps at Al Karama and Qah. My understanding is the ground is gently sloping and sited even in this arid landscape amongst one of the few remaining olive groves. We, with our NATO blue hats on, will be supplying you with food, diesel, and water bowsers on a weekly basis. However, you will have to organise collection yourselves from our military base here at Darat Izza – a 19 kilometre drive eastwards from the hospital. Our borders are closed and under the brokered UN settlement, we can proceed no further into North West Syria'.

As Radek pulled out a pack of Villiger cigars with Kemal taking one, their glasses of 'Raki' were refilled. The men the lit their cigars with the exhaled smoke hanging momentarily in the air, Kemal continued.

'The United Nations through its Refugee Administration for nearly a decade has been attempting to provide critical emergency assistance in the form of clean water, sanitation and healthcare with varying degrees of success in Syria, a country torn apart by a civil war. More than 6 million people have been driven from their homes and remain displaced living in terrible conditions. Whilst the winters are hard where the risk freezing to death is high, the summers are equally extreme with temperatures above 40 degrees celsius. When rain does come, it is torrential so be glad the hospital is being sited on sloping ground otherwise you would be waking up in a large puddle if not lake. In the height of summer, the ground is baked as hard as rock by the sun so flash floods in the camps are commonplace.

Notwithstanding the United Nations Refugee efforts, malnutrition is a fact of life. A staple carbohydrate diet of rice, mealie meal, bread, oats or couscous is of course preventing starvation. Yet without fresh fruit and vegetables, diseases caused by malnutrition are self-evident. Children are of course the most vulnerable group. However, apart from the dangers of a poor diet in their formative years, this group of refugees are even more vulnerable to violence, exploitation, and abuse – particular if they are unaccompanied. Certainly young girls are easy targets of gender-based violence or trafficking'.

Helping himself to more Raki with a splash of water, Radek took a long pull on his cigar, 'Kemal, it seems that my soldiers will have more to guard than just the hospital!' Kemal merely nodded in agreement.

'The biggest impact of such a large and growing influx of internally displaced persons is on the immediate and local environment. It is not just the disappearance of olive groves for wood for heating what are no better than shacks or for simply cooking. Just consider the level of solid waste, air and water pollution, sanitation, and garbage in addition to the depletion of water resources – it is without doubt an environmental catastrophe. These camps have swollen into towns and cities without even in most cases basic infrastructure of a robust sewage system, drinkable water, or electricity supply.

United Nations attempts on behalf of the International Community to provide 'shelter', as it is still unsafe for most refugees to return to their Syrian homes, is still very much work in progress. Tents tend to succumb to the extreme weather after 12 to 18 months and simply rot away. Refugees attempt to patch such rips with material provided by UNHCR but tents are hardly warm in the deepest of winter. As you will see with your own eyes, many displaced families have attempted to build temporary cinder-block houses that are commonly called shacks but to my mind hovels would be a better description. People use materials that they find or from scrap yards or what they can afford to buy from cardboard, plastic sheeting, wooden planks, old tyres, pieces of polystyrene foam and sheets of corrugated iron. Sometimes you will see cinder block walls with no foundation that equally as likely to be undermined and washed away by torrential rain. With a hotch-pot of roof coverings or none atall, these hovels are neither dry nor insulated. In winter these shacks often catch alight as people desperately try to keep warm and even in summer, a cooking stove can similarly cause devastation to such poorly constructed hovels or tents – let alone injury or death to the occupants.'

'What is the security situation I am likely to face in immediate vicinity?'

'I expect your own people have briefed Idlib Province is the last bastion of opposition to Bashir al-Assad's Government. A standoff in the province has lasted for years but since 2015 it has been controlled by Islamist extremist rebels with links to al-Qaeda. The latest Assad offensive backed by Russian Air power began in December 2019. This ended with a cease-fire a few months later after my Country sent thousands of its own troops into the Province in large part to prevent refugees from streaming over the border. Since then, we have been trying to create favourable living conditions simply to prevent more people from crossing or attempting to cross our border. Hayat Tahrir al-Sham, the militant Islamist group controlling much of Idlib, has even been seeking to stabilize the area, albeit as a means to shed its extremist roots and thereby gain international recognition and donations. However, my country does not exert control over the more radical elements of the Syrian opposition, namely the al-Qaeda-linked Hayat Tahrir al-Sham that was previously known as the Al Nusra Front. Our intelligence forecast is that they are more likely to move into the shadows across Syria presenting a new set of challenges to the Assad regime rather than continue to defend the Idlib enclave. People across central and southern Idlib province have fled to the relative safety of areas in the north, along our border, as Idlib Province's centre of gravity shifts from the south to the north. Whilst vast olive groves along our border are disappearing, the precariousness of a refugee's life surviving on UNHCR humanitarian handouts can only be described as 'miserable' with little chance of ever returning to their hometowns and to start rebuilding their lives for many years, if ever.'

'So I am unlikely to face *Al Nusra* jihadis bent on murdering Italian and Polish Medics and nurses.'

'In my view, you are correct. You greatest danger to my mind is maintaining hygiene protocols even within a field hospital. The majority of camps have no access to toilet, shower, and washing blocks. Whilst much of the medical work will be visiting a range of camps under UNHCR guidance to administer vaccines and to carry out minor procedures, overcrowding and poor personal hygiene can only facilitate the spread of disease let alone COVID. The majority of refugees are more likely to take their own lives than the team you are protecting. These people have lost all hope psychologically of there ever being an end to the civil war leaving them with severe anxiety, an inability to sleep, mood swings, and prolonged depression – an unending nightmare with such a tragic human cost.'

'Is there anymore Raki, Kemal? Thousands of kilometres away in Poland it is probably unsurprising my countrymen and I are spared the harsh reality of life as an internally displaced person. This tour of duty will be clearly like no other.'

Chapter 3

The previous two weeks had seen the erection of the hospital within a secure compound. Radek, along with Master-Sergeant Nowak, was awaiting the arrival of the medical teams at Darat Izza. His eyes lit up when he saw Stefan Zysk leaving the first coach. Stefan had been instrumental in saving Alexandra's life back in early 2018 including also unknowingly Maja's.

Stefan saw Radek immediately, waved, and started walking towards him. 'No longer a Captain Stefan – congratulations on becoming a Major.' 'Well your kind words were which more pleasant than my immediate colleagues at the Military Medical Academy Memorial Teaching Hospital in Lodz – they inferred my promotion was entirely due to dating one of General Staff's daughters!'

Broad smiles on their faces, Stefan turned and shouted 'Gabriella ... Gabriella ... Gabriella!' On hearing her name, Maggiore Gabriella Russo turned and began to walk towards the Majors. Radek was trying to decide as she came closer whether Italian Military uniforms for women were deliberately cut to enhance the incumbent's figure or the woman coming towards them was an escapee from a Hollywood movie set. At 174 centimetres tall and probably weighing 52 kilos with an hourglass figure this vision with jet black hair under a jaunty military cap walking on reasonable heels looked so unexpected and out of context at the Darat Izza military base. When her sparkling mediterranean blue eyes arrived in front of them with the broadest of smiles revealing perfect white teeth from a TV commercial, the surreal trance was broken by the formality of 'salutes'.

'Radek let me introduce you to my medical colleague, Maggiore Gabriella Russo of the Italian Medical Corps.'

'Delighted you are joining this humanitarian mission Major though I am not sure your present combat boots will be suitable for visits to the various camps.'

'Maggiore Król, I am Italian and a woman. Just because my superiors have sentenced me to six months with Medici senza Frontiere Italia, let alone being stationed in this 'buco di merda' *(shithole)*, does not mean I cannot for these last few moments enjoy a tight skirt and a pair of heels.'

'Well best we load everyone, your luggage, and everything else you have all brought with you onto the waiting trucks as we head for that 'buco di merda' that will be our home for the next six months' said Radek with a mischievous smile that was returned.

Grzegorz Politczek was sat alone in his 8th floor Rakowiecka Street office. He put down Colonel Hanko's formal report on the reality of the August 2020 Belarus Presidential Election. Even with Grzegorz's experience of living under communism and an authoritarian regime as a young man, the lengths to which Lukashenko, with clearly Russia's encouragement, had gone to, in order to retain power, left him momentarily

speechless. It made him seriously question whether the 9 million or so Belarussians ever had a chance of self-determination. Was it though really a surprise as no election since 1994 has met international standards of transparency and fairness?

The door to democracy was closed if not forever then certainly for the foreseeable future. He began to read again the entire document meticulously making notes.

From the very start of the campaign in spring 2020, Lukashenko loyalists controlled all of the seats in both houses of the National Assembly, all judicial appointments, the media, and the Central Election Commission. In addition to these levers of power, the Belarus KGB, the para-military police brigades, special OMON police units, and the armed forces were all loyal to the President after years of status and benefits - financial and otherwise.

Whilst opposition activists have often been pressured or detained by the Belarussian Government on one spurious pretext or another, Hanko's Report though exposed a more corrupt, sinister, and systematic abuse of State Power.

In May, Syarhei Tsikhanouski, a Belarusian blogger and entrepreneur, announced his presidential candidacy. His canvassing trips by him and his team around the country were immediately highly popular. Gatherings of hundreds of people speaking openly about violations of human rights and economic problems were recorded by a mixture of Belarusian special services and OMON. Tsikhanouski and his team were constantly chased and harassed by police cars and vans yet no police identification, though requested, was

Further political rallies were planned prior to the August Election Voting. However, approval is required by Local Government Administration to hold such meetings in any Belarussian City or Town on public order grounds. No surprise thought Grzegorz that no permissions were granted including revoking some earlier approvals. In addition, confidants of Lukashenko widely pre-booked designated sites for election rallies to prevent independent candidates meeting with people, the electorate. For example, in Pinsk, local authorities provided only one site for meetings with candidates, and this site was booked by a Tacciana Lugina, its Mayor, right up to election day. Again, this Lukashenko stalwart booked the only site in Stolin to election day 08:00 to 22:00 hours. Constant pressure by such authorities was making it extremely difficult for 'Female Solidarity' to unseat Lukashenko's grip on power. Even in the final days of the campaign, local authorities of Slutsk advised a meeting could not be held due to urgent repairs and others, like in Salihorsk, were also cancelled by the authorities at the last moment.

What was more disturbing was those people who had gathered in Slutsk and Salihorsk were asked to leave. Those who refused were not only arrested but also severely beaten. Detained in disparate locations with no information released as to their whereabouts, only served to create despair and worry for loved ones and relatives. Here was the unmistakeable hand of the GRU believed Grzegorz – instilling fear of the unknown into the general public's consciousness.

Just a few days prior to the election, a number of journalists and bloggers were arrested on weak and spurious charges, or were denied accreditation to cover the elections. This was to limit any external scrutiny of the election. Again silencing the free press and controlling the media was very much part of the detail in seeing Lukashenko re-elected.

When Belarus TV channels revealed the results of an exit poll showing a landslide Lukashenko victory, people took to the streets in Minsk and other cities. The para-military Riot Police were ready as unprovoked and violent clashes between peaceful protesters and ordinary police broke out. Social media was soon filled with photos and video clips of people being savagely attacked with batons, stun grenades, and rubber bullets. Grzegorz noted that many internet service providers also lost communication whilst unidentified para-military forces closed down Minsk and other cities.

Twenty four hours later, protesters barricaded the area around the Komarovka Central Market in Minsk. The Government's Security forces response was both harsh and swift with tear gas and flashbangs deployed as protest leaders were seized in baton charges and thrown unceremoniously into unmarked police vans. Meanwhile Tsikhanouskaya was escorted by Belarusian security services from detention to Lithuania. A couple of days later, the Government released a video across State sponsored television media where Tsikhanouskaya read from a script that was clearly filmed under coercion given the content. Subsequently, from Lithuania, on August 14th she published a 2nd video claiming to have received between 60 and 70% of the vote in the first ballot - more than enough to defeat Lukashenko outright. She suggested the creation of a transitional council of society activists, respected Belarusians and professionals to handle the peaceful transfer of power from Lukashenko.

More arrests and violence against protesters were increasingly reported on camera in the week after the election including claims of torture by victims of previous arrests. Words like *'Prisoners of Conscience'* and *'Political Prisoners'* began to describe many of those now incarcerated within Belarussian prisons by Human Rights Organisations like Amnesty International.

With increasing large crowds protesting at what was considered a fraudulent, if not controversial, election result in Minsk and other cities, Lukashenko was forced to call his only ally on August 15th to ask for assistance in restoring security across the entire country. However, immediate and positive implementation of the Collective Security Treaty in terms of military bases in the Hrodno Region and elsewhere was just part of the political concessions Lukashenko had to make to stay in power.

International Reaction was muted and ineffective as peaceful protesters were subjugated to violent beatings and arrest to the horror of Western Television audiences that had dissipated to nothing by the end of August. Fear and incarceration had overcome self-determination.

The September 14th Meeting in Sochi between Lukashenko and Putin, as military drills *(announced in 2019)* began in Eastern Belarus, marked publicly the change in status between the parties. Grzegorz reflected that Moscow may not rush to push its advantage, fearing that siding too closely with an unpopular ruler whose days are numbered, made little sense and could spark a public backlash. Nevertheless, as Russia's 'Boris Pasternak' SU-35s fighter wing were landing at the Hrodno airbase in Western Belarus, there was no disguising the pleasure within Russia's St Petersburg Military Hierarchy as its first ground attack and fighter planes were now in place. Similarly, it was not lost on NATO's strategic planners at the growing concern of the Baltic States to the turn of events in Belarus. Heightened security concerns that the Baltic States could be isolated from Poland and Europe. The 110-115 kilometre wide land corridor between Lithuania and Poland, the Suwalki Gap, connects geographically Kaliningrad *(home of the Russian Baltic Fleet and also a substantial Battle Group)* with Belarus. The threat of an expansionist Russia securing a land bridge between Kaliningrad and Belarus with additional military resources easily and quickly deployed by Russia's Western Military District was suddenly real.

Vladimir Putin also announced that Russia was ready to grant a US$1.5 billion loan to Belarus and the importance of defence co-operation. This served to underline Russia's role as the main guarantor of Belarus's military and economic security. Perhaps the reference to Lukashenko's intention to reform the constitution was a clear indication of pressure to reform and a period of transition from Lukashenko to another, as yet unknown but pro-Russian, 3rd party as a future President. Vladimir Putin's frustrations with decade-long stagnating bilateral integration between Russia and Belarus under the Union State were no doubt voiced privately.

Making final notes, Grzegorz highlighted the provision of a GRU close protection team for Lukashenko during the height of the protests and various overt and covert actions by Russia, Moscow was playing a key role in keeping Lukashenko in power against the wishes of an angry electorate. In addition, the proposed Belarussian constitutional changes would no doubt formally end its somewhat 'artificial neutrality' and remove any restriction on nuclear weapons being placed within its borders. Warning signals were self-evident for the North Atlantic Alliance.

Having been congratulated by his President, Vladimir Putin, on the success of the GRU's 'the Rokossovsky Protocol 8th May 2020', the President outlined a broader strategy.

'Colonel-General Laskutin, you will be well aware of the Ministry of Defence's, Ministry of Foreign Affairs', and my frustration at NATO's continued Eastern Expansion into former Warsaw Pact countries. After the coup against Viktor Yanukovych, what we now see is a determined effort to bring Ukraine into ultimately NATO and the European Union. Frankly, this cannot and will not be allowed to happen.

Belarus is no longer resisting our requirement for a joint military command structure under the Western District at St Petersburg. NATO and the United States now have strategic headache with what is a forward airbase at Hrodno with a rapid deployment battle group being established. The Baltic States Sweden & Finland will once more sense the re-imposition of our sphere of influence. However, in 12 months, ZAPAD 21 will be underway. This quadrennial military exercise to reinforce battle readiness with a variety of scenarios and drills will be commencing. This will provide the cover for the establishment of a large force without creating unnecessary alarm in the West. Many of the top secret drills will be to invade and subdue Ukraine with the timing likely to be, depending on the political response to our demands, in January/February 2022 when the ground will be acceptably hard for rapid mechanised advances. What I need is something to keep the European Union wrong footed and focussing its attention, not on Ukraine's 'frozen war' and the Ukrainian Government's intransigence on Minsk II, but elsewhere.

Your man Yedemsky floated an interesting paper on how some of our embedded agents within the internally displaced people of North West Syria had managed to cross illegally into the Schengen Area via Latvia, Lithuania, and Poland. Their personal mission had been to reach Germany and then embed themselves within radical but dormant ISIS cells. Ruslan, we are missing a trick here. Migration fuels the separating forces inside the European Union more than any other disagreements within the twenty seven member block. We have seen Britain and France openly argue about refugees crossing the English Channel and the Northern European states leave those in South and East to face in practical terms migration alone. What if we make breaches of the Baltic States and Polish Borders fresh entry points for such illegals?'

'Mr President, we will need far more than the minimal numbers who have crossed or attempted to cross into Schengen. What have you mind?'

'Ruslan simply scale. Most of these displaced people only dream of a better life in Europe. If we provide false paperwork implying transit into the European Union, flights to Minsk, and hard cash as a further inducement, do you not think thousands if not tens of thousands cannot be recruited?'

'Mr President, does President Lukashenko endorse this proposal?'

'Colonel-General, you have your President's request'

Ruslan Laskutin felt a trickle of cold sweat run down his spine as he stood putting on his military cap to salute, clicked his heels, turned, and left.

Radek, with Master-Sergeant Nowak, knew that their enemies in this north-west corner of Syria were not bullets but a combination of boredom and the strain of an endless stream of hopelessness. Keeping these experienced specialist soldiers, busy and battle ready would be a challenge.

Life wherever you sleep and work defaults into a routine. Radek, officer or not, was on the night camp guard rota and each morning as dusk broke whatever the season between 05:45 and 06:30 hours led a ten kilometre run. Master-Sergeant Nowak had decided, rather than patrolling the fence line surrounding the hospital, well-placed viewing points during daylight were a better deterrent and protection. At night, and the following day, the positioning was changed relying on their special forces communications electronics with of course night-sights when dusk fell. Within the field hospital grounds outside the GROM units living quarters, a gym had been established with weights and other muscle toning fitness equipment – almost a seven star billet as far as these men were concerned who were more used to deep patrols into hostile territory.

There were three well-travelled UNCHR supplied Toyota Land-cruisers. This meant that at any one time something mechanical would in reality mean two effective vehicles. As the months rolled by, there were always one or two members of the GROM team habitually allocated by Master-Sergeant Nowak daily to the make-shift workshop under some olive trees - rehabilitating one of the inconsistent vehicles.

Fortunately, the Turkish Red Crescent had supplied two mechanically sound Willys jeeps. In addition, the Turkish Military had lent the field hospital cargo trucks to not only transport the Medical Team to Darat Izza but also left them for the weekly restocking of medicines food and water.

At first, it felt strange to all the Polish Military personnel to be swapping camouflaged helmets for the striking blue of the United Nations. Similarly, apart from distinctive 'red cross' across the field hospital and all the vehicles, everything was coloured or painted white.

Major Zysk's and Maggiore Russo's brief was to provide primary health care services. The medical team's immediate priority was to combat the spread of infectious diseases within the nearby overcrowded refugee camps. This meant raising the rate of vaccination coverage for children from virtually zero and also for women of childbearing age. Subsequently, the UNCHR hospital was also to begin providing family health services, including family planning, counselling and care for pregnant women, and ultimately provision of dental services whilst raising overall health awareness within the refugee communities.

This worthy objective was somewhat compromised by the realities of camp life. Some 32% of camp populations are below 14 years old with disrupted education at best and questionable literacy and numeracy levels. 80% are female with more than 25% of child bearing age. Child marriage among Syrian refugees is four times higher than it was in pre-crisis Syria. Consequently, many of these girls have multiple children before they even reach adulthood. As adolescents, the risks to mother and baby are substantially higher than for women over the age of 20. Whether Syrians feel obligated to have a lot of children to compensate for the family and friends killed in the civil war is an open question. Nevertheless, many women and girls are pressured by their husbands and families to avoid contraceptives and continue producing children without adequate time for recovery in between births. Only limited camps have shower and washing blocks with even less having diesel to power the delivery of hot water. Similarly, 30% or more of the camps do not have adequate sanitation provision either through waste disposal services or latrines. When one considers inadequate shelter from the hot sun, the rain and bone chilling winds in winter with rats for company, severe malnutrition is only staved off because of potable water and food handouts from UNHRC and other non-government organisations. Generations of Syrians have been displaced with seemingly not even a glimmer of stability or a better life in the foreseeable future.

Nevertheless, even allowing for these insurmountable odds no different from expecting the tide not to come in, Stefan and Gabriella left the hospital daily with the Toyotas filled with vaccines anti-biotics and other life-saving medicines together with nurses and at least one of Radek's men in each vehicle. The Willys jeeps were kept as hospital transports to bring refugees requiring surgery more often than not on stretchers lashed across the back of the jeep. Battlefield communications equipment meant medical emergencies could be addressed with some coordination from prepping an operating theatre to dispatching a jeep.

This was the hospital routine without any let up for weekends or time off. Radek and his soldiers could not help being in awe of the medical teams dedication and indeed respect for the manner in which they fought to save every single life. It was not long before these special forces soldiers found themselves assisting the nurses and doctors in the temporary health centres erected where possible amongst any remaining olive groves. From serving in Iraq and Mali, most of the team could speak enough arabic to organise queues for new-borns requiring initially tuberculosis, hepatitis B, and oral polio vaccines. Delivery of other vaccines for measles mumps and german measles requiring one dose between 12 and 15 months and another for 4 to 6 year olds became a more problematic issue. Assessing how old many of the children were let alone had they received a first dose, with or without any adult present, did not make things easier in terms of administering the vaccines to the most vulnerable. Diphtheria, tetanus, and whooping cough vaccines were easier with new-borns to schedule at 6, 14, and 26 weeks but for toddlers, youngsters and older children with doubts as to age and whether previously vaccinated, it was pragmatism – if in doubt vaccinate. With chicken pox, typhoid, mumps, bacterial meningitis, rotavirus and hepatitis also to be administered, sometimes within a cocktail of other vaccines at different times and to differing age groups was of course never an issue in Poland or other European Countries.

In refugee camps in North West Syria where people had been displaced many times, Stefan and Gabriella were trying to bring order to disorder with zero information – not an easy or enviable task. However such efforts of preventative medicine were complicated by refugees' being already vulnerable to malnutrition, exposure, injury, and infectious epidemics leaving a variety of chronic illnesses amongst these poverty stricken camp populations untreated such as heart disease, diabetes, cancer, and HIV/AIDS.

UNHCR had managed across all the camps to select competent refugees to assist in the distribution of food rations, heaters for cooking, and drinkable water. Anwar Hassan was one such person. A former administrative officer in the City of Homs, he had proved to be capable and reliable. As the month's rolled by, Radek had often, whilst Stefan, Gabriella, and their teams were dealing with patients, strolled round the various camps with him. This led to Radek and his men organising with refugees to dig ditches to take away rainwater from torrential downpours rather than allowing the weather to wash away tented homes. In addition, with Colonel Kemal Erdoğan's assistance together with the Turkish Military, not only had building materials and fittings been provided for collection at Darat Izza but also the loan of cement mixers and a mechanical digger plus sufficient diesel so shower and washing blocks plus latrines could be built in two of the nearby camps to the hospital. Whilst the water supply was not drinkable without being boiled, it was good enough for the blocks until UNHCR could deliver filtration systems.

The medical teams *(and also the Polish soldiers attempts even if only marginally)* to make life better within the camps, had, by dint of those efforts, earnt the refugees' gradual respect and trust. Hence when strangers began to be seen circulating within the camps in early November, it was not long before Anwar brought the matter to Radek's attention.

'Major Król, there are strangers in the camp offering people the opportunity to enter the European Union. Do you believe this can be true?' 'Anwar do you know these people?' 'No Major Król, they are probably Syrians but it is hard to say.' 'Do you think they are traffickers?' 'I do not know - they are not asking for up-front deposits - rather they are offering a new route into Europe.' 'Tell me more please Anwar.' Radek was handed a flyer by Anwar that stated –

Access to a better and safe life in the European Union

Valid personalised transit document from a neighbouring country into the Schengen Area

'Inbound flight' into the host neighbouring country

Designated accommodation in the host neighbouring country while the personalised transit documentation is completed

Transport to the departure airport terminal

Subsistence payment plus transport on leaving the host neighbouring country's pre-paid accommodation

'Do you believe this?' 'No Major Król it looks too good to be true. However, many people in the camps you have visited and even other camps within this region, are thinking very seriously about this new migration pathway into the European Union. What have us refugees to lose apart from the little savings we have left or accumulated, when they can escape these squalid conditions and life?'

'Anwar has anyone been told or learnt who this 'neighbouring country' is?' 'No Major Król.' 'Has anyone been told who is behind this search for 'paying' refugees? Is it the usual suspects – international traffickers or smugglers or other criminal gangs seeking to profit financially from this human misery?'

'Not exactly Major, the response has simply been it is being organised by a major humanitarian organisation within the neighbouring country. It has apparently negotiated with the European Union a special dispensation for the bulk entry of refugees as legal entrants. The prospect of entering the European Union legally is of course very attractive to people in the camps as the threats of arrest and deportation are removed.'

Tragedy is never far away in any refugee camp. It was no different for Stefan, Gabriella, and their medical teams. There were the unacceptable rapes of teenage girls with little or no accountability for the perpetrators. However, that position changed as the young women identified their attackers to Master-Sergeant Nowak. Within a week, the guilty found themselves limping or being carried into a daily camp field clinic for treatment. Sadly it was not just testosterone fuelled teenagers and young people but also related adults males in their forties and fifties who, even allowing for cultural differences, should have known how to conduct themselves. Apart from unwanted and unwarranted pregnancies, the transmission of sexually transmitted diseases including AIDS was an added factor in dealing with the psychological trauma suffered by these victims. Nevertheless, within a month, the incidence of such attacks on women fell to zero as Stefan and Gabriella noted as they sat one evening drinking Raki with Radek after another difficult day at the camps. Similarly, domestic violence, though still occurring, moved from daily to infrequent. It was in mid-November as the summer heat disappeared and winter began that the medical team faced a harrowing tragedy. As weeks had passed, a young woman, Amal Ibrahim, had been bringing her baby and two toddlers for vaccinations to the clinics. With time and regularity, the doctors and medical team had learnt a little about her life. Amal had lost her parents and sisters in a bombing attack by Syria's Airforce on her home city of Aleppo. Her husband and her had fled with their children and ending up in this particular Idlib camp. Her husband had then, shortly after the family's arrival, caught cholera and died leaving her with the sole responsibility of looking after and protecting her two children. Her baby was result of being gang-raped twelve months earlier – was there no end Gabriella thought silently to this poor woman's suffering as Amal was being treated by her for syphilis. Living in a tent as winter approached meant keeping a cooking stove burning to avoid freezing to death during the sub-zero temperatures at night.

When Gabriella and the nurses were setting up for the morning clinic, Anwar brought the news that Amal and her children would no longer be coming for treatment and the next raft of vaccinations. Fire had consumed the family's tent – there were no survivors.

Radek had been visiting nearby camps in the hope of finding just one of the 'salesmen' who were handing out the flyers for this unknown Humanitarian Organisation. However, his search had proved to be fruitless. Colonel Kemal Erdoğan had ensured amongst every weekly supply inventory of food and medicine that a case of Raki was included.

It was already dusk as the serviceable Toyotas and Jeeps returned to the hospital. Stefan had been in the operating theatre since the early afternoon repairing a catalogue of broken limbs, removing inflamed appendices and gangrenous toes, and finally a hip replacement for certain patients.

Radek and Stefan were slumped in deckchairs around a fire enjoying their first Raki of the evening both deep in their own thoughts when Gabriella joined them. The usual bubbly Italian doctor was completely the opposite as she helped herself to a Raki that she downed in one and repeated the process. 'Questo fottuto posto è l'inferno in terra!' she exploded. Neither Pole knew what she had said. However, they caught the drift as her hands gestured her pent up frustration with every word. When she spoke again in heavily accented English muttering 'This fucking place is hell on earth', they simply nodded. Perhaps the tears welling up in those 'Claudia Cardinale' cat like eyes glowering at them both from underneath her flowing black hair kept Radek and Stefan mute. After a day of stoically doing her duty for the living refugees, and controlling her emotions about Amal Ibrahim's tragic life and loss, the futility of her even being in Northern Syria overwhelmed her as she questioned herself and them about what difference their presence had made to the well-being of the refugees. By this point tears were streaming down her face as she told them how Amal and her children had died the previous night. Stefan refilled Gabriella's and their glasses with Raki.

'Why should I care when the rest of this bloody world doesn't give a damn about these people? What difference have we made here? Far better we had all stayed at home and not seen at first hand all this despair. The hopelessness we see in every refugee's face of a life with no future except poverty and death.'

The sight of Master-Sergeant Nowak appearing instantly reminded Radek that he was on night security duty. There was nothing that he could immediately say that would lift her melancholic mood as he left.

Sometimes it is best just to listen especially when a beautiful woman like Gabriella is venting months of pent up frustration and questioning her worth as a doctor. 'Are we fulfilling our hippocratic oath Stefan? Is our inability to protect patients causing harm? Are we already compromised before we even treat the sick?'

It was a clear night albeit somewhat cold. The medical teams and the soldiers not on the security roster had decided to hold a barbecue in the open air. It was not long before the sound of laughter and music was floating across the hospital compound. Stefan took the opportunity to break what had become a very depressing conversation as Gabriella's mood became more and more despondent. If they continued drinking more Raki on an empty stomach Stefan knew neither of them would be fit to treat anyone in the morning.

'Come on Gabriella let's go to the barbecue'. Standing up Stefan held out his hand which she grasped to pull herself out of the deck chair. Pulling magically a clean cotton handkerchief from his scrubs – he said 'Let's tidy you up'. There was no resistance from Gabriella as he gently wiped away her slowing tears and running mascara. By the time they joined their colleagues the barbecue was in full swing with an interesting mix of hot food and free flowing booze. One of the Italian nurses had a blue tooth portable JBL speaker and various songs by Italian Artists were filling the air.

Tracks from Pavarotti's War Child concerts in Modena were playing. Perhaps it was admiration for the man, but when Bono's voice from U2 began slowly to fill the air at the start of 'Miss Sarajevo', conversation stopped. Everyone was waiting to hear Luciano, even the Polish soldiers stood silent. As this great tenor's voice floated into the night air, all the Italians were overcome with emotion. By popular demand it was put on repeat at which point Stefan felt a woman's hand in his. Turning, it was Gabriella, 'Let's dance.' Stefan needed no encouragement to cease chatting with two of the team's anaesthetists about the day's surgery than to gather Gabriella happily into his arms.

How long they danced as romantic italian love songs one after another washed over them, Stefan did not know but who would care. When a woman as beautiful as Gabriella has her arms wrapped round your neck and her head resting on your chest, what man on this earth would want such a moment to pass? Notwithstanding the warmth of her body next to his, Stefan was only in scrubs and he was beginning really to feel cold. As that first shiver shook his body,

Gabriella raised her head from his chest 'Time for us to leave Stefan.'

As they walked effortlessly holding hands back to the tent he shared with Radek, Stefan at least knew they would have the place to themselves and not have to seek out an empty operating theatre. Neither Stefan nor Gabriella were married or had a partner so there were no issues of betrayal. Rather in last five months, they had both been under intense and daily stress leading their medical teams. Yes physical sex as a self-prescribed prescription for stress relief would, without doubt, boost Gabriella's mood and lift her depression. As for Stefan, it was more about the arousal of male lust, if not attraction, that had lain somewhat dormant since they first met back in May. Nevertheless, as they removed one another's clothes alternatively, the rather unromantic setting of Radek's and Stefan's shared military bivouac was of no consequence as passion took over. They sensibly ignored Stefan's camp bed due to its collapsible structure but threw the air-mattress onto the floor with his unzipped sleeping bag forming a quilt. If Stefan had been cold before entering the tent that was not the case now as endorphins and other hormones kicked in raising his blood flow and heart rate. Whilst in other circumstances, especially after roughly a year of sexual abstinence for both of them, either Gabriella or Stefan might have been slightly hesitant at this point. However, this was pure unadulterated and uninhibited animal passion with the earlier consumption of Raki playing its part. His throbbing and rock solid penis found seamless entry into the encouraging wetness of her vagina. Each thrust was met by her vagina pulsating and drawing him ever closer into her. Release for both of them was not far away until Gabriella moved from the missionary position to being on top – all that she was missing was a Cowgirl Stetson. Kneeling, her hands gently pushed off Stefan's chest and slid up and down his thighs as they supported her while she directed with her hand his hot penis once more into her vagina. Gabriella was now in the dominant position whereby she could delay Stefan's release and her climax by dictating the pace, rhythm, and penetration as her vagina gripped him as she moved up and down. Sometimes her movements were slow and then fast coupled with shallow and deep penetration. Stefan's hands were everywhere as his fingers switched from massaging her erect nipples to stimulating her clitoris. Collapsing into each with shouts of ecstasy as he ejaculated what felt like a bucket of semen as she enjoyed orgasmic waves. Within minutes they were both asleep welded together in the warmth of each other and a zipped up sleeping bag.

When Radek opened the tent flap, Gabriella and Stefan were both fast asleep as he arrived to pick up his running kit. Moving quietly as only a GROM trained soldier can, Radek left also picking up his trainers. The task of now leading a ten kilometre fitness run was his immediate task. As he led the soldiers, including Master-Sergeant Nowak, through another surviving olive grove, he decided not to pass any jovial banter on the medical soundness of 'sexual healing'. Hopefully, Stefan's particular treatment to alleviate Gabriella's depression had worked. She was a great doctor doing a fantastic job.

His mind turned once again to his mission and Grzegorz's request *'I need you to be intelligence gathering as to whom or what is promoting new ways to enter the Schengen Area – particularly with regard to the Baltic States and Poland'*.

Chapter 4

Radek and Master-Sergeant Nowak had agreed two days previously, when on night patrol protecting the field hospital, that one of the 'salesmen' touting this alleged new migration route into the European Union had to be followed to the originating source. Whilst he would in many ways have preferred personally to be accompanied by Bartek Nowak, this would have been a poor command decision whatever the success or otherwise of what was an intelligence gathering mission. Similarly, careering off alone into what in many ways was still a war zone would have been the height of stupidity and poor judgement. Having reviewed the best choice amongst their special forces team, Navy Lieutenant Kacper Jankowski stood out from the rest. At twenty five years old and at two metres tall, Kacper had already completed three combat tours in Afghanistan where he had demonstrated the important infiltration skill of blending into local environments unnoticed.

The third Toyota was now road worthy as were the other two thanks to the efforts of a number of the soldiers and Kacper, a mechanical engineering graduate from Gdansk. It was the perfect undercover vehicle for the mission with its dented bodywork and peeling paintwork. There were places under the rear seating to hide from view their Hecklar-Koch 416 rifles and ammunition plus satellite comms equipment.

The boot contained water plus six jerry cans of diesel hidden under a rag tag covering of dirty refugee clothing only fit for burning. Any signs of fading UNHCR white paint and red cross signage were removed to the extent the vehicle uncared for and unloved by whoever the previous owners had been. It would not look out of place anywhere in Syria or Iraq.

Radek's and Kacper's Glock 21s with suppressors ready if necessary and a spare cartridge clip were discreetly hidden under their clothes. Both men had grown beards whilst in Northern Syria and when Anwar returned with cheap and third or fourth hand clothing from Idlib market, their disguise became complete as they put on traditional Syrian head-scarfs.

Two weeks later the Toyota came to a halt a few cars behind a bus that was letting off passengers close to the centre of Idlib. With Anwar's assistance, they had identified and photographed some twelve or more 'salesmen' in local camps, including the one nearest to the hospital. Radek overheard and recorded a few of their sales pitches to an increasing number of refugees that were unsurprisingly more than ready to listen.

Kacper adjusted his headscarf to cover his earpiece and microphone then stepped out of the Toyota. It was the end of the day with dusk beginning to fall. Some seven of the 'salesmen' had exited the bus and were now walking purposefully towards a café across the square. In the meantime, Radek had eased the Toyota into a parking spot on a side street leading back into the square with a clear view of the café. Kacper had on entering the square moved diagonally to a fresh fruit stall and bought an orange then appearing somewhat absent mindedly to peel it while heading also towards the café. Radek locked the Toyota and headed towards the café from the other direction whereby Kacper and he appeared to be old friends meeting after a day's work. Radek ordered two fresh mint teas and two shots of Arak passing on the traditional *'Nargila'* pipes that other café customers were clearly enjoying without any regard for their health. Kacper could understand arabic but any attempts to speak would immediately identify him as a westerner. Radek's fluently spoken arabic on the other hand indicated more of a Lebanese accent on some words as opposed to anything else. A table at the front was occupied by a suited Syrian man with a half empty bottle of Aryan *(a cold salted yoghurt drink)* in front of him. The 'salesmen' were gathering in front of him. 'What news?' said the suited man. The apparent leader of the 'salesmen' replied 'Sir *(sayedi)* the people are interested but wary. They need proof that this new route into the European Union works.' 'How do you believe that can be achieved?' 'We discussed amongst ourselves - refugees who have successfully arrived in Europe always make contact with their relatives and ultimately remit money to them. If you can achieve this with a few migrants from Northern Syria then word of mouth will do the rest.' The nods and murmurs of agreement to their spokesman's words met the seated man's gaze. Standing up, he pulled out a money clip containing US dollars and then proceeded to peel off a number of bills. He handed each 'salesman' a fifty dollar note which was more than most Syrians could expect to earn in a month.

Radek and Kacper, being only a table away, had heard quite clearly even above the café's general hubbub the conversation between the seated man and the 'salesmen'. Kacper had left so as to be ready to tail this Syrian man wherever he might go. Radek sat quietly sipping another fresh mint tea. The 'salesmen' had left as soon as the dollar bill was placed in their outstretched hands leaving the suited man to once again to be seated. Was he going to pay the bill and leave or order another drink? If the suit orders another drink thought Radek then he is waiting for someone or perhaps he already has such company. The answer was not long in coming. Whilst there were some darkish corners, it was the burst of light from a cigarette lighter that alerted Radek to there being someone else with an interest in the suited Syrian. Steadily into the café's half-light emerged a bald man in a dark grey suit smoking a cigarette. As he passed Radek's table, the strong smell of russian tobacco hung in the air as the man exhaled smoke from his lungs. Joining the seated Syrian, the bald man's ill-fitting suit jacket revealed the bulge of a weapon in a shoulder holster. So it was the Russians orchestrating and scheming after the tell-tale smoke from an AD40 cigarette. The conversation between the Syrian and Russian started in arabic but reverted in parts to solely russian. The next step would be for the bald russian to report. That would decide Radek's and Kacper's next move. A party of Syrians arrived to celebrate the birth of a son to one of them. Their jovial and noisy conversation prevented any likelihood of gleaning any further information from the suited Syrian and Russian. Radek left the café keeping his back to them as he slipped into the safety of an unlit square. Kacper met him with the camera – he had returned in order to take bursts of shots of the suited Syrian to then have been fortunate enough to capture on camera also the Russian. As they left for the Toyota, Radek correctly saw little benefit in following the

Russian either to the Tartus Naval Base or more probably to the Hmeymim Air Base. Both bases were within the Latakia Region that was fully under the control of the Syrian Government and its military. Apart from dodging numerous check points, the Russian bases would be heavily defended and guarded. Learning what the bald russian would report was broadly a given and to whom would now fall to the skills of Rakowiecka Street's Cyber Listening team.

Lieutenant-Colonel Hanko saluted and took off her military cap. 'Well Weronika what more can you tell me after reading Major Król's report?'

'General, we have identified the russian as Cappitan Konstantin Makarov of the GRU and the Syrian as Kadyn Suleiman. Kadyn is a mid-ranking officer within Syria's General Intelligence Directorate and already identified by the European Union as a leading participant, if not organiser with others, of human rights abuses and killings in Dara as the city was finally retaken by Government forces in 2018. From our monitoring of GRU communications out of Hmeymim Air Base, we were able to identify Makarov's coded signature on a report into Moscow Central. What was more interesting was subsequently an encrypted phonecall a matter of hours later from Colonel Igor Yedemsky to, we presume, Makarov.'

Grzegorz Politczek turned to Colonels' Jan Chmura and Kuba Pawlukowicz who had also seen copies of Major Król's report. Kuba was the first to speak.

'Weronika have you any ideas as to what our russian friends might be planning?' 'Colonel, it is a fact that the GRU are looking at creating, probably temporarily, a new migration route into northern Europe. An assessment is now being made of refugee appetite for taking such a route and how to give such migration scale. According to geography, the only non-European Country to fit as the host transit point can only be Belarus with its land border with Latvia, Lithuania, and Poland. If we factor in Russia's dominance of Lukashenko and his government since August, with a new base in Hrodno and joint military drills in Eastern Belarus, the so called 'neighbouring country' can only be Belarus. In my department's view this will mean during the first quarter of 2021, a concerted effort will be made to incentivise and actively to assist a 'pathfinder' group of refugees to make illegal entry across this northern border to Schengen. In the knowledge Yedemsky is involved, we have to assume Laskutin and GRU are following a directive from President Putin. If our intelligence assessment is correct, during the summer, we will see increasing numbers of refugees in their hundreds, if not thousands. They will seek to cross either through illegal forest routes or at formal border crossing points as successful *'word of mouth'* stories feed back into the sales pitches.'

'What do you see as the key issues to be addressed for us to address in regard to our border with Belarus?' asked Jan Chmura.

'General, Colonels, most of our border runs through dense forest and in part the Bug River with adjoining marshland. It is not secure. This means that our entire 416 kilometre border will need to be both physically strengthening and have substantial manpower added to our Border Guard if it is to be policed properly. The same will apply to our Latvia and Lithuania neighbours. In the interim, Brussels has categorically denied that a transit agreement has been negotiated with Belarus or any neighbouring state to the European Union – either in the past, now, or indeed planned in the future, it is all complete rubbish.'

'So we have a clear and imminent danger of something related to a new northern migration route into the European Union. Colonel Hanko please organise a video conference with my counterparts in Latvia and Lithuania for later today' 'Yes general' said Lieutenant-Colonel Hanko as she stood up donned her cap, saluted, and left. Standing up Grzegorz walked to his desk hitting the intercom button to his aide de camp, Major Adamski, 'Pawel I need an appointment with the Interior Minister tomorrow morning if possible.'

'What do you think the Russians are really playing at Grzegorz?' 'Minister, one certainty is that 'Ivan' is not seeking to create a permanent northern migration route through Belarus into Poland. This very recent interest in internally displaced Syrian refugees can only be to self-serve a wider Russian political objective. Lest we forget, since 2015 the Russian Air Force and Navy has had no second thoughts about bombing and shelling indiscriminately civilian areas in support of Bashir al-Assad's military.'

'What's your current best guess?'

'Lukashenko's problems this summer have played into President Putin's plans for a much closer union. Russia now has Su-35 fighter wings permanently based in Hrodno, currently winter drills in Eastern Belarus integrating

Belarussian army groups, and its troops are now being regularly rotated through new bases on Belarus soil. Next year its Western Military District will be holding its quadrennial military exercise, Zapad 2021. Hence there will be large movements of military equipment and troops in the second half of the year. There will be a new President in the White House with immediate problems at home of COVID and of course exit from Afghanistan. We cannot ignore United States Foreign Policy is becoming more Asia Pacific / China centric rather than Europe. Therefore, an influx of refugees at our Borders will be initially seen as our problem rather than a smokescreen for any Russian geopolitical play. Will it have anything to do with Ukraine's *frozen* war in the Donbass or possibly to create additional instability across the country?'

'Any thought as to our immediate response to this border threat?'

'My recommendation is that we have to develop a contingency plan with the Border Force, Military, and your department as to securing the border plus processing likely volumes of economic refugees.'

Radek was contentedly asleep as the C-17 lifted off for Gdansk from Incirlik air base. He would be home for Christmas. Master-Sergeant Nowak checked on his soldiers who were seemingly following their Major's lead before he did the same. As for Major Zysk and Maggiore Russo, they had already been in the air on a Boeing 737 for twenty minutes as it headed for Rome along with the *Medici senza Frontiere Italia* medical team. Stefan was going to spend

Christmas with Gabriella and her parents. The lovers had been inseparable since waking together in that sleeping bag.

Chapter 5

When Radek had left for Syria in the Spring, Poland was waking up from the hangover of its first COVID lockdown. Commercial and private Life was beginning slowly to return to some semblance of normality. His return though marked the country's extension of the existing restrictions introduced in connection with the coronavirus pandemic until at least mid-January. After Christmas, further restrictions were introduced. From December 28th, shopping malls were to be closed again; restaurants could only operate in take-away mode; and hotels were in effect permanently closed just like the ski slopes. Whilst there were no restrictions on movement during the Christmas Eve holiday, there was a limit on the number of guests that could be invited into your family home; a maximum of five guests in total, except for those who live together permanently. As for New Year's Eve, there was a travel ban throughout Poland from 19:00 hours on the 31st to 06:00 hours on the 1st.

Most of the European Union had instigated similar if not tougher regulations from curfews to complete closure. This was Christmas unlike any other – it was cancelled. Television news channels showed repeatedly dozens of ambulances queuing to enter hospitals with suspected COVID cases. New York, Birmingham, and St Petersburg were just a few of cities and towns worldwide facing the same challenges to their respective overwhelmed health systems.

The only good news was after successful clinical trials of the Pfizer-BioNTech and Astra Zeneca vaccines, and subsequent formal emergency medical approval in both the United States and the United Kingdom, there was at last the prospect of a weapon against the COVID virus for 2021.

Grzegorz Politczek had returned to Warsaw after spending Christmas Eve and Christmas with his youngest daughter and her husband in Wroclaw. It had been a welcome break from his intelligence responsibilities at ABW for Poland. A widower of some four years since his wife lost her battle against breast cancer, he had adjusted to living alone. It was New Year's Eve. Grzegorz lit the fire in his study and opened a new bottle of Glenfarclas 25 year old. Pouring a measure into a stuart crystal tumbler, he settled into his worn leather armchair and sipped his whisky. Unanswered questions began to enter his thoughts and set his mind thinking. What were the Russians planning – surely establishing a new migration route was not their objective or indeed to embarrass the European Union? There had to be more to this intelligence threat.

Whilst COVID may have resulted in three hundred thousand or more deaths, the Russian economy had clearly suffered. However without nationwide lockdowns, the National Wealth Fund had increased by nearly 60 billion US dollars to 180 billion dollars with Central Bank Reserves now topping 600 billion with the rouble being allowed to float. This strong position was only going to become even greater Grzegorz mused looking at the burning logs. Energy demands for fossil fuels would outstrip market supply as world economies reopened. President Putin must be feeling both confident and rather smug. His conservative prudent fiscal policy since 2014 meant accumulated reserves to weather whatever was thrown 'left field' at Russia like the COVID pandemic. Nevertheless, the major reductions in Government Expenditure had not deflected the increased spending year on year since 2007 of completely modernising Russia's Armed Forces from training to payroll to equipment to battle readiness as Colonel Hanko had remarked at the monthly intelligence meeting with the Prime Minister and Interior Minister in late November. There had to be more than simply saying Russia is handling the pandemic far better than the United States, the United Kingdom, and most of Europe.

Another large measure of Glenfarclas was poured into the tumbler sitting on the side table next to his armchair. He slid forward, partially stooping, to place fresh logs on the fire before slipping back into the welcoming comfort of his armchair. A warming sip or two of this speyside nectar and Grzegorz was back again attempting to figure out what Russia's Foreign Policy objectives truly were.

Was it a seminar or a podcast or from Colonel Hanko where he first heard Ivan Krastev's quote? *Authoritarians only enjoy those crises they have manufactured themselves. They need enemies to defeat, not problems to solve. The freedom authoritarian leaders cherish most is the freedom to choose which crises merit a response.* Had the absence of United States leadership over the last four years, the West's need to re-boot United States and Russian arms control, and the substantial growth in energy supplies into Europe coincided with the pandemic to provide the perfect moment for

Russia's thinking on foreign policy to match its political ambition?

The European Council's inability in Brussels to coordinate and maintain the free movement of people as border controls re-emerged within the Union at the beginning of the pandemic in Q2 2020 sent messages of self-interest in a global world. Although European Union countries have subsequently come together with an impressive economic response package, normalised freedom of movement, and seen reopening of borders between states, did Russia perceive that this underscored the dangers of globalisation over self-reliance? Had Europe's 'just in time' inventory issues for manufacturing been compromised by logistic supply problems whether via ports, rail, air, or road? Certainly Western Governments around the world have had to assert themselves, whether they wished to or not, as the key players during the pandemic by providing financial lifelines for businesses and people.

According to our deep cover agents in Sergey Lavrov's Foreign Ministry, the Kremlin Establishment believes there is no one worth talking to within the European Union about Russia's security concerns. Macron does not speak on behalf of Europe and playing the international statesman benefits perhaps his own ego rather than political future at home; German Chancellor Angela Merkel has already announced she will not be seeking re-election; and as for US president-elect Joe Biden why should Russia seek to engage with the incoming administration in 2021 as his policies are unlikely to last beyond his one term in office. In general, Russian diplomacy has few incentives to reach out to Europe unless sanctions are gradually removed and lifted. However, that is highly unlikely, if not unrealistic, as between Russia and the West since the annexation of Crimea in 2014 in breach of International Law. This has created somewhat of a siege mentality within the Russian Elite he pondered. With the common disaster of the pandemic, there was initially the prospect of engagement with Russia in the fields of healthcare and the environment. Nevertheless, with the novichok nerve agent poisoning of Alexei Navalny in August and also Russia's support for Lukashenko's brutal crackdown on Belarussian protests around the same time made any outreach impossible from either side.

What is Vladimir Vladimirovich Putin planning? Grzegorz was no nearer an answer even after seeing he had consumed nearly half a bottle of his favourite whisky! Maybe he wondered is President Putin, to quote Winston Churchill, simply *'a riddle, wrapped in a mystery, inside an enigma'*? Churchill went on to say about Joseph Stalin's Russia in 1939 *'... an inscrutable and menacing land that plays by its own rules, usually to the detriment of those who choose more open regulations ...'*. Has so much changed today wondered Grzegorz?

Certainly, Russia was not slow in anticipating the need for close engagement with Belarus for strategic reasons. Its involvement in Syrian Civil War has been both a military and political success. Russia's economic strength and self-confidence must also have had some bearing on forcing Saudi Arabia to accept, without Russian involvement, any attempt to control the oil market was doomed to failure. As for its other Foreign Policy goals, President Putin and President Xi Jinping have continued, even before the pandemic, to bring their countries ambitiously closer together. Does this mean autocracies uniting against liberal democracies with disinformation and other elements destabilising democracy? Is this a forerunner of some future agreement – Russia will take Ukraine and China will take Taiwan with neither party objecting to one another's action and protecting each other with the use of their 'Veto' in the United Nations Council? An axis of convenience if not connivance he mused.

A knock on his study door broke his line of thought, 'General, the night security guard are now in place. Thank you Kapitan.' Finishing the remaining contents of his tumbler, Grzegorz left for his bedroom with his questions unanswered – what were the Russians' real objectives and who would be his eyes & ears across the border in the Białowieża Forest over the coming months?

Radek had returned to the loving arms of Alexandra and his parents in Niepolomice just in time to celebrate Christmas Eve Wigilia Supper with them all. After his Syrian posting, his orders were to return to Gdansk for arctic warfare training with the Swedish Rangers inside Sweden's Arctic Circle. Although not part of NATO, Sweden has, since Russia's actions in Georgia in 2008, territorial takeover of Crimea in 2014, and more recent covert actions in Belarus, been upgrading its military's defensive capabilities including integrated training with NATO members. His orders were to report at 12:00 hours on Thursday February 4th to GROM Military Headquarters Gdansk. Alexandra's and his expectations were that he would be back well before Easter at the beginning of April, probably mid-March.

A telephone call from Colonel Kuba Pawlukowicz was to bring Radek's furlough to a halt some nine days earlier. He was to report to Rakowiecka Street in thirty six hours and understand that he will be incommunicado for some months.

Alexandra was understandably worried after only just having her husband back at long last from North-West Syria. In addition, Kuba's request to only report in his dress uniform with no luggage meant only one thing to her with her former M-16 experience that Radek was going somewhere as a deep undercover agent within a new operation.

After saluting and removing his military cap, Radek was motioned by a wave of Colonel Pawlukowicz's hand to sit in one of the armchairs.

'Radek, the intelligence you gathered in Idlib has us all concerned on two counts. The volumes of refugees will have an adverse impact at our borders from containing illegal entrants to processing legitimate ones; and what are Russia's real reasons for financing a new migration route.

Bearing in mind these uncertainties, your mission is to observe, watch, and report what you learn from being undercover in the Białowieża and Damačava forests.

From now on you are Sergey Antonovich Petrov. Here is your identity card, VTB debit card, details of your home in Gomel, photo of your family with names, birth certificate, details of your conscription into the military after school, and your academic record.'

'Is there a Sergey?'

There was – he was a drifter taking casual manual jobs. His family have not seen him since he left the military fourteen years ago. Sergey met an untimely death on New Year's Eve freezing to death in a Brest park after consuming enough vodka to sink a battleship.'

'I like him already' smiled Radek somewhat facetiously 'and the family?' 'Parents are dead only leaving a sister who was five years old when he left. Not a perfect cover but matches your age and build.

You are going to be met in Białystok at 19:00 hours this evening in McDonalds. When you see a policewoman enter who purchases two takeaway meals, you must follow her. She will drive you to the edge of the Białowieża Forest and point to a path for you to follow. After half a kilometre, the path will disappear into fallen deadwood and bushes – this is where you will meet your guide, and future employer, to take you across the border into Belarus. Eryk Shevchenko is a sixty one year old Belarussian smuggler like his father and grandfather before him. Originally the family name had been Polish but at some point during of World War II, a decision had been made to become, at face value, Belarussian. This had paid off as the family's sawmill remained in their ownership and control untouched by any commissar. The Soviet Secret Police and later the Belarussian GRU occasionally either requested Eryk's father or him to guide people through the forest in either direction or to smuggle one kilo tins of beluga caviar on their behalf. After the collapse of the Soviet Union, Eryk was briefly arrested in Białystok's market. This led to the Polish Intelligence service turning him into an asset and undercover agent. Earnings from both the saw-mill plus his other unseen activities for

Poland enabled him to equip and buy a second mill in the forest near Damačava to the south of Brest. You will be casual labour in either sawmill with an unchallengeable reason for roaming around both forests under Eryk's direction. We are expecting, based on your and other intelligence, that by the spring if not sooner, illegals could well start to cross into Poland from Belarus. You will be very much our 'on the ground' early warning of what may well develop.'

'How long are you expecting me to be in hostile territory Colonel?'

'Hard to answer Radek – but I have direct orders from the General to ensure your wife is kept sufficiently in the loop as your mission grows. The Quartermaster has your kit waiting for you in the Basement Armoury & your departure timetable to Białystok.'

Radek rose from the armchair, put on his military cap, saluted while saying 'Sir' as he clicked his boot heels, and headed for the Quartermaster's basement office.

'Good afternoon Major, I have been expecting you – please follow me.' Kapitan Piotr Okolski led the way into a side room where the Head of Clothing was waiting. On a table, a variety of clothes, thermals, boots, gloves, parka & backpack were laid out.

'Major, please pick up a set of underwear and change into them alone. Your Military Uniform should be left in the changing room together with any residual items including laundry.'

After Radek was stood barefoot in his recently acquired underwear that, whilst cotton, had Chinese labelling. Similarly every item could only have been purchased in Belarus or Western Russia. His boots were identical to those worn by Russian Special Forces. His Chinese wash bag contained Belarus toiletries but with the odd European Union item readily purchasable in Brest and Minsk. His jeans were seemingly Levis 501s but in reality were Chinese copies.

His perfectly spoken russian did have the slightest of accents. Nevertheless, it fitted perfectly with someone who had grown up in Western Russia and East Belarus. With less than 10% of the Belarussian population speaking Belarussian in their *'day to day'* lives and less than 23% even understanding the language, Radek was protected. His Polish though would enable him to broadly understand what was being discussed even though he would sensibly stick to Russian – this was not a social visit or someone on vacation.

The Head of Clothing removed his uniform, dress boots, cap, and other items assuring Radek as he left that everything would be cleaned and ready for his return.

Kapitan Okolski continued his part of the briefing as Radek packed the back pack with his recently acquired wardrobe. Nothing was brand new, nothing was ironed though clean, and Sergey Petrov was after all a drifter of no fixed abode. Handing Radek a money belt with russian and Belarusian roubles plus close to a thousand US dollars, all in well-thumbed and used notes together some Belarusian coin, for which he duly signed to keep at least ABW's Accountant happy, Radek was now ready to leave.

It was already dusk at 15:35 hours as the mercedes people carrier with blackened windows left ABW's underground car park and entered the bustling Warsaw traffic. Radek noticed that the driver made a couple of deviations in order to be sure no over-inquisitive foreign agent was following the vehicle. The comings and goings at Rakowiecka Street were always of interest to 'Ivan'.

Snow flurries were being borne on a chilling northerly wind that had crossed the freezing waters of the Baltic Sea. There was no moon and once in Europe's last primeval forest, anyone risked in that darkness falling over deadwood or meeting worse. If you tripped and broke a leg, your survival became doubtful if you were alone. Radek stood looking at what seemed dense foliage of overly large holly and rhododendron bushes with the path having come to dead end. The only noise was the creaking of the tree boughs as increasing gusts of wind shrieked and howled around him. That said, the military grade russian parka was keeping him dry and warm as he waited patiently in the all-consuming darkness.

Standing still in such conditions after fifteen minutes or so, even with thermal gloves and a wind proof beanie under the parka's hood, the wind-chill saps one's energy as it seems to claw its way into your very bones. After thirty minutes, you need to move or find shelter out of the wind. Radek's previous Arctic Survival training missions had seen him looking for such cover shortly after arriving at the path's end. Pulling a heavy duty three millimetre thick survival sack from his back pack, he pulled, what was like a large dustbin bag over his entire frame, prior to settling down out of that swirling cold wind behind the remains of a fallen oak to wait for Eryk Shevchenko. The sack kept him dry and warm to the extent after nearly an hour of waiting Radek was already grabbing some sleep unrelated to any symptom of hypothermia.

In spite of the gale whipping through the forest canopy masking all sounds including those of wandering bison or other animals moving through the forest, Radek's eyes were suddenly fully alert whilst his entire body remained inert. Thirty or more metres to his left there was a stationary shape crouched low to the ground. His mind was racing but coldly evaluating – was that shape there before, is it moving, could it be his guide Eryk, was it an unknown party or nothing? His Glock 19 with its fitted suppressor was resting on his lap. Nevertheless, his winter gloves were too bulky to ensure for an accurate headshot so without seeming to move, he gradually eased his right glove off so his hand could grip the pistol butt and turn the weapon towards the perceived threat. The dark shadow remained motionless.

Radek was beginning to think he had been imagining things when the shadow moved in a blink of eye behind what seemed to be an impenetrable thicket of seemingly coppiced woodland. He had to assume the shadow had seen his wrapped shape in the survival sack. Stay and die or move and live were the thoughts passing through his brain. Quickly removing the sack, Radek ran to where the shadow had been taking cover behind some evergreens as he moved. When he reached the spot, he dropped immediately pointing the Glock along the sight line to the rear of the thicket. No shadow – nothing seemingly in the darkness then a voice above a whisper floated towards him in the swirling wind. 'A woodcutter needs a sharp axe…' Radek answered '…to clear the fallen trees.' From the darkness the shadow emerged, it was Eryk Shevchenko. 'Some trouble Eryk?' mouthed Radek as they shook hands. Walking to where his backpack was, Radek repacked the survival sack as Eryk explained why he had been so late for the rendezvous. A political prisoner had been detained since late May under Article 342 of the Belarussian Criminal Code ie the organization of group actions that grossly violate public order. His crime had been organising the collection of signatures in support of Tsikhanouskaya's nomination as a presidential candidate the previous year. Whilst this innocent man had been brought before the Leninski district court of Hrodna that morning for purely sentencing after being held for seven months without trial, he had managed amazingly to escape his captors after the verdict - the passing of a six year sentence in a high-security Belarus penal colony. This had resulted in a major manhunt throughout the Grodno Region with Russian GRU Special Forces Units entering the Białowieża forest in support of the policing effort.

As the snow flurries intensified and the wind howled through the trees, Eryk took the lead whilst Radek followed a constant six metres behind. Their movement was cautious and slow with the intention of remaining unseen by anyone or anything in the forest. This meant movement was slow and deliberate. As dawn was beginning to break, they were in the warmth of a log cabin within the sawmill buildings. This unit would become Radek's home during the entire mission. As for Eryk, his initial task would be to integrate 'Sergey' into the mill's small workforce of two and simultaneously familiarise his charge with a smuggler's knowledge of the forests many secrets. For now both men needed sleep.

Chapter 6

Oleg Yedemsky was feeling rather pleased with his plan to begin creating a major distraction on the European Union's northern border.

A private Syrian Airline, Cham Airlines, had agreed, in principle, to establishing direct flights to Minsk from Damascus at the beginning of March, even though the majority of passengers would most likely have only purchased outbound tickets within the package created. Financial compensation for potentially an almost empty inbound flight back to Damascus had been agreed by Cham with the Belarussian Authorities on the basis of fortnightly flights. Similarly, the Ministry of Foreign Affairs had agreed to the provision of seven day extended transit visas for each refugee from Syria, Iraq, Kurdistan, Yemen, and even Afghanistan subject to an inclusive consular and service fee of US$400 per tourist visa. Application documentation had also been simplified requiring only completion of a one page application, a passport sized photograph, and details of pre-paid accommodation in Minsk with a guaranteed five day turnaround by the Ministry.

Oleg had been very careful to ensure Belarus remained front and centre in the entire matter with no chance of a publicity blowback on the Russian Federation for weaponising the plight of desperate refugees. This distraction had politically to be owned by Belarus. Minsk's GRU office, with the full compliance of President Lukashenko, had also negotiated specific reciprocal direct flights between Belavia and Turkish Airlines in respect of Istanbul International and Minsk airports for the spring. This would provide the additional loading capacity for what was envisaged as ever increasing demand. Iraqi Airlines had also been approached for flights into Istanbul International along similar lines to Cham Airlines. Thus his expectation was that by early summer, with also direct flights to Minsk anticipated from Erbil, word would be spreading in Aleppo, Damascus, Idlib, and Raqqa that the easiest and fastest way to reach the European Union was a flight to Belarus.

The refugees on the first Cham Airlines flight would be bussed to various hotels for at least one or two nights before being taken to Belarus's borders with Latvia, Lithuania, and Poland. Human Trafficking Smugglers would act as guides not only in successfully leading their charges across the border but also delivering them into Germany before abandoning the refugees to claim asylum. The extra cost of US $1000 would be paid to the smugglers by the Belarussian handlers as to 50% initially & the balance on their return after safe delivery into Germany.

Oleg expected possibly some 70% or more might be picked up and arrested by the various countries border patrols or whilst heading towards Germany. Nevertheless, those few, who did reach Germany, would via instagram and snapchat messaging to family and friends back in refugee camps remove any remaining doubts and suspicions about the viability of this new migration route. The tsunami of refugees arriving in Minsk would then begin.

'Word of mouth' alone would not be sufficient on its own to create sufficient demand for such a deluge of humanity to arrive on the European Union's northern border. Human greed to profit for a piece of the US$3500 in cash paid by each desperate refugee had to be brought into play. Syrian Intelligence Officers would begin briefing travel agents across the Middle East just before the start of the Eid Festival (Ramadan) and known traffickers of this profit opportunity. Both parties will have been working with many people for months if not longer looking for any alternatives to enter successfully the Eurozone without the need for a Schengen visa. It would not take long for the word to be out Belarus was issuing visas.

All the airline carriers had been briefed as to their initial response to any complaint from the European Union. If a passenger has a valid passport and visa how are they to distinguish between a valid tourist and a prospective migrant? The thought brought a smile to Oleg's face.

It was highly likely the ingenuity of travel agents once alerted from Lebanon to Dubai will find flights to reach Belarus given so many are still prepared to make the perilous journey into the unknown. When the experience of living in refugee camps in Lebanon and elsewhere is often far worse than the destruction and disruption suffered to their previous lives, who would not take an opportunity to escape such despair and poverty proffered by Belarus? Would it be human trafficking as it was simply a ploy to achieve a wider political objective for Russia? Clearly 'Yes,' thought Oleg. However, people, fleeing wars and poverty, will simply never stop finding other ways to reach Europe. For those very few who seek asylum and achieve it, maybe there is the slightest mitigation in what he had deviously concocted against the weak and vulnerable for his President.

During February, Radek was put to work in the mill removing logs that had been naturally and systematically drying under cover into a kiln to complete the process. The work was physically demanding and by early March he was once more fully fit with his Christmas sabbatical in Niepolomice a distant memory. His early morning runs had also enabled him to gain a working knowledge of the immediate area around the mill for six or so kilometres in any direction. Running through the woods, his only company were the forest animals albeit on sighting wild boar he gave them a wide berth apart from looking for a climbable tree. When Radek was not drying timber, his duties revolve around stacking cut planks using one of Eryk's fork lifts or bringing trunks to other machines to strip the bark prior to cutting.

His weekly wages were paid, in Belarussian roubles, was the equivalent of US$80 as his accommodation and meals were provided. This was all part of establishing, in addition to his daily work, the cover story for *'Sergey Antonovich Petrov'* as fact.

At the end of the month, an OMON Police Unit arrived in a Lada Largus at the Mill. Radek could see that he was about to be interviewed. Eryk was talking to two of the policemen who had stepped out of the Lada. His gestures plus the officers' looks in his direction made that abundantly clear. Eryk had forewarned Radek that from time to time he should expect to see unannounced Police visitors and he should not be surprised if his living quarters were searched. This would test the strength of Colonel Pawlukowicz's cover story as the final two OMON officers emerged from the Lada. Radek reminded himself that he was a drifter of no fixed abode with only a secondary education – he had to stay in character and not raise any 'red' flags with the police.

Radek carried on moving logs on a fork lift as the officers approached. Eryk deliberately turned back to organising the turning of cut oak beams seemingly oblivious to whatever OMON's interest in *'Sergey Antonovich Petrov'* might be.

OMON 1: You, Petrov, here now
[Radek vaguely heard something through his ear defenders but the sound of the diesel engine made it indecipherable. He decided to carry on placing the beech planks as his back was only visible to the approaching officers]
OMON 1: Petrov *[shouted but with all the other mill noises including a local radio station being played through a tannoy system his voice was drowned out]*
OMON 2: *[having walked in between the drying wood stacks of planks now faced Radek on the turning forklift making a neck cutting gesture with his right hand across his throat. Radek turned off the diesel machine, removed his ear defenders, and stepped down from the forklift facing the other three police officers]*
OMON 1: Identity Card
[As Radek pulled out his wallet, he could sense eight eyes watching his every move as he removed the card handing it to OMON 1]
OMON 1: You are a long way from home Sergey?

[Radek did not respond keeping his body still and face unchanged – a look that was neither defiant nor subservient more the pose of a vagrant who has been stopped and questioned many times]
OMON 1: *[handed Radek's (or rather Sergey's) identity card to OMON 4 who went back to the Lada to check the details including access to an up to date crime-sheet if there was one and a crosscheck to the current 'wanted' list of criminals and politicos]*
OMON 3: Take us to your cabin Sergey
[Radek led the three officers to his cabin noting this was not a request and remembering Eryk's words, if OMON visit, rather than the para-military police, you will feel the underlying menace of their presence. They can kill you without blinking and suffering no consequences – maybe even receiving a commendation from their superiors]
OMON 2: *[picking up his backpack emptied the entire contents onto the floor then kicked them around with his snow and mud covered boots]*
OMON 1 & 3: *[proceeded to trample over his clothes as they tossed the entire cabin looking for anything incriminating. Even his drying washing was unceremoniously dumped onto the floor as his bed was stripped and mattress turned. It was a humiliating experience for anyone, even a real 'Sergey']*
OMON 4: You have been stopped before and jailed overnight for vagrancy Petrov
Radek: Yes
OMON 4: This dump must be a pleasant change after sleeping rough in parks, underground pedestrian passageways, and multi-storey car parks
Radek: Yes
OMON 1: Let's stop wasting our time on society's dross

With that, the police left the shambles of the cabin and left as quickly as they had arrived.

Radek closed the cabin door and walked back to forklift resisting any temptation to glance at the departing police. He had reacted impassively to OMON's provocative style as any vagrant would. Being hassled by authority is an occupational hazard for such people. 'Sergey' would have learnt long ago that mouthy comments or objections would only result in a severe beating. He was resigned to being defenceless against such authority.

Nevertheless, the interview had served its purpose. He was now entered onto the central computer by one of the OMON team as living and working at the Shevchenko Mills. This would mean the authorities would expect to come across him in the forests as he was ostensibly there working for either Mill. The secret compartment containing the glock and suppressor, cartridge clips, combat knife, and most importantly his satellite encrypted communication gear remained just that - hidden.

Shortly after OMON's visit, Eryk began to educate Radek on the landscape of each forest. Whilst, in both cases, some 95% of the surface area was covered by trees of various varieties, the remainder comprised of abandoned fields, meadows, some tracks, wastelands, flowing streams and standing water. Eryk was an excellent tutor as Radek began to understand how the differing soil conditions would decide where specific tree varieties would be found. 50% of the forests were home to Norway spruce and Scots pine evergreens with deciduous species of black alder, beech, oak, birch, Norway maple, poplar, and elms contributing to the special natural habitat. Eryk would normally lead off on a quad bike with Radek trying to keep up on his machine. Both men would have chainsaws, axes, rope, and chains strapped on the rear of the bikes plus also when Mrs Shevchenko's larder needed filling with meat, hunting rifles across their shoulders. Radek knew from his days hunting with his father that roe deer meat was simply the best. Lean, fat free and delicious to taste, his mother's venison winter stews bore witness to such a statement. Whilst bison moose red deer would generally move away, wildcats and wolves were not so accommodating. The noise of a quad bike would generally scare animals away unless they were all protecting their young. There was talk that brown bears were once more moving around the forest but so far Eryk had seen no tracks to support alleged sightings.

By mid-April Radek was a familiar sight in both the Mills and forests more often than not working alone. Police at temporary checkpoints would wave him through and the occasional roaming military forest patrols were more likely to enjoy a cigarette with him. His cover was firmly established.

Russian and Belarussian GRU handlers began the process of dealing with the first exploratory flights from Damascus and Erbil to Minsk. Some two hundred mainly Syrian and Iraqi refugees were directed from the plane towards the five empty buses standing on the airport tarmac. The buses then took the people who were predominantly male to a variety of one star or less Minsk hotels for their first night in Belarus.

The following morning the migrants re-boarded the buses that then split up heading for villages close to the Latvian (one bus), Lithuanian (two buses), and Polish (two buses) borders. Over the next six nights, migrants were shepherded across the border in groups of six or seven by local smugglers and Belarussian Police Officers. The migrants were accommodated in barns and farm sheds with minimal facilities if any. Their quest to re-settle in Western Europe, particularly Germany, where some already had relatives, and the United Kingdom, had become one driven out of despair rather than hope of a better life. The Migrants unease was heightened by the Belarussian overseers treating them more like cattle than human beings.

Latvia's 130 kilometre boundary with Belarus had no hard border so it was a case of avoiding the regular Latvian Border patrols. Lithuania's 679 kilometre border was not much better than Latvia's with both being sieve-like. Poland's was slightly better but again there was no hard border along much of its 418 kilometre length some of which passed through dense forest like Białowieża, the last primeval forest in Europe and a national park spread across the border of Poland and Belarus.

Radek had begun to question why and for what his masters in ABW had sent him undercover here. Surely, his time with Eryk was not to turn him into a woodsman or smuggler. Eryk had though been approached by officers of either the Belarussian or Russian GRU to smuggle some people into Poland. However, with his wife about to go into hospital, he was able to turn aside the approach without raising any suspicion by such agencies.

Nevertheless, this alerted Radek that his daytimes in the forests would soon turn into nights watching and reporting such movements without being discovered.

It was mid-afternoon. Radek had felled a large Norway spruce in the Białowieża Forest and was in the process of lopping off all the branches to reveal the trunk. Enjoying a mug of warming soup from his thermos flask and finishing the remaining ham roll from his lunchbox, he sensed the approach of people. Turning towards the increasing sound of human voices, he saw military uniforms, a gaggle of civilians who were clearly not Europeans, and a presumably a local Belarussian who was in the lead.

Showing complete disinterest, he finished his snack sat on the felled spruce's trunk and as the group came closer, lit a cigarette.

'Privet Sergey' called out one of Belarussian Border Police forcing him to turn as the somewhat breathless group arrived. Walking around or over fallen trees with spring undergrowth and brambles did not make for speedy progress. Although the Belarussian forest guide and Border Police were still relatively fresh, their charges were not in such good shape. There was no short cut around a seventeen kilometre hike across this terrain that was made worse for the migrants simply because of their clothing. Track suits and trainers were simply inappropriate. Radek felt more than a moment of remorse as he looked at the six refugees with so reminiscent of the faces he had seen in Idlib camps less than six months ago.

As he offered the Border Police and guide cigarettes from his packet of Java Gold, Radek knew that he needed to ask some questions without arising any suspicion.

Nodding in the direction of the migrants who unsurprisingly looked pretty depressed, began to seek some answers.

'Who are that lot?'
'What is it to you Sergey?'
'Absolutely nothing but they looked completely knackered'
'What do you expect from Iraqi and Syrian refugees?'
'Well they are hardly wearing the right gear for crossing this forest.'
'I told you Gennady – Sergey's right' interrupted the Guide. 'We are not a branch of GUM! We are just tasked to make sure you deliver our charges to a waiting vehicle on the map (as he tapped a pocket on his military cargo pants) and not directly into the hands of the Polish Border Guards.'
'I thought you had arranged for their attention to be diverted elsewhere' uttered the Guide stubbing out his cigarette.
'You are being well paid so you stick to your job and my colleagues will do theirs.'

The conversation was over and the group moved off with dusk some hours away.

Latvian, Lithuania, and Polish Interior Ministries were receiving daily reports from their respective Border Guards of migrants seeking asylum.

A week later, Colonel Pawlukowicz was looking at a copy of an Interior Ministry Weekly analysis. The migrants were predominantly Iraqi and Syrians whereas in earlier weeks the make-up was Belarussians, Russians, and the occasional Afghan. Every Border Patrol seemed, as he read the detail, to have almost been fed the migrants by some unseen hand. The result was then the Border Patrols were overwhelmed time-wise delivering and processing the captured illegal entrants to Refugee and Migration Centres. In the days covered by the report, Kuba also noticed from the separate Podlaskie, Lublin, and Masovian regions' migrant filings, police had seemingly found themselves arresting migrants in Białystok and Lublin together with small villages closer to the Belarussian border where again tired, dishevelled, cold, and hungry refugees had surrendered to local villagers. Was this a deliberate distraction of the Border Force to hide something else or was the sheer weight of numbers crossing illegally highlighting a resource issue he wondered?

Kuba also had the benefit of Radek's Report dealing with the chance meeting in the Białowieża Forest over a week ago. Unlike his previous undercover reports that simply said 'Nothing to report', this was different.

Monday 26th April 2021
Contact timed at 15:50 hours Moscow Standard Time
Encrypted Message

Six males, four being Syrian and probable two Iraqis (maybe Kurds) from listening to their arabic, were being guided through the Białowieża Forest by a local smuggler. They were, I consider, being escorted by two GRU Russian Special forces from their accents initially but possibly more from their general attitude towards the guide. What is more the rendezvous on the Polish side was to a waiting vehicle indicating that further assisted travel was involved. Later, in the early hours, I position myself close to where I had encountered this group only to see unobserved the smuggler and GRU soldiers returning alone. From my recent time in Northern Syria refugee camps, the talk was always about Germany as the preferred destination. Hence it might be a reasonable assumption that this was the refugees' final destination. I am unaware whether or not other migrants from Syria/Iraq have as yet been crossing the border. It is strange to see GRU personnel shepherding six dishevelled refugees to a waiting vehicle unless delivery to their ultimate destination had specific relevance.

This is still a puzzle to solve Kuba thought as he lifted his telephone handset to dictate Radek's orders.

'Please spend more time in the locale of Damačava and its forest observing but retaining your cover'.

When Radek asked if he could spend more time legitimately in the forest closer to the other Shevchenko mill, Eryk was very accommodating. It fitted with the spring marking of trees by foresters as suitable for felling. His current mill foreman could not defer his mandatory military eighteen month military service any longer. As a result of the May conscription for all males between eighteen and twenty seven, he was already undergoing basic training at the Hrodno military base. Radek knew enough to temporarily fulfil the foreman's role whilst Eryk searched for a replacement so it worked for both men.

The only immediate drawback was moving his communications gear in daylight but Eryk took care of that problem amongst a delivery of spruce planking.

Whilst Radek would clearly miss Mrs Shevchenko's lunchboxes and ready-made dinners for the microwave, the local Damačava cafes and bakery would, as things turned out later, proved almost better than his observations and surveillance exercises.

During May, Radek was often on one of the sawmill's Minsk dirt bikes during the day seeking out where particular stands of tree varieties had been marked for felling. This gave him the ideal opportunity to learn the various trails throughout the entire forest. As the weeks passed, he came across increasingly larger and larger groups of migrants being shepherded by Belarussian Police and its GRU officers towards the Polish border as dusk was falling. On one such outing as he returned to ride on tarmac back to the Shevchenko Damačava sawmill, Radek noticed activity a large warehouse. It had previously had a much weathered 'To let' board and according to Eryk had been vacant since it was built - 'another unnecessary investment built by the State with Chinese money' was his cynical commentary as they passed. Yet now the sign had gone. Men in military uniforms were unloading trucks containing hundreds of palliasses. These items were being hurriedly carried inside the warehouse through many of its loading bays. What were the Belarussians up to thought Radek as he slowed the motorcycle for a delivery truck to exit.

During the next week, whether passing the warehouse on either a dirt bike, quad bike, or truck, he saw buses full of middle eastern men disembarking and going inside the warehouse. It was reasonable to assume Radek thought that the majority were Syrians and Iraqis.

Kuba Pawlukowicz read the report from ABW's undercover agent at Minsk International Airport. The man was a baggage handler and thus ideally positioned to report unusual activity.

From mid-June he had reported daily flights were arriving for the very first time from Basra, Damascus, and Erbil. The passengers were off-loaded from the planes directly onto assembled buses on the tarmac without entering the terminal building.

Kuba then re-read Radek latest report concerning the apparent housing of large numbers of middle-eastern people being mainly men but with some women and young babies - time to report to Lieutenant-General Politczek.

Grzegorz waved Colonel Pawlukowicz to enter leaving Colonel Hanko's report on his desk making his way towards an armchair. Her analytical report on the recent diversion of a regular commercial Ryanair flight between Athens and Vilnius whilst in Belarussian airspace would have to wait.

'Well Kuba what is so important before I have even had time for my second coffee of the morning'.

'General, we have been seeing increasing numbers of illegal refugees entering Poland from Belarus. A large number have been detained by our Border Guard but even with recent arrests in Germany, it is clear a number have avoided our security. From reports from Major Król and Minsk 'eyes', I am convinced our border is about to be subjected to a major attempt for 'illegals' to cross our borders by sheer weight of numbers, thereby overloading our existing Border Posts and limited physical fencing'.

'Well Kuba it looks as if the Interior Minister and Poland has run out of time'.

'What makes you say that General?

'The Minister has in principle agreement I believe to begin construction of a temporary two and half metre-high, razor-wire-topped fence where the border protection is at its weakest, particular in the forested areas. However, I suspect it will be late summer before any construction can start. The Border Guard Agency has already tabled a formal request for a permanent fence of some five and a half metres high to be equipped with cameras and motion detectors, among other things. The cost is likely to be in excess of €350 million to build. Understandably, the Government believes that the cost of protecting our eastern border, yet also the Schengen Area's northern one, is not only Poland's burden but also the European Union's as a whole. In my view, it will thus be late autumn before Legislators in the Sejm can gain parliamentary approval to a suitable proposal. In the interim, we are going to face major disruption along our northern border into 2022. Any thoughts on what I should be advising the Government to be doing in the interim Kuba?'

'The shared border with Belarus runs along only the administrative borders of the Podlaskie and Lubelskie voivodships with the Grodno and Brest regions on the Belarusian side. The Border Agency will require Military support and an exclusion zone for ten kilometres. We will be dealing with 'illegal migrants' whose displaced status from the Syrian, Daish, Iraq or other wars has been weaponised by Belarus. Hence, we need a new law or some formal authority. Any foreigner, after crossing the Polish border illegally, will be obliged, using force if necessary, to leave Polish territory. Waving a completed asylum application should not deter either the Border Guards or Army from pushing illegal entrants back into Belarus. It is difficult to see how their life and freedom has been threatened rather they have become political pawns. An exclusion zone is very important as 'Human Rights' groups and other humanitarian organisations will disrupt what will become a military operation and encourage migrants to keep attempting to cross our border. There will need to be a prohibition against access to all media and non-residents. If you are right about the timing of a permanent fence, the winter months will make our treatment of these political footballs seemingly inhuman for a democratic country. The United Nations Refugee Agency (UNHCR), along with others, will undoubtedly demand, as months pass, that we provide medical assistance and shelter. However, we have to face the reality. In my view, the Government has to be ready to issue a State of Emergency over the Podlaskie and Lubelskie voivodships. Additionally, the Ministry of Defence must allocate and send sufficient troops to support the Border Guard including the establishment of checkpoints on all roads and tracks leading into and out of such an exclusion zone'.

'Do you believe Belarus is deliberately orchestrating this influx in retaliation against European Union sanctions over Lukashenko's disputed Presidential Election last August and the subsequent crackdown on dissent before and after voting or something else'.

'General, I believe, after Lukashenko's somewhat miraculous survival, that whatever happens now within Belarus is controlled and directed by Vladimir Putin and his regime'.

'Kuba – please put your thoughts into a suitable paper that I can present at my regular monthly meeting tomorrow with the Prime Minister. Oh, and pull Radek Król out of Belarus, his job is done'.

Chapter 7

Grzegorz returned to his desk and Witoria Hanko's report.

On May 23rd, a Ryanair Boeing 737-800 (Flight 4978-Athens to Vilnius), operated by the Polish subsidiary Buzz, carrying six crew members and one hundred and twenty six passengers, was diverted to Minsk National Airport. The aircraft had entered Belarussian airspace at 12:30 hours local time when its Air Traffic Control (ATC) told the pilots at 12:33 hours there was a security situation with reports of a bomb being on board. The Boeing was 45 nautical miles (eighty three kilometres) south of Vilnius and 90 nautical miles (one hundred and seventy kilometres) west of Minsk, albeit in Belarusian airspace. Nevertheless, the pilots were instructed to divert to Minsk.

The device was, according to ATC, set to detonate when the plane entered Lithuanian airspace.

When the Investigation Team of the International Civil Aviation Organization checked the server, it found the email notification had been sent at 12:56 hours, some 23 minutes later, and it mentioned only that the device would explode over Vilnius. Yet the Department of Aviation of Belarus claimed that the email was received in the generic mailbox at 12:25 hour's local time and yet ATC still insisted the plane should be diverted to Minsk even though a Lithuanian airfield was closer.

We, Hamas soldiers, demand that Israel cease fire in the Gaza Strip. We demand that the European Union abandon its support for Israel in this war. We know that the participants of Delphi Economic Forum are returning home on May 23 via flight FR4978. A bomb was planted onto this aircraft. If you don't meet our demands the bomb will explode on May 23 over Vilnius. Allahu Akbar

This message was sent separately to the airports of Lithuania, Athens, Sofia, Bucharest, Kyiv and Minsk, with the first five sent while the Boeing was flying over Ukrainian airspace and immediately prior to entering Belarussian airspace.

Lithuanian Authorities confirmed, immediately prior to the plane's diversion, the details of a recorded telephone conversation timed at 12:34 hours. The Belarussian ATC had advised an altercation between passengers and a member of the cabin crew had forced the pilots to request permission for an emergency landing at Minsk somewhat in contradiction of the earlier and purported mail from Hamas.

Upon landing in Minsk, the Belarussian opposition activist Roman Protasevich was removed from the aircraft together with his girlfriend, Sofia Sapega, a Russian citizen. There was apparently no explanation as they were removed from the plane then the remaining passengers were allowed to disembark. Protasevich and Sapega were led off the plane by OMON police officers with two other passengers bringing up the rear.

Having used ABW's facial recognition software on all boarding passengers at Athens, Major Sergei Ogarkov and Kapitán Nikolay Anishin were identified as members of Russia's GRU Intelligence Service. When the Ryanair boarding passenger manifest was checked, neither Ogarkov's nor Anishin's names were identified. There was an early assumption that these individuals were undercover Belarussian KGB officers travelling under pseudonyms and fake passports. The presence of these GRU operatives who have identified in previous kidnappings means either a joint operation with Belarus or Moscow's hand was behind the entire orchestrated diversion to Minsk.

Passenger reports taken by Lithuania's State Security Department (VSD - *Valstybės saugumo departamentas*), when the Boeing landed some eight hours later, all made the same comment. Belarusian security officers at Minsk airport made a great show of searching for an explosive device with Bomb Disposal personnel both inside and outside the aircraft with the hold luggage being unloaded and checked. Similarly, earlier reports that MIG fighter jets were scrambled and escorted the Boeing to Minsk were untrue. No passenger, crew, or pilot mentioned in any of the VSD interviews seeing such warplanes at any time whilst in Belarus airspace.

Protasevich, a Belarussian citizen, faces charges of being behind civil disturbances that followed Lukashenko's a disputed re-election in August 2020. He was a key administrator of the Telegram channel Nexta-Live that covered the mass protests denouncing the official results of the election. Protasevich is listed as a wanted terrorist and faces if sentenced to fifteen years. Sapega, a Russian citizen, edits a Telegram channel, the Black Book of Belarus. It has published Belarussian security officials' personal information and the channel has been designated an extremist group. At this moment the charges she was arrested for are unclear. Sapega has, it would seem, been caught in a political battle as Belarussian security forces targeted her boyfriend, Protasevich, for his activities. After what appeared to be video confessions obtained by the Belarus authorities under duress, Protasevich and Sapega were moved from the prisons where they were being held to house arrest together on June 25th.

In summary, this was a message to all perceived enemies of the greater state that now includes Belarus that they can and will be hunted down. It is very reminiscent of the attempt in August 2020 on Alexei Navalny's life with Novichok in being a further indication of a wider policy to erase the prospect of any political dissent in or outside today's Russia aided by its aggressive 'Foreign Agent legislation'.

Grzegorz put down the report and walked over to look across Warsaw. Hanko's last words echoed inside his brain 'to erase the prospect of any political dissent' for what grand purpose Mr Putin?

Pouring himself a coffee, he then pushed a button on the desk handset 'Pawel please ask Colonel Hanko to come and see me as soon as she is free'. He walked back to once more deep in thought gazing across Warsaw whilst sipping his third coffee of the morning.

'Witoria, remind me about President Putin's use 'Foreign Agent' legislation to silence independent news and opinion in today's Russia'.

'General, the legislation was introduced to counter threats to National Security from political activity. According to the Russian Government being designated a 'Foreign Agent' does not prevent freedom of speech and merely ensures transparency about who is speaking. The regulations have a strong chilling and silencing effect on the entire panoply of independent media. For example, failure to highlight such designated 'Foreign Agent' status by the authorities when quoting such organizations and individuals in any broadcast or publication results in high financial fines by Roscomnadzor *(federal executive body responsible for control, censorship, and supervision in the field of media, including electronic media and mass communications)*; similarly even omitting a legal disclaimer on a social media share of someone else's post has the same financial penalty.

Criteria for the designation are extremely broad and vague, from actually receiving foreign grants to participation in an international conference with accommodation at the expense of the organizer to a gift from friends or relatives living abroad or even transfer of your own funds from an account in foreign currency.

Non-profit organizations can be declared a 'Foreign Agent' if they participate in political activity in Russia and receives funding from foreign sources. Political activity is defined as any influence to public opinion and public policy. During any legal proceedings a person or business distributing printed, audio, or audio-visual materials can be declared as performing the functions of a 'Foreign Agent' even in the absence of representation in Russia. As for individuals, political activity by Russian citizens, foreign citizens and stateless persons can also be designated a 'Foreign Agent'.

Several prominent international organizations have been targeted, including Amnesty International, Human Rights Watch, and Transparency International including having documents seized during office searches. According to our records more than 60 organizations in 16 Russian regions have been subjected to this process. Raids conducted often with photo-journalists who subsequently air programs accusing opposition activists of pushing the interests of the West.

Meduza, a Latvian media outlet, publishes materials on its website in Russian and English. Two months ago, the Russian Ministry of Justice designated Meduza as foreign media performing the functions of a 'Foreign Agent'. It should be noted Meduza does not have branches or representative offices in Russia.

This 'Foreign Agent' legislation has been part of Kremlin's war to remove any opposition to Vladimir Putin's regime in the written and verbal media. It cannot be looked at in isolation.

Boris Nemtsov's political assassination in February 2015 on the Bolshoy Moskvoretsky Bridge as he crossed the Moskva River should have been the warning to the West of a revanchist Putin. Nemtsov was a fierce critic of the Kremlin's increasingly authoritarian and undemocratic regime while also exposing the widespread US$30 billion embezzlement and profiteering ahead of the Sochi Olympics. He had also previously published in depth reports detailing the corruption and cronyism that only led directly to Putin. Nevertheless, his harshest and most vociferous criticism was for Russian political interference and military involvement in

Ukraine including the 2014 annexation of the Crimean Peninsula. Nemtsov was working on a report demonstrating that Russian troops were fighting alongside pro-Russian rebels in eastern Ukraine, which the Kremlin had been denying immediately prior to his death and is still doing so. As part of that political struggle, Nemtsov was in Moscow to participate in a rally against the Russian military intervention in Ukraine the following week. Whilst a group of Chechens were found guilty, the question of who gave the order is still an open question for some. However, the poisoning of Alexander Litvinenko in 2006 was judged a killing by the Russian State to silence another highly vocal critic of the endemic corruption within Putin and his regime.

No conversation about opposition to Putin's Regime and its methodical silencing of any criticism would be incomplete without mentioning Alexei Navalny.

In 2011, Navalny christened Vladimir Putin's United Russia political party as 'a party of crooks and thieves'. He founded the Russia of the Future as a political party and the Anti-corruption Foundation. Navalny was the face of the liberal opposition. Detailing corruption on social media channels led to nationwide protests against Putin's rule. However, two trumped up embezzlement charges, considered by the European Court of Human Rights to have abused Navalny's rights for fair trials, enabled the Central Election Commission to rule out his candidacy for the 2018 Presidential Election on the grounds of those prior criminal convictions. The same playbook was of course used by Lukashenko in his Election last year to disqualify any credible opposition candidate running even before ballot tampering.

On August 20th 2020, Navalny was of course hospitalised in serious condition in Omsk after being poisoned on a flight from Tomsk to Moscow. He was medically evacuated by air to the Charité Berlin Hospital on August 24th. On September 2nd, the German government announced that Navalny had been poisoned with a Novichok nerve agent, from the same family of nerve agents that were used to poison Sergei Skripal and his daughter. As a result of this 'unequivocal proof' from toxicology tests, the Russian government was again asked for an explanation only to be met with silence. Navalny accused Putin of being responsible for his poisoning and a subsequent investigation implicated agents from the Federal Security Service (FSB).

On January 17th this year, Navalny returned to Russia and was detained immediately on accusations of violating his parole. Conditions imposed as a result of his 2014 conviction because he had failed to report to Russia's Federal Prison Service (FSIN) twice per month during his illness. Amnesty International has unsurprisingly heralded Alexei Navalny as a prisoner of conscience. Following his arrest, the release of the documentary 'Putin's Palace' accusing Putin of corruption resulted in mass protests across Russia. On February 2nd, his suspended sentence was replaced with a prison sentence of over two and half years' detention in a corrective labour colony in Vladimir Region. While in prison, Navalny and human rights groups have accused Russian authorities of using torture against him and his life being under threat.

Navalny's Anti-Corruption Foundation has been added unsurprisingly to the Justice Ministry's list of 'Foreign Agents'. The die was cast for its closure back in 2019. At issue was a video containing allegations that a service supplier to kindergartens and schools had not complied with sanitary standards, forged documents, and delivered poor-quality food. A lawsuit filed by the service provider, a food company associated with businessman Yevgeny Prigozhin, a close associate of Russian President Vladimir Putin, obtained damages against the Anti-corruption Foundation of US$1.2 million. This crippling fine forced the closure of the Foundation and its many offices across Russia

Foreign Agent' legislation is needed to protect Russia's Autocracy as far as the Regime is concerned from foreign meddling and to silence any opposition.'

Grzegorz lit a cigarette and then stood to pour Colonel Hanko & himself a coffee. Putting the cup in front of Wiktoria, he walked to look once more across Warsaw.

'Would it be fair to say freedom of speech and information within Russia has been and is being methodically muzzled since Putin's rise to power?'

'Yes General. Perhaps Navalny's remark prior to his poisoning throws us a warning *…it is difficult for me to understand exactly what is going on in Putin's mind. 20 years of power would spoil anyone and make them crazy. He thinks he can do whatever he wants…*'

'Colonel, what do you foresee over the coming months?'

'The Russian Duma has consistently, at Putin's clear bidding, strengthened through amendments the 'Foreign Agent' legislation. There is a clear direction of travel. It is expanding the application of this law to the remaining few entities and individuals voicing an alternative or opposite view to the Regime's and State Media's pronouncements. Criminal sanctions will be significantly raised for non-compliance with these regulations making even the minimal free exercise of the civil and political rights impossible. However, Putin's Russia has hardly been a democracy since he rose to power. The stigma of the 'Foreign Agent' designation will be used to ban individuals from entering public service and forcing employers neither to retain nor hire such designated persons. Increasingly criminal prosecutions leading to the deprivation of liberty or threat of such action against journalists of the very few remaining independent television and radio channels will force ultimately their closure. This growing crackdown on independent media has the chilling and hidden effect of driving away advertisers, who make such media financially viable, because of increasing legal troubles with the government if not also being classified as a 'Foreign Agent'. Access to advertising revenue from many such companies in Russia will evaporate fearing a backlash for affiliating with someone perceived and unfairly tarnished as working for the enemy. There is no good outcome here General. The country today is being run by the graduates of the Soviet Union's most feared and hated political police, the KGB.'

Chapter 8

Grzegorz walked through the marble entrance hall to the Chancellery on Avenue Ujazdowskie. The building houses the Polish Government including Ministerial and Administrative offices. His appointment with the Prime Minister had been hastily arranged earlier that afternoon by the PM's Chief of Staff.

Following the Deputy Chief of Staff down a long corridor, he wondered what had caused not only the need for this meeting but also his presence.

Entering the Prime Minister's conference room, Grzegorz realised he was the last to arrive, nodded to the Prime Minister, and took the remaining seat at the table. He recognised everyone from the Ministers of Defence, Interior, and Special Forces to the Minister of Foreign Affairs and the Generals commanding the Army and Air Force.

'Gentlemen, Afghanistan. Our American friends still believe the Afghan National Defence Security Forces (ANDSF) will protect the withdrawal of any remaining Polish citizens including those Afghan nationals who have worked with us over the last twenty years, together of course with their families. They are simply wrong. We are going to face major territorial gains in the coming days and weeks by the Taliban as the ANDSF retreats without in all probability even putting up a fight. This will make the capture of Kabul by mid to late August a certainty and hence we need to act with far greater urgency if we are not to be too late evacuating our own people and indeed our friends in need.'

The Minister of Defence, having summarised this latest intelligence assessment, went on to remind his audience of today's reality.

'The widespread corruption in Afghanistan's defence and interior ministries enables funds for pay, ammunition and food deliveries to be stolen well before reaching the soldiers on the ground. Far too many commanders embezzle money by submitting fund requests for the salaries of fictitious soldiers while actual military personnel are kept unpaid and on duty without permission to leave and see their families for months. Unsurprisingly, the ANDSF has one of the highest desertion rates in the world – an attrition rate per month in the thousands while recruitment rate is in the mid-hundreds. Such embezzlement and corruption has only undermined and sapped morale within the ranks of the army. For unpaid soldiers, the Taliban's offers of amnesty instead of fighting and dying will only lead to a strong preference to save their lives by surrendering. It is no surprise there is deep mistrust towards the country's political leadership. These doubts and suspicions will only further undermine the Afghan soldiers' resolve to resist the advance of the ideologically cohesive Taliban seeking to drive out occupying foreign troops. The ANDSF has clearly no sense of national duty and belonging. When factoring in the continuous political interference and reshuffling of office holders as high as interior and defence ministers, governors and police chiefs, this can only adversely affect battlefield performance. An army needs unity of command and leadership continuity to function properly and fight effectively.'

Silence fell across the room only to be broken by the Prime Minister's voice 'Before you ask, we have of course shared our assessment with NATO. However, I am not prepared to wait for other Intelligence Agencies to gradually reach the same assessment, we do not have the time and we need to act decisively if our exit from Afghanistan is not going to appear as equally shambolic as the United States telegraphed withdrawal is potentially looking.'

The Minister of Special Forces looked across the table 'Grzegorz your thoughts?'

'We should deploy sufficient GROM teams to ensure our countrymen and women are safely brought back to Poland together with those Afghans, and thus their families, who have fought alongside us as translators or served in other capacities. Quite how we fly people out will be an issue. The Americans' decision to hand over Bagram Air base or should I say vacate it last week with literally zero notice is still something I find incredulous.'

'General I will leave you to liaise with my Chief of Staff to make it happen. Now, Gentlemen I want your thoughts on President Putin's essay on the Historical Unity of Russians and Ukrainians, Foreign Minister.'

'Throughout the past seven years of undeclared war between Russia and Ukraine, Putin has reiterated his frequently voiced conviction that Russians and Ukrainians are 'one people' blaming the current collapse in their bilateral ties on foreign plots and anti-Russian conspiracies. Nevertheless, when he openly questions the legitimacy of Ukraine's borders and argues dubiously that much of modern-day Ukraine occupies historically Russian lands, I am very concerned his appetite for further annexation of Ukrainian territory remains unsatisfied. When Putin also declares Ukrainian statehood depends on Moscow's consent and the true sovereignty of Ukraine is possible only in partnership with Russia, my reading is the threat of a Russian Invasion at some point in the next 12 months is real.'

'Whilst being a masterclass in disinformation and blurring of history to support his viewpoint, it is one short step from declaring War - perhaps it is Putin's final ultimatum to President Zelensky airing his perceived grievances in this way. Yet Russia continues to occupy Ukraine's Crimean peninsula and much of the industrial Donbass region in eastern Ukraine in breach of International Law. Belarus and Russia armies are shortly to begin joint military drills and exercises. This autumn Russia will be conducting its quadrennial 'Zapad' military exercises. Both provide ideal opportunities to create under the fog of training assembling a large military force on Ukraine's borders to the east and north. Our Intelligence has monitored a steady build-up of ground troops already in excess of thirty thousand within the Crimean Peninsula. Putin is, in my view, preparing the ground for a major invasion. No doubt amongst our NATO allies there will be some who will call us 'Russophobes' but, unhinged or sane, this treatise is what Putin and his regime actually believe. More importantly, the Kremlin is to my mind prepared to use its military might in order to bring all of Ukraine within its 'sphere of influence' – this is scary to think eighty years after WWII we could be facing war on the European Continent.' As the Minister of Defence finished this statement, the Army and Air Force Generals concurred.

After a few moments as the import of what the Minister of Defence had said was gradually being absorbed by all those in the conference room, the Interior Minister began to speak.

'Moscow cannot countenance letting Ukraine either join at some future date NATO or begin the process of becoming part of the European Union. Such ideas pose a direct threat to Putin's imperialism. Our intelligence briefings have for some months indicated that the hawks within his inner circle are known to advocate the use of force. To my mind, Putin is messaging Russian society and its ruling elite that the Kremlin is determined to defend what Russia perceives as its national interests. The anti-Western mood and the image of the state as a 'besieged fortress' are all elements of the same strategic project of enhancing the regime's legitimacy and rebuilding its great-power legacy. Whether or not the West has left it too late to strengthen Zelensky's Government and Ukraine's ability to choose its own future, I do not know. Nevertheless, we must double and redouble our efforts to stop any attempts by Putin and his regime to subjugate Ukraine to their will by dint of arms.'

'Grzegorz you have been very quiet – do you have anything useful to add?'

'Yes Prime Minister. I have been pondering for some months why increasing numbers of Middle East migrants are being flown from Damascus, Erbil, Baghdad, Basra, and Istanbul to

Minsk. Gradually, we have seen increasing numbers reaching our common border with Belarus accompanied by members of the Belarussian Military and Police forces. These soldiers and para-military units have been assisting these predominantly economic migrants to enter our country. It will not be long before we find crossing points like Kuznitsa under siege from thousands of 'would be' asylum seekers. Having read Putin's essay and listened to the Ministers' comments this afternoon, this border issue is a well-planned distraction by Russia's GRU. The intention is for the European Union to be caught in the highly political and contentious spotlight of Migration. Meanwhile Putin will move unseen his 'pawns and knights' into place along Ukraine's borders with invasion as the end objective. Our eyes will be focussed elsewhere just like the United States has been looking towards Asia Pacific and its trade issues with China. The United States April announcement, with minimal prior advice or discussion with ourselves and other NATO allies, to withdraw from Afghanistan let alone the prior US Administration's telegraphing its intentions to the Taliban during the Doha Peace Talks, has left us now with an unnecessary extraction task along with our NATO allies. In my view, this is a humanitarian disaster in the making thanks to ill-considered actions by the United States Government past and present. Again this is an unexpected windfall for Putin with the West focussed on Kabul rather than Ukraine. Internally, ABW has chronicled how Putin has systematically removed outspoken critics over the last twenty years and tightened the screw on the voice of independent media through ever more draconian amendments to its 'Foreign Agent' legislation. When it is daytime and Russia State Television channels tell the populace it is night, eighty per cent of citizens will go to bed. I am not joking. Putin's disinformation messaging is vital to retaining his grip on power and it is just like the days of the USSR - control the narrative.'

'Thank you Ministers' and Generals' for your depressing but accurate assessments of the threats we face from a revanchist Russia and in particular President Putin. Democracy and the entire post WWII rules based order that has kept the peace in Europe for eighty or more years, is without doubt under serious threat. NATO will have to begin quickly bolstering its Eastern flank. Hence the Ministry of Defence along with our Baltic neighbours will need to decide what additional defensive equipment and troop placements we all require. I have a video conference with our Baltic friends in an hour's time. Somehow we must gain the attention of the President Biden, his Secretary of State, and the Pentagon to this threat even though the withdrawal from Kabul has the likelihood of becoming chaotic and highly dangerous for all those involved.'

'Prime Minister could Lieutenant-General Politczek and I request a few minutes of your time as we are here?' asked the Interior Minister as everyone else stood up and began to leave the conference room.

'Minister, the President has agreed in principle to declare a 'State of Emergency' in certain towns and villages along the shared border with Belarus. However, our assessment is that we should be reactive rather than proactive at this point in time. Your request for a ten kilometre exclusion zone from the borders of the Podlaskie and Lubelskie regions with Belarus is more likely to be three kilometres. We should not forget that Belarus is a signatory to the Geneva Convention on Refugees. All refugees and migrants are obliged to submit requests for asylum within Belarus. Such individuals have no right to cross our border without our visa and will if necessary be returned into Belarus territory by Law. Any foreigner, after crossing the Polish border illegally, will be obliged, using force if necessary, to leave Polish territory. Border Guards should be reminded of the legal position if you have not already done so. Similarly, the Ministry of Defence are deploying a battalion of around six hundred soldiers next week to begin patrols along and within the proposed exclusion zone including establishing future checkpoints. Tenders have gone out to selected contractors to erect a new wall along the Belarus border aimed at deterring future illegal refugee crossings that are currently already over a thousand per week. The 5.5-metre-high wall will run along 186 kilometres of the border with a construction start date at the beginning of January and completion by the end of June.'

'Prime Minister, notwithstanding Belarus is weaponising the plight of migrants as political pawns, Human Rights Groups and the United Nations will seek to paint them as victims and Poland as being inhumane.'

'True but we will hold the line - including with our European Union colleagues placing further sanctions on Lukashenko. I have another meeting about to start with the Minister of Health regarding COVID, so please excuse me Gentlemen.' With that the Premier was gone.

The Turkish Airlines Boeing 737-800 turned to make its final approach into Hamid Karzai International Airport. Radek was not alone when he left Warsaw on a scheduled LOT flight into Istanbul. Apart from Master-Sergeant Nowak and their team, Lieutenant-General Politczek had agreed to his request for Captain Filip Cuda together with Master-Sergeant Kacper Stodola together with their GROM unit to be part of the mission. The good news was the Polish Embassy in Kabul had closed back in November 2014 so they would not be faced with diplomatic staff to extract together with their families. In addition, the last of the remaining 340 Polish soldiers in the recent and final rolling deployment had left Afghanistan for Wroclaw at the end of June in accordance with NATO's withdrawal planning.

Yet this return to Afghanistan brought back dark memories for the majority, if not all of Poland's elite Special Forces soldiers on this flight. Rescue mission or not, was Afghanistan worth the lives of 44 Polish soldiers and close to 200 injuries including loss of limbs and sight to their brothers in arms? How does one square the country's 20 year involvement, let alone the other losses incurred by the United States and NATO military, as being a success? Was the price in blood and treasure far too high when Afghanistan seemed to be heading inexorably back to feudal, if not medieval and tribal, times? Radek had no answer nor did his fellow soldiers.

The Ministry of Foreign Affairs had trawled back through its historic Kabul Embassy records via payroll records and staff files to compile a list of Afghans who merited evacuation. However, the issue was clearly whether the listed addresses within Kabul, after such a period of time, were even current. The Defence Ministry had maintained a list of translators who had served directly with its troops whether in combat or more latterly training roles with their last known locations.

There were of course next to the majority of the listings mobile phone numbers but again Radek and Filip wondered how many would prove still to be active. They, and the Master-Sergeants, noticed that particular members of the Afghan National Army's Special Forces (ANASF), who had served with them on patrol hunting down Taliban insurgents, were unaccountably missing. This omission was not down to an oversight by the Polish Government rather the secret nature of GROM's missions where ANASF personnel were never identified by name. Colonel Chmura had reiterated during the mission briefing that their task was for now 'top secret'. The Government was, whilst anticipating a complete breakdown and collapse of the Ashraf Ghani's administration, not prepared by widely publicising this rescue mission to create a self-fulfilling prophecy. The message from the Prime Minister was '... we do not forget about those Afghan allies *(and their families)*, who helped and served Poland, especially when, because of that service, their lives are increasingly now put at risk. We keep our commitments ...' Master-Sergeant Kacper Stodola's briefcase contained blank 'humanitarian visas' already sealed, stamped, & signed by the Consul-General's Office within the Ministry of Foreign Affairs. Nevertheless, their issue was not simply concluded by writing or rather typing in a name. A passport sized photograph had to be added along with a current Afghan passport. Kacper recognised that obtaining passports, whether for an adult or child, from Kabul's Ministry of Interior Affairs in what appeared to be a rapidly destabilising environment, was going to require something more than money.

Billeting twenty professional soldiers was the first challenge as for now they were ostensibly civilians and not seeking to attract attention. The Turkish Airlines plane had landed fortuitously at night with the GROM teams disembarking after all the commercial passengers had left. Major Gul Wazeer of the ANASF was stood on the tarmac. 'Seagull', as he was known by his fellow special forces warriors, had organised housing in the suburban residential area close to the Airport's North Gate entrance to the military zone. In addition, some Toyota Corolla estates and saloons were placed at their disposal. Neither Radek nor Filip nor anyone else asked knew or speculated who was paid or paying for such on the ground resources. The mission was undercover.

Radek made the decision with Filip and the Master-Sergeants, whilst waiting for their connecting flight to Kabul in Istanbul's airport, they would start by focussing on those Afghans who were purportedly living in Kabul. The team was split into pairs and sent out across the City to find those Afghans and assist them plus their families escape the Taliban.

Radek's and Kacper's first port of call was the Ministry of Internal Affairs and a meeting with Deputy Minister Abdul Habibullah. It was a purely commercial transaction. The price was agreed at US$1200 whether an adult or child. A thin briefcase containing US$1million was opened on the Deputy Minister's desk then closed by him. His cousin, Mohammad Khada was employed as an Administrator entering valid passport details into the Government Records whilst the Deputy Minister's brother in law, Bibi Rahmani was a leading forger and supplier of black market passports. 'An interesting family side to the Deputy Minister' murmured Kacper as they left the Ministry.

After 5 days, the team had located 118 Afghans who were former employees of the Polish Government. With their wives and children, this meant a requirement for over 700 commercial airline seats. Radek through Colonel Chmura, organised the chartering of LOT planes into Kabul over the course of ten days with the in-bound passenger manifests to Poland virtually full. The commercial side of the airport was still functioning though almost each hour check-in desks became busier and seat availability lessened.

As the populace learnt in early July of the Taliban advances on key border crossings with Iran and Tajikistan and the growing threat to provincial cities, people were starting to vote with their feet. With independent news reports confirming over a thousand Afghan Army soldiers had fled into Tajikistan, it was self-evident the Government's forces had abandoned their posts without even putting up a fight. The Islam Qala crossing was one of the biggest trade gateways into Iran, generating an estimated US$20m in monthly revenue for the government. The Torghundi border town was similarly one of two trade gateways into Turkmenistan where again the general public was also learning the Taliban fighters had seized five districts in Herat with the Afghan Army once more putting up zero resistance.

Nevertheless, as quick as the Polish Special Forces team located and processed the Afghans and their families, after the first week of August, it had become a losing battle organising LOT flights or indeed seats on any flight. The Taliban's lightning advance was absorbing Provincial City after Provincial City and thereby heightening fear throughout Kabul of life once again under its rule. Increasingly the few remaining civilian aircraft were successfully heading for

Pakistan, Uzbekistan, or any neighbouring country. Chaos, lawlessness, and panic were in stark evidence at Hamid Karzai International Airport - its Security was losing control of the Terminal Building.

The team had meanwhile identified specific Afghans who had assisted the Polish Military on missions as translators in addition to those who had fought alongside GROM units. However, this meant extractions from Mazar-i-Sharif in the north across Taliban held territory. Yet there was no voice within the GROM doubting or wavering as to the necessity of their rescue. It was a debt of honour for not only their bravery on the battlefield but also the many Polish lives their actions had saved.

There was no doubting the will to sacrifice their lives but Radek needed a plan to mitigate the risk. Travelling by road was courting danger. More importantly, the extractions were not of just 1 or 2 people but entire families where a bus would have been more suitable transport. It had to be helicopters. Whilst a chinook would be the bus, it was an unprotected asset. This meant cover from Blackhawk attack helicopters. However, the only glitch was the United States Military and NATO had passed control of such equipment to the Afghan National Army.

'Seagull' had requisitioned the equipment at Bagram Airbase and confirmed to Radek the kit was 'locked, fuelled, loaded, and ready.' Nevertheless, having the necessary tools was of no use without combat pilots familiar with such helicopters. Fate decided to intervene. As Master-Sergeant Nowak was returning from shepherding two families from check-in to the flight gate in the airport terminal, he bumped into Jean-

Philippe Bernard together with Bruno Müller and other 'rotorheads'. Bartek had flown missions with them all on previous tours and convincing them to undertake another mission was pushing water downhill.

The fall of Kunduz on August 8th highlighted that the Taliban had captured 26 of the 34 provincial capitals in Afghanistan in less than two weeks. It was becoming clear Herat, Kandahar, and Mazar-i-Sharif would shortly follow with the fall of Kabul then a matter of days if not hours. There was not a moment to lose and as night fell the chinook escorted by two blackhawks took off from Bagram heading north to Mazar-i-Sharif, the country's largest city in that region and well-known anti-Taliban stronghold. Nevertheless, they could all feel the security situation worsening before their eyes every day since their deployment. Ashraf Ghani's Government was in freefall.

Abdul Ahmadi, a father of four daughters, had served with distinction both as a translator for the Polish Military and a soldier on special missions with GROM units in Helmand. With the Taliban sweeping the country with little if any resistance from the Afghan Army, he had no illusions that the Taliban would have him on its kill list and his family would be terrorised if not murdered in cold blood. No one in Mazir-i-Sharif or elsewhere across Afghanistan had forgotten the Taliban's strict interpretation of Sharia, or Islamic Law when it was in power from the mid-1990s to 2001. Its rule was widely condemned for beheadings and massacres against civilians, harsh discrimination against religious and ethnic minorities, denial of United Nations food supplies to starving civilians, destruction of cultural monuments, banning of females from school and most employment, and prohibition of most music. With his daughters' future schooling at stake, he had no choice but to leave Afghanistan. Similarly, Abas Mohammad, who had previously been an Afghan Army Special Forces sergeant attached to the Polish Military, had fled Kunduz immediately prior to its fall with his wife and their three children to the comparative safety of Mazir-i-Sharif. His six year old son had fallen ill during the journey that was made even more difficult by the numerous Taliban checkpoints. Asal Nasrin was a student on summer vacation from studying Law and International Politics at Herat University. Her late father was Polish and had served with the Polish Special Forces. He had been killed on a mission in the mountainous north east border with Pakistan. She along with her younger brothers and mother knew they had to leave the country before the Taliban captured Kabul.

Having flown back into Bagram, 'Seagull' was waiting. His face told Radek that all was not well. 'Intelligence indicates that Kandahar will fall tomorrow and Mazar-i-Sharif if not then the following day. The Afghan army is not offering any resistance. The Taliban's offer of amnesty is meaning the military is just fading away either by laying down its arms or simply disappearing. Ashraf Ghani is organising his exit to the United Arab Emirates for this Sunday on the expectation that the Taliban will be at the gates of Kabul. Ghazni was captured last night bringing their frontline to only 100 kilometres from here. It is over my friend.'

'What are you going to do?' 'Don't worry about me Radek, I have three helicopters being refuelled and my people, their families, and I will be in Pakistan before you are all back in your billets – good luck.'

Even though it was early morning, there was more traffic on the roads back into Kabul than one would normally expect. As their convoy weaved its way through the centre, it was clear the traffic was increasingly heading for the airport. There were people walking, holding, and leading young children whilst carrying or pulling suitcases.

Colonel Jan Chmura listened to Radek's summary. 'You are now no longer undercover. Please ensure you are all in full battle-gear and armed. The Pentagon is deploying three infantry battalions from the Marines and Army, to Hamid Karzai International Airport within the next 24 to 48 hours. You will have coded access to the airport's North Gate once the airport is secure. The intention is to restore security to the airport and its perimeter so evacuation planes can land. We will be sending on rotation Hercules C130 transports for you to police and fill with the remaining Afghans you are processing plus NATO journalists and other personnel looking legitimately for flights out. A meeting is taking place tomorrow in Doha between high ranking Taliban and American officials. The United States had previously asked that they, the Taliban, refrain from entering Kabul given the deadline for the planned withdrawal by August 31st and the need for all those with ties to the States and NATO to be evacuated. The Taliban had agreed as it sought to maintain the administrative functions of the Afghan government by staff remaining in post and to ensure a peaceful transition in authority from the government of President Ashraf Ghani. It is now becoming self-evident a vacuum of power is highly likely, especially if the strong held feeling on both sides that Ghani and his ministers will flee does actually come to pass. If the Taliban encounter as little resistance as seen in capturing the Provincial Cities, the chain of command among government security forces has clearly broken down. The United States will not take responsibility for Kabul's security. Hence the expectation is the Taliban will be forced to enter Kabul to protect property as well as the dignity and lives of the people. In accepting this highly probable new reality on the ground, we are told American, NATO, diplomatic staff, military, and Afghans seeking to leave will not be delayed or interfered with by Taliban fighters. Their roles are simply to maintain security outside the airport and not within the perimeter. So Radek, you need to ensure, although in uniform and armed, no aggressive postures by your team or responses whatever the provocations. The mission remains the same.'

When the news spread Jalalabad had fallen overnight then Mazar-i-Sharif that morning without a fight and later Ashraf Ghani had fled Kabul during Sunday afternoon with his wife initially to Uzbekistan, tens of thousands of Afghans began rushing to Hamid Karzai International airport in a desperate attempt to board any outgoing flights. This increasing panic was only heightened as Taliban fighters began to enter the completely undefended city. By Monday, the seething mass of humanity flooded the Terminal and flowed out onto the tarmac trying to force themselves onto packed planes. This was when the world witnessed several Afghans plunging to their deaths in the chaos as they clung to the landing gear of departing aircraft. This brought about the closure of the airport out of a sheer caution. United States and NATO soldiers then began slowly to clear the runways of people and restore order within the airport perimeter and Terminal building. American Military transports began subsequently to land with the expected additional troops who immediately joined the other soldiers dispersing the huge crowds that had earlier stormed the airport. Later a German evacuation plane landed as night began to fall heralding the start of a concerted evacuation over the coming days.

Gosia Bronski and Maja Stanek were graduates of the Institute of Oriental Studies at Krakow's Jagiellonian University. They had been enjoying a summer spent across India and South Asia as part of their Indology Masters' degree theses. With the Taliban fighters in the city, they had become increasingly nervous as single, if not unattractive, women and also knowing its doctrine towards women. To be fair, neither woman was wearing 'Kylie Minogue' shorts, nor make up, nor looking, in any way by western standards, provocative. Nevertheless, out of caution and respect, they had started to wear the hijab and cover their bodies with long-sleeved tops and trousers in the form of jeans in a serious attempt not to cause any offence. Hence, they were unsurprisingly eager to leave Kabul by August 26th. Walking with their backpacks towards the airport, Gosia and Maja were part of an ever growing crowd that was increasingly harassed at hastily arranged Taliban checkpoints forcing long delays. Whilst these young women had been studying the languages, literature, history, art, culture, different religious traditions and much more across India and South Asia, they were suddenly faced with the tragedy of tribal Afghanistan. The first checkpoint was manned by fighters from the north, Tajiks, speaking 'Dari'. When the women had shown their passports, they made the mistake of trying to speak 'Pashto', the dialect of the southerners. This was open sport as their ethnolinguistic gymnastics caused much banter and laughter before finally being allowed to pass. With fourteen or more tribes and different languages rather than dialects, it was seemingly only the extreme interpretation of the Quran that united the country under Taliban rule as these Tajiks clearly did not consider themselves as 'Afghans'.

The women witnessed Afghans being beaten and intimidated as they waited to pass further checkpoints by Taliban fighters. They noticed none of the victimised Afghans revealed any identity papers or other documents like a passport. Did it mean, they whispered to one another that it might have revealed they were people who had now become after two decades being the hunter now the hunted?

When Gosia and Maja could finally see the main entrance to the airport from the rear of a huge throng of people seeking to escape, the scene was anarchic. There was the smell of tear gas and cordite in the air as United States (U.S) Marines had been forced to repel an almost unstoppable onslaught of humanity. Taliban fighters were also attempting to hold back this swarm of humanity by in their case, firing live rounds directly into the crowd unlike the Marines who shot skywards. There were thus an untold number of dead civilians to step over. The open sewage culvert running along the part of the southern perimeter and under the bridge to the airport terminal entrance and Abbey Gate entrance was full of people some of whom were attempting to scale the wall with U.S Marines either looking down on or actually assisting them with an out-held hand. These Afghans were in the main those waving passports and visa paperwork ostensibly entitling them to be flown out of Kabul as those nationals who had assisted and worked for U.S or NATO countries. This spooked the women as if they were not frightened enough. They had flown in from Karachi and seriously doubted if the Polish Government even knew they were in Afghanistan. Certainly, there was no way they could be on a list of evacuees. Seeing that there was no crowd movement towards or through the main airport entrance, the women started to follow a number of Afghans with children clutching papers, presumably visas or other documents, working their way towards the Abbey Gate entrance along the protective southern perimeter wall of the airport. They had just entered what was a seemingly penned area full of Afghans and families with a number of U.S Marines circulating trying to find those people with legitimate rights to be flown out and gathering the relevant paperwork. There were many who had applied for U.S visas years earlier but their applications had been stalled for lack of an administrative confirming document. In this mass of clamouring humanity that had in effect been camped for days desperate to leave Afghanistan forever, was Abdul Rahman al-Logari, a lone suicide bomber and an Afghani. Quite how this bomber had managed to get past numerous Taliban security checkpoints will always be an unanswered question. Yet in the tightly packed crowds at Abbey Gate, this man was within 5 metres of a gathering of U.S soldiers, translators, and even some Taliban fighters before detonating his explosive vest. The deadly explosion spread shockwaves through the tightly packed crowd at Abbey Gate for over fifty metres from the detonation site. The Polish women were thrown unharmed to the ground by the force of the explosion but covered in the blood of the Afghan Family that had been stood in front of them. As a subsequent U.S investigation would reveal, the device was particularly lethal. It was made with about 9 kilograms of military-grade explosives and ball bearings. Even those U.S Marines, inspite of their body armour and helmets, could not avoid catastrophic injuries by such bearings on unprotected areas. As the dust cleared, the only sounds were the moans of the seriously injured and dying. The Islamic State-Khorasan, an affiliate of the Iraqi/Syrian terrorist group, subsequently claimed responsibility for inflicting the carnage on U.S troops, the Taliban, and far too many civilian Afghans and their families. As the blood splattered women got to their feet, 12 U.S marines were dead with one later dying from his injuries, 45 marines were injured and medevac'd out of Kabul, and 170 Afghans lay dead with many more injured.

In the previous, 12 days, the U.S Marines, with some remaining NATO Special Forces units, had over-watched the successful processing and evacuation of over a 100,000 people. The Taliban had given the United States until August 31st to withdraw its troops, evacuate its citizens, and those Afghans with documents to leave. During this period, President Biden had stated, as wars end, neither one side nor the other can guarantee everyone who wants to be extracted will be able to. The final number did exceed 115,000 including 6,000 U.S citizens.

Hearing the deafening explosion outside the Abbey Gate entrance, Radek, Filip, and the GROM teams left the processing area and the comparative safety of being within the airport perimeter. The sight that greeted them was one of horror with dead parents and children, the cries of the dying, body parts, dead in the open sewer, and of course the priority of finding their brothers in arms whether alive or dead. For Gosia and Maja it was like waking from a bad dream or nightmare to then hear Polish being spoken by soldiers in Kabul. They were just too shaken and too far to see their flag patches. As Radek turned, he saw the young women running towards them shouting 'Help help we are

Polish Citizens' *(Pomoc pomoc Jesteśmy Obywatelami Polskimi)*.

As the Polish Airforce Hercules C130 cargo door closed, Radek reflected on the last 5 weeks in Afghanistan. A total of 52 military and 15 civilian flights had brought 1,232 people to Poland. Most of the military rescue flights had travelled through air corridors with stops in Tbilisi in Georgia and Navoi in Uzbekistan. As for the Afghans who had assisted and worked with Poland's Military, some six hundred and their wives and children had also been saved. His Team had also successfully evacuated employees of the International Monetary Fund, people working with the Permanent Representation of the European Union in Kabul, as well as others employed by the governments of Germany, the Czech Republic, Lithuania, Estonia, and even one Dutch citizen with their family plus sporadic Polish citizens like Gosia and Maja. Radek was under no illusion that the Taliban would exercise retribution on anyone who had in any way served U.S and NATO forces in spite of the announcement of amnesty. The executions had already begun and darkness was once more covering this land-locked country. Radek recalled the faces of those Afghans who had shared their food, advised, and protected his team's patrols in the Hindu Kush, and were just kind to them all. How many of these unofficial heroes had they been forced to leave behind? It did not sit well with him or any of the Special Forces soldiers on this mission. The unstable and rapidly changing situation was not an excuse. Everyone dreaded the return of the Taliban, especially the young. They believed in the West and had studied growing up in what was still a fledgling a democracy for all its failings. Radek could not stop thinking about all that effort, the lives lost, the promises broken, and all those dreams destroyed as he drifted into a fitful and troubled sleep.

Chapter 9

Their orders were to stay on the C130 and not to disembark at Wroclaw where Polish Television was waiting to interview the evacuees. The Hercules's next stop was Mielec one of the flight crew had let slip to Bartek when he asked. As the cargo door was about to close, Colonel Kuba Pawlukowicz stepped into the plane's hold. 'Officer on Deck' shouted Master-Sergeant Nowak above the roar of four Allison T56 turboprops springing into life as the cargo door was closing. Bleary eyed GROM Special Forces soldiers sprung from the horizontal to the vertical standing to attention in one movement purely on instinct at hearing those words of command. 'Stand Easy, Master-Sergeant' 'Yes Sir Colonel - Stand Easy'

Colonel Pawlukowicz dropped his kitbag and sat between Radek and Filip Cuda. 'Radek, please wave the sergeants to join us in the huddle *(a military term for developing a plan where matters on the ground are developing within a wider battlefield brief)*.'

'With every passing day, the security situation in our part of Europe is worsening. We are sensing that President Putin is planning something far more sinister regarding Ukraine's future as an independent and sovereign democratic country. The quadrennial Zapad military exercises are beginning across Western Russia including joint drills with the Belarus Military whereby large battlegroups will be formed. UK intelligence, and belatedly the Pentagon, concurs with our assessment that much of the equipment and troops along Ukraine's eastern and northern borders may well not return to their home barracks. Hence, you will shortly all be stationed across our border with the Ukrainian Army. Your mission will be to sharpen their Special Forces skills against an invading force, in particular focussing on warfare battle strategies that disrupt extended logistical supply lines. Before your deployment, Radek and his unit will spend the rest of this month until mid-November assisting our Border Guards who are already under tremendous pressure. Radek spent time undercover in late winter and early spring within the border forests, hence we want to capitalise on that 'behind the lines' intelligence by disrupting the Belarussian Authorities efforts to weaponise illegal migration. Filip, your team will proceed from Mielec to Ukraine and be joined by Radek's unit and him in mid-November. After which, dependent on external factors, we would expect rotation within your units for timely 'R & R' back in Poland.'

'What's been happening on our border with Belarus?' asked Kacper Stodola innocently.

'Whilst you have all been in Afghanistan, we have had some major issues with Belarus. Illegal attempts to enter from their territory into Poland alone, and thus the European Union, have risen to over 4000 per month. Indeed with the benefit of Radek's undercover work and other supporting intelligence, our Government was suitably forewarned. Tomorrow, September 2nd, our President will formally declare a State of Emergency along a 3 kilometre strip abutting the border in Podlaskie and Lubelskie regions. Our Interior Minister legalised last month immediate expulsions with a new regulation whereby any person, crossing the Polish border illegally, are simply to be delivered back to the border and Belarus. There are to be no exceptions even for people seeking protection under International Law. In addition, under the State of Emergency, the 3 kilometre area along the border remains restricted. This means in effect no access for human rights and humanitarian organisations, lawyers and media. This means only those living in villages or justifying movement for work will be allowed through checkpoints. The Government is already experiencing 'blowback' from these groups as to the lack of accountability, transparency, and failure to provide humanitarian and medical aid to these stranded people at the border. Nevertheless, Lukashenko's regime, or we now believe more strongly on the orders of Putin's GRU, decided to organise and push these hapless people onto Polish, Lithuanian and Latvian territory. The purpose is to destabilise the European Union's northern border. Our Government has deployed around 12,000 soldiers, 8,000 Border Guard officers and 1,000 police officers in the Kuźnica area, and now Radek and his unit, to assist halting this activity. Work had begun on laying a razor wire border fence but this has been partly destroyed with attacks on border guards, police officers and the military. Tear gas and water cannon have already had to be used to pushback these illegals at various crossing points. Where we have arrested and detained these illegal refugees prior to sending them back into Belarus, there is a common theme. While in Belarus, they had been beaten and threatened by its security forces. The Belarusians forced them to cross the border, instructing them when and where to cross while preventing people from leaving the border area to return to Minsk. This escalating level of violence and harassment from beatings, kicking, setting dogs on these migrants and then theft involving phones, money and documents was far too often the repeated experience at the hands of Belarus's security police.'

'Surely Belarus must have realised that this action will ultimately fail?'

'It depends how we define failure Filip. If the purpose is to distract the Western Powers from the amassing of a major military force on Ukraine's borders, I would suggest the distraction, especially with the added benefit of the U.S's and its NATO Allies bruising exit from Afghanistan, has to a large extent been successful. Since the early spring of this year, Lukashenko's Regime has cynically exploited the anxiety of European Leaders and their societies concerning migration. The Belarussian Government has been issuing visas to thousands of internally displaced people from countries afflicted by war. Their intention may have been seeking to polarise the European Union by provoking political divisions similar to how societies responded to the 2015/16 Migration crisis. We know from Radek's assignment in North West Syria that the GRU are behind luring these desperate people to buy visas to Belarus; a country that is now beyond doubt Russia's vassal state and ready to do its bidding. However, polarising European political attitudes would have been an unintended but positive consequence for the Russian Federation had that occurred. ABW's and the Government's view is that Putin is determined to keep Ukraine within his sphere of influence by force if necessary.

That is why Poland and NATO will need you all to be in Ukraine – this is about democracy and freedom of choice.'

The Białowieża primeval forest was once more to become home to Radek. Eryk Shevchenko had, as he was schooling him in the ways of the forest last March, shown him some caves within a rocky outcrop covered by evergreen trees and surrounded by deep undergrowth, marshes, springs, and mixed impenetrable forest even to Bison. It had been a long forgotten and lost partisan fortress from WWII. This was to be their base camp for the mission. Eryk met Radek and his team, who were all laden with extra-large Bozeman Military grade backpacks, and then led them in daylight to the caves. As Master-Sergeant Nowak entered the entrance to the first cave, of the cave and tunnel complex, and removed the weight of the backpack, he was covered in sweat. Looking back, out of the cave entrance masked by silver birch branches, he knew instinctively that this was a very defensible citadel, especially as the climb up the rocky incline was seemingly on a non-existent trail suitable only for mountain goats. Eryk proceeded to lead them deeper into the complex to a large central cave. Perhaps the biggest surprise was the cast iron stove that had been previously disassembled by those WWII Partisans and then brought piece by piece into this safe space. The flue needed some obvious repair but Eryk assured them all it could be brought back to life. In a side cave without an exit, there were metal bars with hooks to hang freshly killed game. Apart from the freshwater spring in another cave, numerous empty hurricane oil lamps were left scattered throughout the entire cave complex. Eryk proceeded to show the unit where two escape tunnels surfaced within deep undergrowth. With winter approaching, nights were already falling below zero so becoming 'luxury' cave dwellers seemed somewhat of a holiday for this hardened group of warriors. Eryk's grandfather and father had shown him this place during Soviet times as somewhere to be safe. However, after eighty years, the other Partisans were long dead so its very existence had been lost in the annals of history. The first week was spent protecting any trails leading vaguely in the general direction of the caves. This did not mean placing claymores or creating stick booby traps rather using today's technology to warn the unit of a hostile presence. With so many wild animals moving around during both day and night, motion detectors linked to day & night vision cameras, all suitably camouflaged and hidden, proved to be the most effective warning system for a one and half kilometre protective zone around their citadel. At one kilometre incendiary explosive charges were laid in such a manner that an area of fifty metres or more from the point of detonation would be completely destroyed. Amongst the other equipment and weapons drawn down at the Mielec Special Forces armoury were Ravin 29RX Sniper Cross bows with a kill range of 70 to 100 metres. All this protective communications equipment, night vision systems and battlefield sensors required an enhanced Portable Power System. There were no plug sockets or charging points in the caves. Military Technology came to the rescue with kit consisting of a 55-watt solar panel, a charge controller, an AC/DC adapter, plugs and charging-related gear.

Before disappearing as dusk fell, Eryk had indicated on a Białowieża Forest regional map two disused warehouses in Glyadovichi south of Grodno. They were being used in a similar manner to one they had seen in the Damačava forest back in the spring. Radek's orders were clear 'disrupt without discovery'.

Tomek Jureki had been taught by his grandfather how to hunt live game. When he appeared with a freshly killed gralloched wild boar carcass, Radek's decision that field rations, apart from kilo bags of rice, would be unnecessary on this mission was vindicated. Piotr Vrubel had shown himself to be an excellent chef both in Idlib and Kabul. When he had managed to surprise the team by resuscitating that cast iron stove, life in the Białowieża Forest was definitely looking up. Tomek hung the gralloched carcass in the cold side cave for Piotr to butcher when ready. When Radek asked Tomek what he had done with the boar's disembowelled parts, he confirmed the kill had been over 2 kilometres away and had been hidden beneath undergrowth. A sniper cross bow had nailed its first victim.

With the entire group including Radek enjoying the pleasure of sweet and sour pork with rice, his thoughts turned to their mission. He decided not to question Piotr as to where the local supermarket was for jars of such sauce. Sometimes it is better not to ask or even know.

The team, with a bottle of Belvedere vodka mysteriously appearing, listened to Radek explaining the problems they faced in executing their mission successfully.

'Our mission is to disrupt the Belarussian effort to use migrants as a distraction along our border. Our problem is to achieve this result without alerting either the Belarus Authorities or indeed their Russian Masters. From Eryk's briefing, increasing numbers of migrants are flying into

Minsk and then bussed to the 3 warehouses on this map. Daily buses take these illegal refugees to differing crossing points into Poland. In addition, whilst Belarus border gates are opened, our Border Guard are faced with hundreds of people running if not charging towards them. Other refugees are being shepherded towards other points where fencing can be breached with the active help of Belarussian Border Police, the OMON units, and Riot Police.'

'What happens if we deplete the number of serviceable buses?'

'Tomek, I am not saying we should not do that but the wholesale disruption of the entire bus fleet might flag our presence – stealth and remaining unseen are the guidelines for whatever disruption and havoc we can create.'

So we are stuck Radek to adding water to diesel tank of every 10th bus?'

'Maybe Tomek'

'What about removing the migrants' shelter – nights here are becoming colder.'

'Not a bad idea Pawel. However, seeing one of your warehouse hotels burnt to the ground may seem bad luck but a second would be seen as more than coincidence' interjected Bartek.

'We might have no choice but to flag our presence. Nevertheless, destroying the migrants housing could result in refugee camps in the woods along the border, especially close to crossing points. It would make things worse for our Border Guards in the short term but just might force the Belarussians to repatriate them Radek.'

'Kacper you make good points. When I was here back in Spring, small groups of Syrians Iraqis and the odd Afghani were being guided and escorted to the weakest points in our border security. That steady flow through the forest has been replaced by now buses full of illegals. This has made crossing the forest with so many people impractical according to Eryk. Buses are driven apparently to forest clearings that are 200 or so metres from a border crossing point. With this forced adaption of strategy, the demands on the Belarussian Border Guard and OMON Police Units is such that there is no longer time in their work rotas for random patrols through the forest looking to catch and be bribed by smugglers.'

'Does this mean Radek, accepting there is always risk when in enemy territory, daylight sorties as opposed to solely disruptive night attacks are also on the menu?'

'Yes Bartek I think so.'

'Whilst we were in Syria last year, the ordinary Belarussians had demonstrated against Lukashenko's staged re-election. Tsikhanouskaya is now in exile in Vilnius giving interviews and speeches to those who will listen. The Belarus citizens have been subjected to such brutal force and suppression such that an uneasy calm has been restored.'

'Carry on Kuba' said Radek as the man momentarily hesitated.

'What if we become the militant wing of the Democratic Movement? It would provide us with the cover to destroy buses, warehouses, and indeed if necessary kill. We would, as far as the 'silenced' Belarussian public is concerned, be 'Partisans' fighting the injustice and oppression of Lukashenko's regime.'

Nods of approval circulated round the cave fire.

'Kuba this is a solid way for us to disrupt what is going on here – as it is your idea how do we make the Authorities believe a militant group is behind explosions, fires, and death?'

'Radek, there is one name across the Russian Federation that stands for freedom and justice, now more than ever with Belarus just a subservient region. It is Navalny. Amnesty International has designated him a political prisoner and man of conscience. We will not have time to write his name but, in Russian his name is *'Навальный'*, we should spray paint 'Н' on everything we can.'

'Agreed – and ABW's own propaganda can leak the disinformation via various social media channels and connections. I will speak with Colonel Pawlukowicz.'

The next few weeks into October were a combination of reconnaissance and familiarisation with the forest terrain including the various animal and smuggler trails. The entire team put a great deal of time listening to and learning from Radek. They all had to be able whether it was day or night to know where they were and how to return to their protected 'Citadel' without leaving any trace that could be followed.

The dark and forbidding Białowieża forest was to be their protector and become their enemies' nightmare.

Radek decided that the first target had to be a building in Brest. It would seem to be the opening salvo by Belarussian Patriots prepared to take up arms. The ballot box had failed to change autocracy into the start of democracy leaving no alternative but to fight for that freedom. This would be the disinformation message. Attacking a Police Station would resonate with all Belarussian citizens and protesters who had been beaten, clubbed and imprisoned by Lukashenko's security services last autumn. The days were already becoming shorter as the nights were drawing in. Another 10 days before the clocks were to be turned back an hour on October 31st. Radek and Kuba Michnik had stolen a few hours earlier a fairly old and sad looking Lada van. Kuba and the other GROM members of the team had been provided with some basic Belarussian identity papers and a back story. Radek was once more Sergey Antonovich Petrov. Kuba was selected because he was also the explosive expert of the GROM team plus his spoken Russian was even better than Radek's *(one of the benefits of having a Belarussian mother who had married his Polish father)* plus it was his idea!

Dressed as casual labourers in the half light, they were slouched in such a way on the bonnet of the Lada that may or may not have even been theirs. They were seemingly enjoying a takeaway burger and beer after a hard day's labouring to anyone who took even the slightest bit of interest. Kuba and Radek were looking for cameras either on the targeted Police Station or across the street from its public entrance. The van was suitably packed with an adequate amount of military grade semtex around cans of flammable diesel with a remote timer. It was then four OMON security police strode out of the Police Station and headed across the road towards them. 'Shit' said Radek under his breath. 'They look like the bastards who tossed my quarters at the end of March.' Kuba casually stood and walked towards these military security policemen while taking bites out of the cooling hamburger and slurping somewhat even colder takeaway coffee. The security police were in fact stopping next to what was in fact an un-marked OMON police saloon and preparing to leave. They turned to see a shambling builder walking in their general direction but did not stop and they drove away leaving Kuba in a cloud of black diesel exhaust. A vacant parking spot in front of Police Headquarters for the entire Region appeared in what was seemingly a blind spot of the surveillance cameras. In addition there was no nearby street lighting. Radek as an added measure turned the vehicle round so he could reverse into the spot then simply step out of the car with his back to one camera of concern. After closing the driver's door, he knelt down next to the front offside wheel and slashed the tyre. He had already ripped out the ignition wiring immediately after he parked. The van was truly immobilized and now parked outside an uninspiring Stalinist designed building with the rather grand title of the Department of Internal Affairs of the Administration of the Moscow District of Brest. Radek's concern was that blowing out the windows of the Police Station did not cause unnecessary damage to nearby private property and also importantly the explosion did not injure or kill civilians. Eryk had feigned a need to stay in Brest overnight through an excess of vodka the previous week. He had spent the entire night watching the police station. The shift change took place at 22:00 hours and from 01:30 to 04:00 hours no one went into or exited the building.

Kuba and Radek left the scene taking the opportunity to paint with aerosols some 'Hs' when they were as far as they knew unseen. They stayed as they left Brest in the shadows choosing to pick up a local bus to Kamieniuk from a bus stop outside town.

Shortly after 03:00 hours, the silence of the night was broken by the Lada Van rising vertically in the air before simultaneously being consumed by a large explosion with flames shooting skywards and outwards. As the molten dismembered chassis crashed back to earth, the sound of breaking glass could then be heard along the entire street. Most, if not all, of the Police Station windows had been blown inwards with also some damage to shop fronts immediately across the street. However, the falling burning metal and the searing heat created a chain reaction as other parked vehicles caught fire and then exploded with the remaining ones not on fire emitting the wailing noise of anti-theft sirens. Whether it was the explosions of the other parked vehicles' petrol or diesel tanks or the molten shrapnel of the disintegrated Lada Van, the result was the Police Station was on fire.

As the on-duty Police were, with the handcuffed prisoners from the cells, running from the building, sirens were heralding the imminent arrival of the Brest Fire Brigade and numerous Police patrols. It was then that matters took a turn for the worst in terms of extinguishing the fire as flames were already licking up the exterior of the building. The rat-ta-tat-tat of exploding bullets began to be heard making the Fire Chief stop his firefighters from entering the Police Station that was already developing into an inferno in less than five minutes from the initial explosion. This forced Brest

Fire Brigade to be playing streams of water onto the building through a variety of hoses while other firefighters from supporting tenders were attempting to extinguish the blazing parked vehicles with foam. Deep inside the building, there was a large explosion as the gas main into the property melted thereby creating with the heat, a secondary explosion. It removed the entire rear of the building leaving a flaming torch from within the rubble. It took until dawn to bring the blaze under control by which time the Department of Internal Affairs of the Administration of the Moscow District of Brest was a smoldering ruin within its remaining unstable walls. The street itself took on a macabre feel with burnt out vehicles and metal strewn across the cobbled road.

Members of the Belarussian State Forensic Department and Officers of Almaz Special Anti-Terrorism Unit (SPBT Almaz) had been dispatched simultaneously from Minsk around 05:00 hours and were now observing the complete devastation. By mid-morning, in conjunction with Brest's Fire Chief, it was agreed the attack had commenced with the explosion of a vehicle that was probably a van. The Forensic Team concluded the explosive was C4 (Semtex) that was used as the triggering device for probably 100 kilos if not more of Ammonium Nitrate with a fuel accelerant of probably diesel or petrol to create this level of destruction. Whether there was any chemical trace in the C4 used that might determine its place of manufacture would require the burnt out chassis to be removed to the Forensic Laboratory in Minsk and this necessitated the evidence was not compromised during transportation.

At around 11:00 hours the Belarus State National Broadcasting Channel on Makayonka Street in Minsk received the following message on its website-

At 03:00 this morning, a bomb was detonated outside the Brest Police Station - a symbol of Lukashenko's oppressive regime that declared war on innocent protesters last summer. Belarus is becoming a Region within Russia against the wishes of all Belarussians. Every instrument of oppression, from institutions to individuals, keeping this Regime in power is on notice they are now legitimate targets. Navalny is in jail for highlighting corruption and seeking freedom of speech. Non-violence does not work in a Police State only insurrection and armed resistance.
The People's Commissars of Belarus

It was lunchtime in Moscow when the news of the total destruction of the Brest Region Regional Police Headquarters reached Igor Yedemsky. The Belarussian GRU had reported to their GRU colleagues that it would be a few days before a detailed forensic analysis would be available. In addition, 'the People's Commissars of Belarus', who had claimed responsibility for the explosion, were as of now an unknown terrorist cell. However, with all known activists, radicals, and protesters in penal colonies since sentencing the previous autumn, there were, at this time, none of the usual suspects still at large. Any clues, apart from numerous capital letter 'Hs' adorning various walls referencing presumably Alexei Navalny as the political motivation, much will depend on the forensic analysis in terms of providing clues as to the perpetrators. The surveillance cameras and records were completely destroyed by the fire but camera records within the immediate vicinity area are being reviewed especially where 'Hs' appear.

Oleg had been to date delighted, as was his President, with just how well the gathering tsunami of refugees from the Middle East had been disrupting the calm along the Polish and Belarus border. However, the European Union was now looking to diplomatic channels to successfully block the arrival of further groups into Belarus through collaboration with governments and airlines. When European Union Leaders declared in October the Union would not accept any attempt by third countries to weaponise migrants for political purposes, the scene was set for the next Council Meeting in mid-November to amend its sanctions policy. In future, individuals and entities, organising or contributing to these activities by the Lukashenko regime facilitating illegal crossing of the EU's external borders, will be specifically targeted. Nevertheless, whilst the disruption along the border would gradually come to an end, the distraction of the European Union had to a large extent worked whilst ZAPAD 21 was being undertaken by the Russian Military, even though the unity rather than disunity had been the unexpected outcome to the Migration provocation.

As for 'the Peoples Commissars of Belarus', Oleg saw this as purely a Belarus anti-terrorist investigation and left for the day.

An encrypted message timed at 08:19 hours was received the following morning from Rakowiecka Street onto the cave dwellers' Communications Unit –

Satellite imagery reveals complete destruction of the Brest Regional Police Station. Exercise caution

A day later, Eryk, with his quadbike loaded with a sack of potatoes, onions, and carrots from his own vegetable garden, made an unannounced visit in the late afternoon.

Leaving the bike well outside the perimeter and camouflaged, he waited for 30 minutes or more listening and watching. Similarly, inside the cave, one of the GROM team was watching not only Eryk but also constantly checking all the other hidden cameras for any signs of hostile forces. Since the encrypted message, the entire unit had been on alert. Notwithstanding it being daylight, Radek considered it necessary to launch the Anafi USA thermal imaging drone with zoom camera capability from 5 kilometres to 1 centimetre. After completing a series of circular sweeps revealing no external threats, Radek left with one of the team to meet Eryk.

Radek sat quietly as Eryk briefed him on what had been happening in Brest since the destruction of its Police Headquarters. Wotjek Tarnowski watched the 'comms' screen inside the main cave as the Drone continued its surveillance whilst keeping his eyes searching for any sign of movement from the other camera feeds.

'OMON military and riot police are now on every street corner demanding that people's identity papers be shown. The City is under a night time curfew from dusk until dawn with police foot patrols moving about all night. House to house and apartment to apartment searches in residential blocks are underway with street and area closures. The Local

Police force has, I am told, been bolstered by, in addition to a few hundred security police on the ground, the Belarussian State Forensic Department and Almaz Special Anti-Terrorism Unit were at the scene within hours of the explosion. This has resulted already in the burnt out and shattered chassis of your van being transported together with other debris to the Forensic Laboratories in Minsk. The anti-terrorism unit is clearly behind the orderly and systematic demand for all the records of commercial and private surveillance camera systems not to be deleted and be provided to the authorities. These surveillance camera records are being viewed frame by frame in what was previously a vacant 3 storey office block which is for now the Regional Police Station for the foreseeable future. Temporary checkpoints have also been put in place on every entrance into Brest and citizens are being asked for any video clips from their mobiles if they were filming in the City the day before the explosion. I might add the border crossing to Terespol in Poland was closed for 24 hours.'

'Anything else Eryk you think we should now?'

'Belarus Television reported a major gas leak had caused damage to a number of parked cars and buildings. Fortuitously no loss of life was a result of the prompt action of the Police and Emergency Services. That said, it was almost a footnote at the end of a lengthy newscast special focussed on Lukashenko's very public hobby of playing ice hockey. However, whilst this implies the Regime is, as far as the populace is concerned, downplaying the ostensible 'terrorist act' but in Brest clearly the opposite is the case. Whilst I know the intention is to destroy the present migrant housing outside Grodno, it might draw the authorities' entire attention directly onto the western borderlands, including the Białowieża forest, unless you can create a false lead.'

'Well in many ways OMON, Belarussian GRU, and other Police units with Border Guards are already there Eryk.'

'That may be for now. Unless the destruction is somehow shown to be 'an Act of God' then Radek you can expect thousands not hundreds of security personnel combing the entire region looking for you all. Remember you are, as far as the Regime is concerned, an active terrorist cell and a threat to its existence; maybe even a frustrated element and militant arm of Sviatlana Tsikhanouskaya's Democratic Movement.'

With that, the men shook hands and parted with Radek carrying that sack of vegetables back to the cave.

By the 4th day of the investigation, the Almaz Team believed that two men occasionally caught on surveillance footage and in the background on some video clips were the most likely suspects. It was not that any frame showed a clear facial shot in fact it was more the efforts made by them to keep to the shadows, including avoiding any bright street lighting. It was impossible to draw any conclusions as to their age except to broadly guess 20 to 50. From the glimpses of clothing, the men appeared to be construction workers or people worked outdoors for a living. Nevertheless, no reliance could be placed on such an assessment more that these terrorists were professionals rather than just amateurs with a bee in their bonnet.

The Minsk Forensic team had identified the van as a Lada from a piece of the chassis found some 34 metres away from the detonation point. Remarkably, the manufacturer's vehicle identification number had survived intact. Police vehicle records had identified the owner who was not only a Brest resident but had reported his vehicle as stolen during the morning of the explosion. This did not mean that the 58 year old electrician did not have to endure a very unpleasant interrogation a few days later with members of Almaz and the Belarussian GRU lasting over 24 hours. The Forensic laboratory had found no chemical marking agent in the Semtex to indicate where the plastic explosive had been manufactured. This might indicate, they reported, that it had been acquired on the black market from stocks known to have been previously supplied to Libya, Iraq, North Korea and Syria. They also reported that the Semtex had been used as a trigger to detonate probably 100 kilos or more of ammonium nitrate with an incendiary element provided by diesel. This combination caused the deadly force of the device coupled with the damaging fire.

For now the investigation was stalled until the terrorists continued their bombing campaign when hopefully they would unwittingly leave further clues that would lead ultimately their identities and arrest.

The Grodno out of town warehouse complex near Glyadovichi comprised of two large buildings that had been temporarily converted by providing simply mattresses for the increasing flow of migrants landing daily in Minsk. For the GROM unit who had been in Syria, Lukashenko, no doubt at his Kremlin's Boss's instruction and urging, was no different to a scammer and thief. Misleading desperate people with false promises of a new Life far away from Syrian and other refugee camps in the European Union was, for them all, a new low for this undemocratically elected and authoritarian Regime. Innocent people will be belatedly finding out that after paying thousands of dollars they have been deceived and cheated.

Around the fire that night in the cave, with temperatures falling outside in the forest below zero, the conversation turned as to how 'the Grodno Hotels' could be taken off the table without flagging their presence except as 'the People's Commissars of Belarus'. There was no magic wand for an answer.

The Neman River flows through Grodno and then travels in a southerly direction before making a long turn to the east creating a large lake. A flood prevention embankment had been built in decades past to prevent heavy winter rains or melting snow upstream raising river water levels where, prior to the embankment, the Neman River's excess water would naturally flow onto its flood plain.

As a detailed topographical map was passed round, the Grodno out of town warehouse complex had, it was clear to everyone, been built on the flood plain. If a section of the embankment was breached, the buildings would be directly in the path of the Neman River. The complex itself was standalone with no nearby housing or commercial property so should the decision be taken to blow up part of the flood prevention embankment, the river water would be contained across the flood plain farmland.

The more this proposal was debated it seemed to provide the level of disruption that such a terrorist group would be seeking to cause, especially after the destruction of the Brest Police station. However, such militants would, they considered, be looking to attack infrastructure and institutions but not injure fellow Belarussians. Their argument was with the State not the majority of its citizens.

Nevertheless, the debate now centred about timing. Would it be better for the river water be flooding the 'hotels' and surrounding farmland during daylight or at night? From surveillance the unit had already carried out, migrants were often bussed at night in addition to daytime sorties to points along the border. Radek could not see with any certainty as to when during any 24 hour cycle the buildings would be completely unoccupied. Hence, the decision rested on protecting the security of his team which possibly meant travelling and returning in darkness. The Grodno Region had of course become a forward base for the Russian Air Force and also for an Army Battle Group during the current year. In normal circumstances, there would be a heightened risk of being stopped by random Police or Military patrols anywhere close to those bases. Fortunately, Glyadovichi is some 80 kilometres to the south of the nearest of those closed military areas.

Belarussian GRU were continuing to escort a smuggler and a small group of migrants through the forest to gaps in Poland's Border Security on at least a weekly basis. These journeys would normally commence in daylight and it would often be almost dawn for the Belarussian security to return. This provided an opportunity for the GROM team to live up to its nickname of being 'unseen and silent'.

A police transit van pulled to a halt in a wooded parking area on the fringe of the Białowieża Forest. A group of male migrants stepped out of the vehicle as a Belarus GRU Toyota Land Cruiser pulled up alongside. As the transit pulled away, the GRU officers led the migrant group into the forest to meet a Polish smuggler close to the border.

The unoccupied Toyota with its police markings was the prize. Radek led Kuba and two other GROM soldiers towards the vehicle. Whilst their Polish military fatigues were somewhat different to those of the Belarussian Army, in the dark if they were stopped at a checkpoint, such differences would have been lost in the darkness. Shoulder flashes had been substituted with those of the 5th Spetsnaz brigade; a unit known for its brutality the previous year when subduing protesters in the streets of Minsk after Lukashenko's re-election. In addition, arm patches of the notorious 'Valhalla' unit would make any sentry think more than twice about asking any questions of those in the vehicle. The drive to Glyadovichi took just over one and a half hours.

After an hour, the Toyota slowed as a tailback of vehicles indicated an accident, breakdown, or a checkpoint. Flicking on the siren and its flashing blue lights, Radek accelerated into the oncoming traffic lane. It was by now raining quite heavily as both the queuing traffic moved closer to the kerb and the occasional oncoming vehicle mounted the verge. No one argues with a speeding Police vehicle unless you envisage life in a savage penal colony doing indefinite hard time. As the Toyota slowed easing in to the front of the queue, the soldiers at the checkpoint just waved them through and on their way. However, with ponchos failing in such a rainstorm to keep them dry let alone warm as the night-time temperature was falling close to zero, there was no effort to note the Toyota's registration as it disappeared into the darkness. Radek weighed as to whether it would be prudent to take an alternative route or anticipate that by the time of their return the checkpoint, which was clearly temporary, would have moved to another location if not abandoned in such weather.

The trek across recently ploughed fields was exhausting as the sodden earth was increasingly like adhesive glue wrapping itself, layer after layer, underneath and around their combat boots. As the four of them were carrying 50 kilos of semtex explosive each in their military backpacks, the going was extremely tough with lashing rain and slippery heavy ground. At the embankment, Kuba directed where the backpacks should be placed and then he set about linking all the backpacks with primacord whereby a 100 metres of the retaining flood embankment wall would be removed. Recent heavy autumn rains had the River Neman flowing fuller and faster than normal for the time of year. In many ways, Kuba would have preferred to have controlled the detonation rather than rely on a digital clock timer set for midnight. However, this was a necessity if they were to return to the comparative safety of the forest unscathed.

Master-Sergeant Nowak was watching the car park for any sign of a Belarussian Police or Military presence. Tomek Jureki was like a silent panther tracking its prey. His role was quite simply that if the Belarussian GRU officers back-tracked earlier than expected, they were to be dispatched to Valhalla! With ear pieces, modern comms kept Nowak and

Jureki as the eyes and ears of this operation whilst Wotjek created his bomb kilometres distant.

By midnight the entire GROM unit was once more relaxing in the central cave and drying off from their endeavours.

The Toyota engine was already cold and its ignition wires suitably repaired. Radek had insisted on each of them taking separate paths from the car park back to their undercover base. They all removed their tactical combat boots replacing their footwear with smooth soled boots that Master-Sergeant Nowak distributed before they all left the forest car park. The soft ground on various trails and tracks made for perfect boot tread impressions. Whilst some might simply be washed away by the night's rainfall, the GROM unit still had to remain unseen in hostile territory even though its mission in Belarus was coming to a close.

At midnight, those individuals in the two warehouses were momentarily woken by a distant crump and an ever so brief short tremor. The majority of the inmates who had woken were soon once more asleep but not for long. A 100 metre wide or more torrent of 3 metre high river water hit the end elevation cinder block wall with such force the wall just crumpled. Migrants were heading for the exit but their sodden palliasse straw bedding was creating an artificial dam. Water will always follow the line of least resistance and as the weight of river water increased by the second, loading bay mechanical shutters were simply wrenched from their housings. The plus was that no migrant drowned even as the building's loading bay became an impromptu swimming pool. The interior and exterior lighting was still functioning until the river entered the sub-station. When the development was completed two decades earlier, the regional authorities took the opportunity to replace an ageing electrical sub-station. In doing so, the area supplied was expanded to include all the villages within a 12 kilometre radius. Water and electricity do not mix as the sub-station explosion confirmed, creating an immediate blackout. For the OMON security detail, they were no different than rabbits caught in the headlights except they were now stumbling around in total darkness and struggling to swim. The empty parked buses were soon turned into battering rams as they struck the second warehouse. It was dawn before the authorities began to grasp what on earth had taken place during the night. A large lake had been formed at the bottom of the downward slope that rolled into a shallow valley. The roads were submerged and some wild ducks had taken up residence on the lake. It was a disaster

At around 10:00 hours the Belarus State National Broadcasting Channel on Makayonka Street in Minsk again received this message on its website from the People's Commissars of Belarus

At 24:00 last night, a bomb was detonated near Glyadovichi. This enabled the River Neman to destroy some warehouses. These were being used to house illegal migrants from Syria Iraq and other countries at the bidding of Lukashenko's masters in the Kremlin. Enticing and encouraging desperate refugees to cause border issues with our neighbours underlines just how low this Regime has sunk. Such activity is against the humanitarian wishes of all genuine Belarussians. Remember non-violence does not work in a Police State only insurrection and armed resistance.

The Belarussian State Forensic Department and Almaz Special Anti-Terrorism Unit arrived together from Minsk at midday. However, their vehicles had to be left some 50 metres from where the road disappeared into what was now a huge lake. As the officers of both teams made their way across increasingly soaked ground in continuing rain, waterway engineers were attempting, initially with sandbags, to rebuild a level of protection and seal the breach. With the forecast of rain for the next few days, the River Neman would soon be rising again and become a swift following river. The engineers were fighting against the clock. Whatever evidence there might or might not be, it was most likely washed down the slope by the force of the river after it breached the protective embankment. The water levels would need to be substantially lowered before their investigations could begin. What evidence there might be, if any, would be inevitably under layers of silt and earth. As for the Grodno Regional Power company, it had an even bigger problem. Its sub-station, or what was left of it, was still underwater. Pumps were attempting to lower a large pool covering where the sub-station was expected to be with so far limited success. Electricity was unlikely to be re-established to those previously supplied villages for 2 to 3 weeks at least. Something that the Authorities could not keep quiet, especially when sewage pumps no longer had power resulting in raw sewage spewing out across the village streets and gardens. A health hazard had been created with the Ministry of Health and Grodno Regional Health Authority considering evacuation as the only solution until normal life could be resumed. The disruptions to supplies of clean water, wastewater treatment, electricity, transport, communication, and threats to health rather made the destruction of the Brest Police station seemingly a minor terrorist event.

The Almaz Unit had also brought the State's Professional Dog handlers with them to see whether through this almost sea of devastation there were any clues or tell-tale signs. Over what was left of the ploughed field abutting a farm track, they found boot imprints but the heavy rain had removed most of any identifying tread. Piecing together the differing treads, these appeared to be combat boots and possibly a group of 4 people. A vehicle had been parked at which point the trail went cold. The terrorists had nullified any use dogs might have had by putting distance and time in their favour with also the weather helping to obliterate any scent.

As for the displaced and somewhat damp migrants, they were all suffering to a greater or lesser extent from hypothermia. The cold river water being only a few degrees above zero and the nightly temperature drop into low single figures made them all understandably ask if they could return to Minsk for a flight back to the Middle East.

Following the declaration of a state of emergency along the Polish Border, attitudes had hardened during October. Belarusian GRU uniformed officers were forcibly leading into the forest groups of 100 to 500migrants along the entire border. The OMON riot police officers then assisted the Security Police to push, shove, and beat migrants with riot truncheons through razor wire fencing to enter Polish Territory. The majority are then apprehended by Polish Military and Border Guard patrols. They are then forcibly brought back to the border and pushed through temporary gaps in the razor wire fencing for that purpose far from official border crossing points between the countries. The practice of 'pushback' in Migration Policy had become formalised; a process that was applied indiscriminately to the elderly, women, children, men and the sick.

This had led to the creation within the Belarussian side of the forest, albeit 300 metres or more back from the wire, of an ever increasing refugee camp of 1000 or more people by early November. The Belarussian GRU and OMON riot police officers had added to the human misery of life in the forest by the sheer violence used to force migrants to cross again and again into Poland. Migrants had thus become trapped in the border area between both countries as hostages in a seeming political game; the Lukashenko regime on one side and Poland with the European Union on the other. The Belarussians prevent migrants from returning to Minsk or their countries of origin, while the Poles prevent migrants from entering and applying for international protection.

Against this background, by November 8th, patience and tempers on all sides, especially amongst the migrants were on a short fuse. The Belarussian Authorities had decided to direct by far the largest group of migrants in excess of 3,000 people towards the border crossing in Kuźnica Białostocka, an official border crossing point. The migrants had intended, if refused entry, to hold a peaceful protest in order to draw the world's attention to their situation. The root causes of their displacement including the motivation of the Belarussian regime rather than just today's consequences of the 'ping-pong' game played with them, as human beings, being the ball being repeatedly being pushed back and forth across the border.

The Polish Authorities had organised, either with prior knowledge of what might take place or as standard operating procedure, to have water cannon, tear gas, stun grenades, rubber bullets, and anti-riot protective gear from shields to clothing to helmets. The Belarussian Authorities, in the knowledge the World's Press would be covering the event from particularly the Belarussian side, had ensured piles of rocks and stones were conveniently placed under the guise of forthcoming remedial roadworks. Once bus-loads of migrants had been assembled in front of the Belarussian Border post, the gates were thrown open. Belarussian GRU officers, suitably dressed to blend in, were within the crowd as agent-provocateurs. Their first act was to run towards the Polish Border Post. For those in the crowd behind them, the instant conclusion was that Poland had opened their border so they stampeding through the Belarus crossing as well. Their second action was to peel off letting the crowd pass them in the knowledge that this mob hurtling towards the Polish Border would be repelled with extreme force if necessary. Loud speaker announcements were repeated stating that unless they were Polish Citizens or with valid visas plus EU approved COVID vaccination certificates, they would be refused entry. The message was repeated in Arabic as well as Russian and Polish. Border Police assisted by the Military pulled spools of razor wire in front of the Border Post. The Migrants were now less than 50 metres from the Polish Border when the water cannon exploded into action sweeping people off their feet and for a moment halting the mob. Then a flurry of one or two stones were being hurled, no doubt from the undercover Belarussian GRU officers, before seemingly the mob, in spite of its sprint to freedom had been inherently peaceful, then became full blown rioters. An hour of tear gas and stun grenades followed by water cannon washing the remaining protesters back to the Belarus Border Post made for good television news.

This was probably the watershed moment in the border dispute.

European Leaders had previously declared, at their Council Meeting on October 21st and 22nd, they would not accept any attempt by third countries to 'instrumentalise' migrants for political purposes. They condemned all hybrid attacks at its borders and affirmed that the European Union would respond accordingly.

On November 10th, Josep Borrell, High Representative for Foreign Affairs and Security Policy, issued a statement strongly condemning the Lukashenko regime for deliberately putting people's lives and well-being in danger. Mr Borrell also added, apart from stirring up the crisis at the European Union's external borders, it was an attempt to distract attention from the real situation in Belarus where brutal repression and human rights violations are continuing daily and even worsening.

A week after the Kuźnica Białostocka riot, the European Council amended its sanctions regime in response to the Belarussian Regime's manipulation of human beings for political purposes at the EU's border with Belarus. The listing criteria was broadened so the EU would now be able to target individuals and entities organising or contributing to activities by the Lukashenko regime that facilitate illegal crossing of the EU's external borders ie anyone who supports the Belarussian regime's state sponsored migrant smuggling will suffer EU sanctions.

Earlier diplomatic efforts and talks with Middle East countries and airlines by the EU now began to have an effect. Iraq stopped flights to Minsk. Cham Wings airline halted flights from Damascus. Turkish Airlines, Fly Dubai and even Belavia, Belarus's State airline, stopped citizens of Iraq, Syria, Afghanistan, Yemen, Lebanon and Libya from travelling to Minsk. As the makeshift camps in the cold border zone forest of Belarus started to empty, the first of many flights began leaving Minsk returning cheated and exhausted citizens to Baghdad and other similar cities. The promise of illegal access to the European Union had been shown to be a false hope and for some the reality of death in a foreign country's forest. Lukashenko's illegal operation was at long last step by step being closed down.

Chapter 10

Colonel Yedemsky did not touch his breakfast. Those light fluffy and crispy pancakes surrounded by blueberries were ignored as were the toppings of raspberry jam and sour cream. Similarly, the mug of tea flavoured with cinnamon sticks, cloves, and juice from pineapples, lemons, and oranges his wife had placed in front of him was left to go cold. Igor had hardly slept fearing that he might not have much longer on this earth. Whilst his wife realised her husband was worried, Olga had the good sense not to ask. It was better not to know in Putin's Russia. Leaving their central Moscow apartment, he stepped into the waiting limousine.

The previous afternoon Igor had received an order to report to his President at his Novo-Ogaryovo residence some 30 kilometres outside Moscow at 10:00 hours. It was the not-knowing that fed his fear as the car headed west on the Rublyovo-Uspenskoye Highway. Passing through the main guard post into the Presidential compound and forested estate that was in turn surrounded by a 6 metre high wall, his general unease was unchanged.

Two Spetsnaz officers in dress uniforms were stood on the gravel by the main entrance waiting for him as the limousine came to a halt. After exchanging salutes, he followed them up the steps into the Presidential building and was led into a large ballroom surrounded by paintings depicting traditional classical and military scenes. Igor was told to stand in the middle of the room with the two Spetsnaz officers taking up positions a few paces behind him. The doors were flung open and in marched two columns of the Presidential Honour Guard that formed up on either side of the ballroom and immediately presenting arms as President Putin entered the room accompanied by the Minister of Defence, Valery Vasilyevich Gerasimov (the Chief of the General Staff) and Colonel-General Laskutin.

'Colonel Yedemsky, you are here today to receive this Order of Merit to the Fatherland First Class for your outstanding and significant contribution to the defence of the Fatherland. You, like many of your colleagues, are the unsung heroes of Russia. It gives me great pleasure to give you this award in recognition of your service to the State for which I thank you on behalf of all Russians.'

Igor was stood to attention as the medal was attached and then saluted. The investiture was over. Back seemingly in seconds later in the limousine heading back to Moscow, his brief visit to the Presidential residence at Novo-Ogaryovo could only be described as surreal.

With Yedemsky's investiture over, the President's real purpose of this mid-November meeting with his top military officials began.

The Minister of Defence, General Sergei Kuzhugetovich Shoigu, said a few opening remarks before handing over to General Gerasimov who was in overall charge of deploying sufficient military equipment and soldiers for 'Operation Kursk'.

'Mr President, the 41st Combined Arms Army, having been fully relocated earlier from the Central Military District within the Smolensk Region, is now moving and repositioning around Gomel in Belarus some 360 kilometres south west of Yelnya, its previous headquarters. The battle group includes elements of the 35th and 55th Mountain Regiments, the 74th Guards Motorised Rifle Brigades, as well as the 120th Artillery Brigade and the 119th Missile Brigade, and finally the 6th Tank Regiment of the 90th Tank Division. All told, some 700 battle tanks, mechanised infantry fighting vehicles, and self-propelled howitzers together with Iskander ballistic missile launchers will be within 5 to 20 kilometres of the Belarus and Ukraine border. The E95 will provide our main access to the capital, Kyiv. I am looking at using one of the 41st Army's airborne units to secure and occupy the Chernobyl power station. The 1st Guards Tank Army has been steadily moving its nearly 800 battle tanks, a mix of T-80s and T90s, into the Belgorod Region taking up tactical positions to advance on Sumy and Kharkiv with thrusts to Kyiv from the East and also to Kramatorsk from the north and east to secure the Donbass. Notwithstanding our spring and autumn manoeuvres under Zapad 21 that enabled us to create a logistics railhead into the self-declared Donetsk and Luhansk rebel territories, military transports have been flying into Rostov-on-Don with everything from munitions to troops to howitzers so we can create that land link to the Peninsula. As for Crimea, elements of the 58th Army have left their northern Caucasus bases and are already there, including artillery units and land based cruise missile systems. I anticipate us being in strategic positions to launch an operation towards the end of January next year. However, in my battle planning discussions with the Minister, we do have some, if not concerns, then unproven assumptions-

The campaign to subjugate Ukraine is expected to take 2 to 3 days based on the intelligence provided ie we do not expect any resistance from either the local population or the Ukrainian Army-

1. Our primary objective is to secure Kyiv with minimal damage to the country's infrastructure and to arrest or kill the present Government in its entirety

2. The Black Sea fleet directed by the missile cruiser Moskva will blockade the sea routes into Kherson, Mykolaev, and Odesa whilst being ready to launch pre-programmed targeted missile strikes should it be necessary

3. MiG-31K fighter wings from Bryansk, Voronezh, Belgorod, Rostov, and Crimea will control the skies with if necessary use of the wings stationed at our new Grodno and Gomel air bases in Belarus

By the time we are ready in late January, there will be close to 200,000 troops along the Ukrainian border with Belarus and ourselves. Winter is already here and keeping men battle ready when increasingly under canvas does give me concern. There may well be a logistics issue in terms of simply ensuring adequate food and water – an army marches best as we know on a full stomach Mr President.

Nevertheless, satellite imagery will have begun to alert the US and NATO that this deployment is not related to ZAPAD 21. Whilst the military formations might still be unclear as to whether the radar reflection is a self-propelled artillery piece, a main battle tank, or another armoured fighting vehicle, we cannot hide the unusually large military build-up of troops. There are already 100,000 soldiers near Ukraine's Eastern and Northern border and in the rebel-controlled east within the Donetsk and Luhansk Regions. In addition, a further 40,000 soldiers are billeted in Crimea where we already have a basic water problem.'

'Colonel-General Laskutin have you any comments or thoughts on the Chief of the General Staff's mobilisation of our military?'

'Mr President, our responses to the inevitable questions from Governments to Western Press must be consistent and on the same page. In particular, the Foreign Secretary, Sergey Viktorovich Lavrov, and the Kremlin Press Secretary, Dmitry Peskov, must keep to the same script. We have traditionally always kept quite sizeable forces to north and east of Ukraine and to state the obvious, as a sovereign nation, we are entitled to deploy our military as we see fit. In exercising our rights, we are not planning any incursions into Ukraine as things stand unless we are provoked and forced to do so.'

'Noted Colonel-General – you must have more on your mind.'

'Thank you Mr President. Our main foreign policy objective remains to restore control and influence over post-soviet countries. To that end, military coercion - including implicit and explicit nuclear threats, diversionary attacks across many domains from the electoral process to cyberspace, and aggressive disinformation warfare are the tools we employ to undermine those states and deter the West from interfering. In 2014, we were certain about the outcome of the Crimean campaign. We had fully penetrated the Ukrainian political and security apparatus at the time, our Black Sea Fleet was already in Sevastopol, and the Ukrainian government and military were still using soviet communication systems. We knew our chances of success were high even before we acted with minimal pushback from NATO or the US. To date our efforts to penetrate Ukraine's security and political systems have not been as successful as before. The accumulated intelligence from our agents and embedded sympathisers has not provided certainty as to not only Ukraine's reaction but also the World's should an armed conflict become necessary. Ukrainian Intelligence Service has been modernised and reformed whereby we have no idea on the country's plans or indeed Zelensky's or his Government's intentions as the deployment of equipment and troops becomes apparent. Similarly, our inability to penetrate its bureaucratic, political, and economic structures at scale to comprehensively subvert through domestic corruption networks has also been curtailed by the Rule of Law or the threat of it rooting out corruption. That said, since 2014 our agents have helped us steadily amass lists of key manufacturing industrial and other properties to be specifically targeted in addition to hospitals and residential areas.'

'Minister Shoigu updates on our Black Sea Fleet that you have been modernising and expanding even faster than our

Northern, Pacific, or Baltic fleets and in particular its strategic relevance for the Chief of Staff's battle plan.'

'Mr President - the 'Moskva', the guided missile cruiser and flagship of the fleet and two Krivak-class frigates have been joined by three new Admiral Grigorovich-class guided-missile frigates. In addition, 3 Buyan-M-class crafts, carrying 8 Kalibr cruise missiles are among the small craft and patrol vessels together with 7 Kilo-class submarines completing the fleet. There are also three Alligator-class and four Ropucha-class landing ships that can land armoured fighting vehicles and troops on enemy beaches. The Chief of Staff and I are currently considering such a landing might be helpful in taking Odesa. We also have four intelligence gathering ships.

The Black Sea Fleet's long-range strike capability underscores its strategic importance not only for this operation but also others. The Kalibr missile has a range of about 2,500 kilometres and is capable of carrying nuclear warheads. From the well-protected waters around Crimea, we can launch nuclear strikes against targets in most of Europe, with Paris and London being at maximum range. If we include the deployment of roughly 48 land-based mobile versions, the launch capacity is close to triple that number from Crimea alone, our unsinkable aircraft carrier.
Crimea's role as a staging area from which to threaten parts of Europe, and to communicate this threat as part of a wider escalation-control effort, has strategic consequences far beyond the Black Sea region. The renovation and restoration of the nuclear weapons storage site known as simply as Feodosia-13 in Soviet times near the Krasnokamenka base has heightened European fears about the militarisation of the entire area. Such forward deployment and storage of

nuclear munitions close to the launch missile systems dramatically reduces warning times for the West and NATO. Perhaps we should not be surprised that this led to the end of the Intermediate-Range Nuclear Forces Treaty and much subsequent diplomatic tension between the West and Russia. Hence our current conventional military posture is already far beyond a defensive one making other Black Sea states nervous as regards our ultimate intentions.'

'Gentlemen, I met with the Foreign Secretary a few days ago to review the 3rd draft. It was circulated to you all and requires your further comment. It was headed *'Agreement on measures to ensure the security of The Russian Federation and member States of the North Atlantic Treaty Organization'*. In particular, we discussed the timing and method of its release. As one of you has already mentioned, Governments and Western Media will become more and more concerned as the deployments of equipment and military personnel increase along Ukraine's border with Belarus and us in the coming weeks. It is agreed the text will be released in Russian by the Ministry of Foreign Affairs on Friday December 17th in the afternoon. This is immediately before the last weekend before Christian Christmas. From Presidents to doormen, the West will be entirely focussed on the forthcoming festive holiday and New Year's Eve. There will be shuttle diplomacy during January and possibly into February when we will continue to appear more than ready to find, as the Americans will put it, an 'off ramp'.'

1260 kilometres due west of Novo-Ogaryovo, Poland's Prime Minister was in his Warsaw Chancellery conference room having convened an urgent meeting. The Ministers of Defence, Interior, Special Forces to the Minister of Foreign

Affairs and the Generals commanding the Army and Air Force plus Lieutenant-General Politczek as the Head of ABW were all present.

'Last night, the US Secretary of State, Mr Anthony Blinken, and the US Secretary of Defence, Mr Lloyd Austin, in a video call confirmed finally our own worst fears that were reported previously by our Intelligence Services earlier this summer. The Kremlin's latest military build-up is undoubtedly a prelude to an eventual invasion of Ukraine, probably in late January or during February. With the ZAPAD 21 military exercises completed months ago, there is no other rational explanation for this mobilisation. Russia has been willing to use military force before to conduct aggressive actions against Ukraine as we reflect on the West's past inadequate response to the seizure of Crimea and its subsequent invasion of parts of the Donetsk and Luhansk Regions. The Americans have also commented that the Russian Military is making much less effort to hide the current equipment, troop, and battle group movements. This changed behaviour is significantly far more serious than simply wishing to threaten overwhelming force for political ends.'

The Minister of Defence was the first to speak. 'Prime Minister, unlike 2014, we now have strategic intelligence about Russian preparations for the planned invasion. Our military planners are particularly concerned with the movement of the 41st Combined Arms Army which is now closer to the Belarus and Ukrainian border. They believe this eventual massing is more related to a probable military thrust to capture Kyiv and certainly nothing to do with the European Union and our recent border issues with Belarus.

Nevertheless, if Russia did start a war with NATO, the 41st Army's task would be to lead the combined Russian and Belarus armies' advance towards the Suwalki gap. Such an advance would likely be made in conjunction with the 11th Army Corps in Kaliningrad. Whilst NATO military planners have long 'gamed' such a scenario, after 2014 when Russia illegally annexed Crimea, and continued to destabilize eastern Ukraine by supporting the 'so-called' separatists in the Donbass, this triggered the biggest reinforcement of our collective defence since the end of the Cold War. NATO deployed battlegroups in the Baltics and here, combat ready NATO troops, and also raised its presence in the Black Sea. Today's reality is that Russia is preparing militarily to invade Ukraine again. What will NATO's, and particularly led by the United States, further action be to protect and defend its eastern flank from the Baltics to the Black Sea region?'

'If last night's conversation is anything to go by then we can expect an increased US presence from boots on the ground here in Poland within a NATO framework. Foreign Minister, you wish to speak.'

'Thank you Prime Minister - the 2015 Minsk Accords, brokered by France and Germany, stipulated that Ukraine would regain full control of its border with Russia in the rebel-held territories only after the election of local leaders and legislatures. The Rada recently introduced a draft law on such transitional administration after elections under Ukrainian law. The Kremlin disliked the draft legislation because the separatist republics would no longer be under its control. France, Germany, Russia and Ukraine, collectively known as the Normandy Group, were of course formed to settle the conflict. However, my counter-parts in

France and Germany have confirmed the rhetoric from the Russians has been increasingly forceful demanding legislation Ukraine would need to change, what laws it should adopt, which laws it should not adopt, how it should recognise the puppet republics in the Donbass. In other words, Russia wants to have the Minsk agreement implemented only on its own terms. It is now clearly underpinning these demands with military might. NATO is a defensive alliance even though Russia continues to ignore that pertinent fact. Nevertheless, the West has now to send the strongest of political signals to Russia in the coming weeks saying a further invasion of a sovereign country's territory will incur major and irreversible consequences - actions in support of such warnings are the most powerful when we are united.'

'General Politczek.'

'Prime Minister, Russian State Television has begun to portray themselves as the victims of Ukrainian aggression. Thus the country needs to defend itself. Mobilising armed forces in preparation for an invasion is a strategic military activity but starting such an operation of that scale is a political decision. This means that President Putin alone will make that call. We should expect accusations from Putin or his regime that we, the West, have escalated the Ukrainian conflict by supplying lethal weaponry whilst creating an atmosphere of russophobia. Furthermore, it is only since part of its military is stationed along the Ukraine's eastern, northern, and southern border that the West has paid any attention to its legitimate security and other concerns. Undoubtedly, there will be a flurry of Western Leaders seeking to de-escalate the apparent drumbeat towards a war within Europe in the 21st Century. Regrettably, such summits serve only to massage Putin's ego and will not, in my opinion, bring any positive results.

The time for appeasement has passed and history has shown us a bully can only be stopped by force. However, Putin's message to Zelensky and his Government is to my mind clear – do as we say or have war. Like the United Kingdom, the United States, and our Baltic friends we have been supplying Ukraine with military equipment, munitions, and training since 2014. Whatever else we have been doing surreptitiously to date needs to be drastically increased in the coming days and weeks and we need to ask what more can Poland be doing? I am certain the West will be increasingly asked for former Soviet Union heavy armour, jets, and artillery gathering dust in former Warsaw Pact countries' military warehouses in addition to more modern hand held anti-tank weaponry, ground to air missiles, and unmanned aerial vehicles (UAVs) like the Bayraktar TB2 drones already supplied by Turkey. This is not a choice option as the Russian Bear under Putin will be here next and the Ukrainian Army will be fighting for its citizens as well as Poland's. GROM Team 4 is embedded as specialist trainers at the Ukrainian Army's Yavoriv military training base in western Ukraine - some 10 kilometres from the border with Poland and 30 kilometres northwest of Lviv. Prime Minister, I would like permission to deploy GROM Team 6 immediately into northwest Ukraine as requested by my Ukrainian counterpart.'

'Grzegorz aren't you stepping outside your chain of command?'

'No Prime Minister, the Ministers of the Interior and Special Forces have sanctioned the deployment. It is of course led by Major Król. You have asked to be consulted whenever this officer is being placed in the line of fire as the only living soldier holding Virtuti Militari Knights Cross and bar.'

'Agreed General – I suspect this is one time when the less I know the better - continue.'

'Notwithstanding the US intelligence debacle in Afghanistan, our own intelligence supports what the Americans are telling us. Whilst Russia's ongoing troop movements only foster a heightened sense of unease and unpredictability about the Kremlin's ultimate intentions, the ultimate goal is, in my view, the removal of the democratic government and the installation of a puppet regime. We have no time to waste and need to use every channel available to us whereby our military aid, and that of other NATO members, is massively increased.'

'This does rather make a rather important assumption that the Ukrainian Army is capable of resisting a Russian onslaught where it is outgunned and out-numbered. What is the military's view?'

General Piotr Modzelwski, the Chief of the General Staff and Marshal of the Polish Army, responded to the Prime Minister's question.

'Prime Minister, whilst neither NATO as a whole, nor the United States or any other individual member of the alliance, is prepared to risk war with Russia over Ukraine as the last 7 years have evidenced, the Ukrainian Military in 2014, weakened by years of neglect and underfunding, faced Russia's occupation Crimea and invasion of eastern Ukraine. Since that time, the Ukrainian armed forces has adopted NATO standards and received significant training and assistance from alliance members including the U.S. Many of these reforms began out of the experience of defending against Russian aggression in the Donbass. The reforms have ranged from the tactical to the strategic levels and have included transparency, countering corruption, modernizing equipment, defence procurement, reforming command and control, and increasing professionalization. Whilst significant hurdles remain to eliminate corruption, bureaucracy, and needless political infighting, Ukraine had 6,000 combat-ready troops in 2014. Today, the army numbers around 200,000 troops with significantly improved capabilities, personnel, and readiness. Although the army continues to implement reforms in line with NATO standards, it will remain heavily influenced by its Soviet legacy until all its equipment is entirely modernised and its soldiers trained on that new hardware. Perhaps rather than Putin's and his regime's somewhat bizarre perceptions about Ukraine being part of Russia, since Ukraine's Revolution of Dignity exposed Yanukovych as a totally corrupt politician with undeniable links to Moscow, the people's mood began to change from ambivalence to disgust. When Russia later that year annexed Crimea and then fermented an undeclared war in eastern Ukraine, the Ukrainian people's resolve to leave Russia's orbit and to seek closer ties to the West started to become a reality. If a full scale or even a lesser onslaught does take place, Ukraine's collective consciousness will be that Russia is a mortal enemy and there can be no way back for Ukraine to Russia's orbit. In answer therefore, the Ukrainian Army will in our opinion undoubtedly fight with the wholesale support of the civilian population. Importantly, as a student of history, I recall Colonel Hal Moore's response *(later Lieutenant-General)* to General William Westmoreland in November 1965 after the battle of La Drang Valley. Westmoreland commented that the US was going to win the Vietnam War. Moore's response was both simple and direct - 'it is not our land'. Furthermore, the long-term task of occupying, administering, and militarily policing such a vast territory will require an occupation army in excess of 500,000. With an openly hostile population and insurgent resistance, the Kremlin can only believe its own logic for expanding the conflict with a once-friendly neighbouring country.'

'Thank you Marshal, Interior Minister you are unusually quiet today.'

'Not so much quiet Prime Minister rather absorbing what our Cabinet colleagues have been saying. One aspect that we must consider with our NATO colleagues, the U.S, and Ukraine's Government is the consistent manner by which the Russians will seek to create a pretext for an unprovoked assault to widen the conflict. I am also thinking of 'false flag' activities as we all know the Russians will lie and lie and lie. In addition, we have not considered the resolve of President Zelensky and his Government to this very tangible Russian threat.'

'Perhaps I can attempt to answer that Prime Minister' said the Foreign Minister. Receiving the nod to do so, he continued. 'Most of us have by now met Volodymyr Zelensky since his landslide election victory in 2019 where he received on the second ballot 73% of the votes cast. Within days as the president-elect, Zelensky faced his first foreign policy challenge. Putin announced his decision to offer Russian passports to the Ukrainian citizens in separatist-controlled areas of war-torn eastern Ukraine. The Russian-backed hybrid war there was entering its fifth year, and hundreds of thousands of Ukrainians had been displaced by the conflict. Zelensky ridiculed the offer, responding with a Facebook post that extended Ukrainian citizenship to Russians and others 'who suffer from authoritarian or corrupt regimes'. I mention this true story as though the man is still a political novice his capacity to face down Vladimir Putin should no longer be questioned. In September 2019, Zelensky found his administration thrust into the centre of a political scandal in the United States when a whistleblower in the intelligence community lodged a formal complaint about the actions of US President Donald Trump. The matter concerned Trump's alleged withholding of a significant military aid package to Ukraine unless Ukraine initiated an investigation of alleged wrongdoing by former U.S vice president Joe Biden and his son Hunter. Zelensky's transition team declined a request to meet with Rudolph Giuliani over what they saw as a matter of internal U.S politics. Trump admitted that he had ordered the bi-partisan US$400 million military aid package, authorised by Congress, withheld in anticipation of a phone call with Zelensky on July 25th 2019. Trump discussed an investigation of the Biden family and later claimed no quid pro quo was offered or demanded. Those funds were finally released on September 11th 2019. However, Trump's alleged attempt to pressure Zelensky served as the basis for a U.S House of Representatives impeachment inquiry that was opened on September 24th 2019. Political novice or not, we should take further comfort from this example of his ability to withstand political pressure from someone like Trump.

Nevertheless, Zelensky is an actor-turned-politician who capitalised on the success of his production company's popular TV series 'Servant of the People', in which he starred as a high school history teacher who becomes a much-loved president. Whilst he basically turned that show into real life, being President in office was not quite so easy. His approval ratings have plummeted over the first two years of his presidency. His election promise to resolve tensions with Russia have become increasingly impossible to deliver. Zelensky had believed that he could bring peace just by sitting down Putin and talking through the issues. However, Russia's agenda is more about swallowing up Ukraine. Similarly, his other key election promise about rooting out corruption suffered. Though his political agenda with the passage of a law intended to curb the influence of oligarchs had been passed by the Verkhovna Rada effective implementation was too slow. In addition, his relationship with Kolomoisky past and present raised concerns in the electorate.

Ihor Kolomoisky is a household name to Ukrainians. He had acquired in the early 1990s former state-owned enterprises like steel plants to gas wells at fire-sale prices and become a leading Ukrainian oligarch. Kolomoisky displayed a ruthlessness that made even other oligarchs, no strangers to violent crime, blanch. His notorious corporate raiding *(reiderstvo)* and asset stripping across Ukraine was reportedly a function of paying off local judges and magistrates in the process. With strong arm tactics and intimidation, by the mid-2010s, Kolomoisky was one of the most powerful figures in Ukraine. His portfolio enabled him to own one of Ukraine's biggest banks, PrivatBank. When the Bank was nationalised in 2016, it had a US$5.6 billion hole in its balance sheet through shady and imprudent lending practices ie 97% of the corporate loans had been made to related parties of the main shareholders, Kolomoisky and Gennadiy Bogolyubov. Using a myriad of anonymous shell companies and offshore accounts, these entities acquired overseas real estate assets anonymously with no money laundering checks. It was all too easy to defraud PrivatBank depositors. The U.S has sanctioned Kolomoisky for his significant involvement in such corruption and the Ukrainian State had to nationalise the bank.

As an actor, entertainer, and producer, Zelensky had worked for and with Kolomoisky's media network. It had provided him with a valuable platform during his presidential campaign. Zelensky was thus seen unavoidably tarnished as time went on as the Kolomoisky candidate and puppet by the general public with Kolomoisky possibly directing policy behind the scenes.

Today, Zelensky and Kolomoisky appear to have grown apart. Whereas the oligarch once claimed to be a Ukrainian patriot, in recent years Kolomoisky has begun calling for a new partnership between Ukraine and Russia. When that happens, Kolomoisky is quoted as saying 'NATO will be soiling its pants and buying pampers'. After 2014 seizure of Crimea and the war with Russian backed separatists, that is not a remark that will appeal to Ukrainians when the Nation's wealth has been endlessly plundered by a string of similar greedy oligarchs.

Zelensky's political image had long remained indestructible even as Kolomoisky's corrupt business dealings came to light. However, his presidential team made two unforced blunders. A clumsy justification of the president's offshore business holdings revealed subsequently in the Pandora Papers that had in fact been previously fully declared and disclosed during the Election Process. In addition, the ousting of Dymtro Razumkov, former Chairman/Speaker of Verkhovna Rada and the first Leader of Zelensky's Servant of the People Party – a man strongly associated with its election promise to fight corruption. These factors coupled together with energy-related hardships for Ukrainians and a new wave of COVID-19 reduced his approval ratings to 28%. The populist reform platform that swept Zelensky into office appears to be stalled at the mid-point of his Presidential Term.'

'Grzegorz, any smoke regarding Zelensky's relationship with Kolomoisky?'

'ABW does not believe so. We carried out a detailed investigation prior to the 2019 election as we would do for any potential Head of State. The relationship as actor, screenwriter, and producer for Kvartal 95, his company, were all normal contracts for specific tasks with 1 + 1 Media Group. Contracts no different in terms of content or reward where he had been employed by a competitor to 1 + 1. Contract monies received by his Panama companies also matched the contracted amounts. There were no unexplained monies and his tax planning did not breach Ukrainian Tax Law. Kolomoisky is of course still a major shareholder in 1 + 1. Unfortunately for Zelensky some of

Kolomoisky's toxicity has stuck with him in the electorate's mind – guilt by association but not reality.'

GROM Team 6 completed the debrief in one of Gdansk map rooms. They were shown high resolution satellite views of the destruction of Brest's Police Regional Headquarters and the aftermath of the Glyadovichi warehouse strike. Colonel Pawlukowicz was pleased to learn that, in accordance with operational protocols, Radek and his team had removed anything that might lead to there being any suspicion of a Polish GROM unit having been in Belarus. The regiment's stores had also confirmed mines, motion detectors, and cameras were all fully accounted for. The caves had clearly been meticulous checked for any signs of their recent occupation including dis-assembling the cast iron stove as a compilation of the Team's video clips proved beyond any doubt. Master-Sergeant Nowak had similarly filmed the burning of any rubbish. The remnants together with any fire ash were buried in the latrines before they were in turn were covered with soil and ground cover.

Their orders had been to relieve GROM Team 4 led by Kapitan Filip Cuda at the Ukrainian Army's Yavoriv military training base. However, in the light of recent intelligence, both GROM units were given a week's leave before reporting to Colonel Stepan Nalyvaichenko at Ukraine's northern base of its West Military District. With the heightening tension with Russia, the Ukrainian Military were increasingly concerned that its highly forested border with Belarus across its Lutsk and Rivne Regions provided an easy infiltration route. Bearing in mind the majority of the Ukrainian Army is looking to defend its northern, east, and southern flanks, it just does not have the manpower to close off this soft access into Ukraine. The strategic concern is Russian special forces or similar Belarussian units will be conducting missions to force the Ukrainian Army to weaken its other fronts by having to send troops to cover this more recent covert backdoor into Ukraine.

Bartek allowed himself a wry smile as he took the train from Gdansk back to Warsaw. It had to be Radek Król who asked –

'To be clear, we take our orders from Colonel Nalyvaichenko including being sanctioned to use extreme force?'

Alexandra was delighted to see Radek, her man, home in Niepolomice even if only for a week before the Polish Nation had him, and others, once more being placed in harm's way. Maja was now over a year old. Alexandra resented Radek had missed so much of the year but being the wife of a GROM officer and soldier on active service, it went with the territory.

Yet Alexandra was not living in a vacuum as to world events. With her former service as an M16 operative, a sixth sense, or possibly a woman's intuition, was telling her of trouble ahead beyond COVID. Watching on TVN, Ukraine's Foreign Minister and the US Secretary of State give a press conference following their meeting in Washington on November 10th. Anthony Blinken had confirmed the discussions focused on Ukraine's neighbour, Russia, and went on to say Washington was deeply concerned by reports of 'unusual Russian military activity' near the Ukrainian border warning escalatory or aggressive action would be of serious concern to the United States. Russia was also accused by Dymtro Kuleba, Ukraine's Foreign Minister of holding back energy supplies amid record high gas prices. Putin and Lavrov blamed the EU's energy policy intimating supplies can be boosted to Europe once the Nord Stream 2 gas pipeline gets approved. Again Anthony Blinken was firm in his response in that Russia could and should take steps to alleviate the energy crunch by increasing gas supplies. In addition, he said should Russia attempt to use energy as a weapon or commit further aggressive acts against Ukraine, the U.S is committed, as is Germany, to taking appropriate action.

Pentagon confirmed a few days later on November 12th that General Mark A. Milley, the chairman of the Joint Chiefs of Staff, had spoken with Lieutenant General Valery Zaluzhny, the commander in chief of Ukraine's military, to discuss Russia's concerning activity along its borders. When CNN's White House spokesperson that weekend stated American and British intelligence were increasingly convinced that President Vladimir Putin was considering military action to take control of a larger swath of Ukraine, or to destabilize the country enough to usher in a more pro-Moscow government, Alexandra's thoughts crystallised. War might not be inevitable. However, the West had, she thought, to be cohesive and ready to work together, if not then the risk of the Kremlin making a terrible miscalculation goes up. On the other hand, if Russia is so intent on securing a land route between its separatist engineered rebellion in eastern Ukraine and the Crimean peninsula, then whatever the West does or does not do becomes irrelevant, except for giving the Ukrainian Army the tools to fight off any Russian Military incursions or a full invasion.

It was Sunday morning as Alexandra made breakfast for Maja and her. She was listened to a BBC newscast repeating NATO's Secretary General, Jens Stoltenberg, his own warnings about Russia speaking in Berlin on the 12th.

'It is urgent that Russia shows transparency about the build-up of its large and unusual concentration of Russian military forces on Ukraine's border, de-escalates and reduces tensions'.

Her thoughts were interrupted by the compound buzzer. It was a military Mercedes s.500 though it was not painted khaki. The number plate plus a smartly dressed Boatswain in full dress naval uniform did rather give the game away.

Radek was on the front porch. Alexandra had her arms round Radek's neck kissing and hugging him tightly. 'Come inside we're having breakfast' she gasped. The Boatswain had deposited Radek's large leather duffel travels and his suiters in the hall and tactfully exited.

As the morning progressed, Elsa and Tomek came over with the dogs to see their son after attending 'Our Lady of Rosary', the local parish church. With gentle admonishments to Radek to stop feeding cookies to the dogs if he was not going to clear up the mess by Alexandra, laughter tea and family conversation ensued. Elsa demanded that Maja should have lunch with them and Tomek smiled at Radek as they left with a comment out of hearing of the Ladies - 'time Maja had a brother or sister'.

During the whole week Radek was home, Alexandra kept her own council about what she perceived was happening in the

East. She deliberately avoided any conversations with him that might inevitably force her to ask about his next mission for Poland, and in her mind also for Western Democracy.

When the column of 5 humvees arrived outside the compound the following Sunday, she was joined by Elsa Tomek and the St Bernards with Radek proudly holding little Maja in his arms. Farewells and goodbyes are never easy when care and love are in the air. Nevertheless, Alexandra managed to keep her composure throughout. Once the column had left she turned dewy eyed to look at Elsa & Tomek who were similarly close to tears. 'Will he be home with us on Christmas Eve?' asked Elsa. Alexandra and Tomek exchanged glances but did not answer her as they all walked back indoors with little Maja cradled protectively by her mother.

As the Polish column approached and crossed the border, Alexandra and Tomek were alone in the lounge by the roaring log fire listening to the evening news. It was full of the Washington Post's disclosure that US intelligence had found the Kremlin was planning a multi-front offensive against Ukraine in the New Year. Its reporting was based on an unclassified intelligence document and corroborative statements from unnamed Pentagon sources. Officials in the Biden Administration on the basis of anonymity had confirmed the detail of this highly sensitive intelligence information.

Alexandra and Tomek were on the edges of their armchairs lest they misheard even one word as their faces changed from concern to deep worry for the safety of Poland's best.

The newscaster continued that the Russian plan indicated a military offensive against Ukraine as soon as early 2022 with a scale of forces twice what were seen during its snap spring exercise near Ukraine's borders. With a large scale map of Ukraine, a retired U.S military general highlighted for viewers the planned extensive movement of a 100 tactical battle groups with an estimated 175,000 personnel, along with armour, artillery and equipment with frightening arrows showing the most probable lines of attack by Russia's military. There was then with yet another retired U.S General taking viewers through the satellite photos from the intelligence document, now on screen, that showed Russian forces massing in four locations. While Ukrainian assessments consider approximately 94,000 troops are already in near border locations, U.S Intelligence put the number presently at 70,000 but predicted a build-up to as many as 175,000 or more. When asked by the newscaster about the extensive movement of battalion sized tactical groups to and from the border areas by the Russians, the General response was simply their actions were to confuse everyone as to their real intentions and to create more uncertainty.

The newscaster finished this section of 'Breaking News' stating this crisis was provoking fears of a renewed war on European soil after nearly 80 years of peace and in the 21st Century had mankind learnt nothing?

Chapter 11

Colonel Stepan Nalyvaichenko was a 46 year old and active, but rotund, jolly man who had done his soldiering with the Azov Regiment fighting Russian Separatists and Russian Regulars in Donetsk and Mariupol in 2014 and thereafter. Two metres tall, a completely shaved head, a raucous laugh, and a hand like a meat cleaver greeted Radek and Filip.

'I am going to have you police the width and breadth of the Pripiat-Stokhid National Park together with peripheral forests. The Ruskies will believe the flat topography of Prypyat and Stokhid rivers meanderings has, as far as we are concerned, formed a natural barrier to covert entry. Swamps, bogs, peatlands, wetlands, and riverine islands are not easily traversed, especially in the absence of local knowledge. Nevertheless, the rivers do feed into the Dnieper River downstream as they flow through the middle of Ukraine. The outer boundaries form a long and thin shape running west-to-east for 50 kilometres and north-south for an average of 10 kilometres. In the spring, our Ministry of Ecology and Natural Resources financed the construction of a number of observation decks and towers, which will aid your control of the entire open flatlands. There is an old waterman's cottage set back from the natural park in light woodland. This will be your base. It is dry and warm with log burning stoves for heating and hot water. There are also two medium sized ribs so you can access the lakes, rivers, and flooded areas. The pantry is stocked with basics though there are wild boar and deer with of course fish to be hunted. You have oil lamps and candles. I will expect a nightly report even if nothing to report via the radio set in the building. I will give you the encrypted channel protocol and call sign. Anything else you want to know?'

'How long do you see us being on this mission?' asked Filip. Stepan furrowed his brow, lit a cigarette, and with a chuckle 'Until after Orthodox Christmas by which time we will need to refill that pantry!'

'Colonel, I am going to ask a dumb question what are our orders regarding any Russian or Belarussian forces found on Ukrainian territory?'

'If they are those mercenary Wagner bastards, part of Russia's GRU, then the Ukrainian Army does not want them as prisoners of war after the war crimes they committed in the Donbass. Similarly, should Russian or Belarussian special forces units cross our border, they are not entering Ukraine to play bridge or take us out to dinner. These covert actors, that might even include Kadyrov's Chechen murderers and rapists, are attempting to infiltrate our land solely to destabilise this country for which there can be no forgiveness or quarter. Your unofficial motto within GROM is, I believe, silent and unseen – those are your orders. Are you clear?'

Snow was falling as the humvees came to a halt outside the Waterman's cottage. Both Radek and Filip together with their teams all agreed 'cottage' was a mis-description. It was a building that still felt to them as if it had room to spare even after all 20 of them had found their bunks in 5 different but large bedrooms formed in the roof space. The building sat in a slight hollow surrounded by a mixture of shrub and evergreens – unless you knew it was there it was not there. There was no cellar unsurprisingly. No doubt the water table made such construction difficult, if not impossible. A long wooden barn became a convenient garage and workshop. It was also where the diesel generators and oil storage tanks were housed.

Radek, Filip, and the Master-Sergeants Kacper Stodola and Bartek Nowak strolled round the cottage's outer perimeter thinking about how to protect their new home base from a surprise attack. The conditions were unpleasant as snow turned to sleet then rain before starting the entire process again in reverse. With the wind coming from the north and north-east, these were not the sort of conditions to be outside even wearing proper arctic kit.

Whilst it was on the one hand, a bonus, given their mission, the cottage was unseen and unknown. On the other hand it exposed them to the threat of an unseen attack. After pouring over a plan of the buildings for half an hour, a decision was made to rely on motion detectors linked to 'day & night' vision cameras, all suitably camouflaged and hidden. All this protective communications equipment, night vision systems and battlefield sensors were linked to a laptop. With winter approaching, this was a better alternative to an hourly watch rota through the night that would over time wear everyone down. The Master-Sergeants agreed, which was not always the case, any covert entry into the park would be during the shorter daylight hours. The risks of sinking into swamps, quicksand, deep stagnant pools of water, small lakes, and even the rivers during the night were high, especially with temperatures increasingly below zero, at this time of year and at night. This made night infiltration into and across the Pripiat-Stokhid National Park very high risk particularly if heavy snow or blizzard conditions persisted.

Within hours of their arrival, Tomek Jureki had returned with a freshly gralloched deer carcass. Piotr Vrubel had obtained 50 kilo bags of potatoes, carrots, onions, and baking flour from the Lutsk Army kitchen before the column left Lutsk. The GROM team might have to brave chilling wintry conditions during daytime but at least they would not be force to consume dull and tasteless military rations day after day.

Master-Sergeant Stodola was smiling as the gear was unloaded from the various humvees enjoying Bartek saying 'Good call Kacper at Mielec, we definitely need all our Norwegian artic gear and those digital snow camo coveralls.'

That evening after dinner, Radek discussed Colonel Nalyvaichenko orders as bottles of Belvedere were passed round.

'Gentlemen, we are all professional soldiers. Some might even say we are members of an elite group of soldiery. Today we are operating under the instructions of our Government once again on Foreign Soil. This mission is unpublicised and highly sensitive politically. We are deployed to assist the Ukrainian Army in stopping any infiltration by clandestine operators along its border with Belarus. It is clear that Belarus is, after the last 18 months, clearly now a vassal state of Russia if not simply a large region. These individuals or groups will seek, if they can, to undermine the Ukraine Government. Colonel Nalyvaichenko has dealt with the cruelty and inhumanity of the Russian Army since 2014 in the Donbass. Hence, anyone entering Ukrainian Territory without passing through an authorised crossing is an enemy of the State. Nevertheless, I am uncomfortable about us implementing a 'shoot to kill' policy as the Colonel considers appropriate even if they happen to be Kadyrov's Chechen scum. Whilst accepting the military necessity to stop such covert intrusions, the intruders will undoubtedly be Russian agents. Nevertheless, I do not see this as a justifiable reason effectively operate a somewhat murderous policy of execution on 'shoot to kill' orders. If Democracy is, for all its faults and inconsistencies, to survive, it will not do so by joining Russia in the gutter.'

'Whether or not the Ukrainian Army or its Border Guard will accept prisoners, I do not see how we could cope in and around the cottage holding such personnel under guard. It would have the potential to be an increasing nightmare and security risk. GRU and FSB people, especially those attempting to be here undercover, will know the risks in so-called peacetime' uttered Piotr Vrubel.

'Would you think differently if Ukraine was at war with Russia Piotr?' pondered Filip Cuda looking directly at Vrubel and the others.

'As far as Ukrainians are concerned the country has been at war with Russia since the annexation of Crimea and its manufactured insurrection in the Donbass' uttered Kacper Stodola.

'Whether we are on our own ground or elsewhere we have a Code of Honour based on ethics and historic Polish Chivalry. We are not barbarians and if good is to triumph over evil, we should not abandon those values Radek' voiced Bartek.

A period of quiet ensued with each man taking a shot or gulp from one of the bottles of Belvedere vodka circulating whilst considering what they had been asked to do by Colonel Nalyvaichenko and what they should do.

The silence was broken by Radek.

'Gentlemen, I have no wish to look in the mirror and ever be ashamed of any past action whilst serving my country. We have no idea who will cross into this region but they are likely to be hostile. My belief is that we should attempt to see these individuals surrender, return lethal fire if fired upon, and take the survivors or injured to the nearest Border Guard Post.'

The shot glasses were refilled, raised, and some clinked together as in one voice the toast was *'Zgoda, Polska na zawsze'* (agreed, Poland forever).

Winter was coming to Pripiat-Stokhid National Park as in the following week intermittent flurries of snow during the day forewarned of heavier falls during the night.

Recognising that they were on foreign soil, the unit decided to speak in Russian, especially when using their comms.

Although the built-in encryption should protect all their internal communication, a slip into Polish could result in serious political embarrassment for Poland's Government. Every item of clothing was checked to ensure no Polish badging. The humvees had already been suitably doctored in Mielec whilst they were in the armoury and clothing store.

The observation towers proved to be the best points to watch for movement during the shortened daylight hours. However, being up high with little movement risked anyone freezing to death unless rotated. Therefore, the decks were used to check on the absence of any unknown presence in the general area of a patrol and used to overview the safety on return. With snow clouds increasingly lessening visibility, 4 man foot patrols with varying patterns became the way forward. This helped to familiarise everyone with the terrain, its dangers, and ultimately the decision to break out the cross-country skis.

In these conditions, during daylight, they were using Revision's helmet in arctic white with the facemask seamlessly integrating the goggle and balaclava. However, for extra capability to observe and manoeuvre in all weather conditions during limited visibility and under all lighting conditions they had been provided with ENVG-B goggles (enhanced night vision goggle) to trial. These were purported by the manufacturer as enabling them to see and understand more quickly than other troops what is going on around them. These yellow tinted lens goggles should also allegedly make it easier for soldiers to differentiate between potential enemies in front of them and the background they might be hiding in. The goggles also had a double-tubed binocular system for better situational awareness and depth perception with higher resolution thanks to their phosphorescent white colours used in a fused thermal imager with augmented reality and wireless interconnectivity. Well thought Bartek, if there were a mission to trial these goggles, this was it. After handing out this kit, the Master-Sergeant also provided the leader of each 4 man unit with a high resolution military grade telescope specifically for arctic conditions.

The week was spent getting more used to their new equipment and dealing with the harsh environment even for the properly equipped. The silent enemy was boredom. After enjoying Piotr's pork stew, the result of a hapless wild boar running into Tomek Jarocki during a patrol earlier in the day, the radio was their only link to the outside world.

Pawel, Mr IT, gave a loud shout for everyone to listen bringing even those who had crashed upstairs on their bunks downstairs. The US Secretary of State, Antony Blinken, was giving a Press Conference in Washington before departing for Latvia and an OCSE meeting in Sweden.

'The US analysis of Russia's plans is based in part on satellite images that show newly arrived units at various locations along the Ukrainian border over the last month and supporting intelligence. This clear evidence shows Russia has made plans for significant aggressive moves against Ukraine and there would be severe consequences, including high-impact economic measures, if Russia were to invade. Our President has stated, his Administration, in conjunction with our European and NATO allies is now preparing measures to raise the cost of any new invasion by Mr Putin's regime. The President has also affirmed it will be the most comprehensive

and meaningful set of initiatives thereby making it very difficult for Mr Putin to go ahead and do what people are worried he may do. We don't know whether President Putin has made the decision to invade. We do know that Russia is putting in place the capacity to do so on short order should Mr Putin so decide. We must prepare for all contingencies and be ready to forestall any attempts by Russia to false flag actions in Ukraine as a pretext for a military invasion. In these circumstances, we are also urging Ukraine to exercise restraint because, again, the Russian playbook is to claim provocation for something that they were planning to do all along.'

One could hear a pin drop in the cottage as Pawel held up his hand for continued silence – there was more to come.

A State Department official made her way to the lectern.

'During 2021, there has been a dramatic escalation of both President Putin's and his Regime's rhetoric regarding Ukraine. US Intelligence's analysis is that Russia is laying the groundwork for an invasion. The Russian government has also been waging a propaganda campaign against the United States. In the past month, Russian proxies and media outlets have started to increase content denigrating Ukraine and NATO in order to focus, on them, the blame for Russia's military escalation along Ukraine's borders. The Kremlin media narrative emphasizes continually that Ukrainian leaders were installed by the West, harbour a hatred for all things Russian, and were indeed acting against the interests of the Ukrainian people. Russian Foreign Minister, Mr Sergei Lavrov echoed his President's this week repeating his warnings about US military equipment and activity

encroaching on Russia's borders inferring, in his words, 'the nightmare scenario of military confrontation is returning'. Mr Putin has commented that recent drills by US Strategic Air Command over the Black Sea posed a nuclear and security threat to Moscow in addition to the US defensive missile systems in Poland and Romania. Mr Putin also expressed concern about NATO deploying missiles on Ukrainian territory with a flight time of less than 10 minutes to Moscow. This latter remark is complete fabrication and untrue but is indicative of a wider strategy to justify the Regime's future actions.

The sudden mobilization of reservists does not have a credible explanation. Whilst Russian officials have defended the reserve mobilization as a necessary measure to help modernize the Russian armed forces, it defies credulity. US Intelligence has raised concerns about the 'sudden and rapid' programme to establish a ready reserve of contract reservists numbering an additional 100,000 troops to those deployed now. Mr Putin could quickly order an invasion of Ukraine and this is why the State Department and others in the President's administration have been sounding alarms about the threat of an imminent invasion.

The Regime continues of course to dismiss our warnings as mere rumours without any foundation. Russia has apparently no intention of threatening anyone. Such statements are of course part of the Kremlin's wider policy of continuing deflection from the truth.'

'Anything else Pawel maybe on another frequency?' asked Filip. As Pawel twiddled the knobs, there was a loud but soft screech as he tuned into Ukraine's Radio Liberty, the programme was just finishing, in Ukrainian, what had just been voiced by the US Secretary of State and a senior official of the Department in Washington.

The Radio Presenter had clearly interrupted an interview with a Government spokesperson.

'I would add to what Washington has just voiced. Our Intelligence Service has been certain for some time that the military exercises have allowed for equipment and munitions to be left behind at various training facilities. This enables an even more rapid build-up and deployment for yet a further attack on Ukraine. Importantly, these exercises conducted this year near our borders have without doubt helped the Russian Military rehearse for an invasion. Our Intelligence suggests the issues of creating strike groups, logistical support, and transfer of significant military contingents from within Russia have had the benefit of being worked out in real time on the ground. Whilst its military planners may be seeking to engage our Army on multiple fronts, perhaps the Kremlin's objective is not so much territory but capitulation by our democratically elected Government. It is important to remember where this provocative action is coming from. It is not the United States. It is not NATO. It is not the EU and it is definitely not Ukraine. Since 2014, we have been in effect locked in a frozen war with Russia but have sought, and continue to do so, to live in peace with our larger neighbour, Russia. Our Government's mission continues to be the removal of the daily grind of poverty and build a better life for all Ukrainians in a peaceful country.'

The silence was broken by one of the youngest GROM soldiers, Rafal Dudek, 'Well that's a relief – we are here to kill Russians - that rocks my boat!' There was both applause and laughter across the room as a fresh bottle of Belvedere appeared.

Piotr Vrubel had just climbed up the observation tower. It was nearly 08:30 hours but visibility was still poor even for a shorter December day. It certainly did not feel like dawn more like the start of an arctic night. The wind was from the north-east and bitterly cold. Notwithstanding he had only left the cottage 30 minutes earlier on skis, standing on a platform some 20 metres above the ground made you seriously exposed to the elements. Your body, though warm from the recent physical exercise and protected by layers of protective clothing, is being told by your brain not to remain where you are. Piotr pulled out his thermos of strong black hot coffee pouring a cup full. Insulated gloves once more cradling carefully the thermos top, he began to cast his eye across the expanse of forest, wetland, and lake. A wedge of geese exploded from the far side of the lake. However what had suddenly encouraged or startled them to take flight was unclear as they quickly landed on clearer lake water metres away. Ducks similarly and again briefly took flight before landing again. Finishing the last mouthful of coffee and then adjusting his protective balaclava and face mask, he fished out from lightweight pack the telescope that Bartek had previously handed him 10 days earlier. Adjusting the focus definition, Piotr saw a man in a small wooden boat with an outboard emerging from the water-reeds. At 2.5 to 3 kilometres distant it was difficult if not impossible to observe much more. He continued to watch as the boat and its helmsman made progress towards the small wooden pier. Having docked, the man was clearly feeling the cold as he waved his arms and stamped his feet to regain some circulation and heat in his body. After a few minutes, he began to walk along the lake's edge before disappearing behind a stand of fir trees. Maybe 4 or 5 minutes had passed before the man re-appeared running and stumbling in the snow back to the pier.

'Hawk 2 to base. Unknown visitor leaving the lake in a hurry – suggest Patrol 3 see what the panic is about.'

That morning Patrol 3 was led by Radek. Working their way through the snow covered ground, some 40 minutes later spoke through the comms in his arctic helmet also covered by his snow-cam outer-gear to halt. Unclipping his skis, he walked to the edge of a small water-logged bog. There were three men who had seemingly fallen into this quagmire during the night. Whether they had tried to help each other escape the bog's clutches or not, the result was 3 rather ghost like heads and shoulders covered in that frost of hypothermia with abject horror in their eyes as they awaited death. No wonder the helmsman ran like a startled chicken thought Radek.

He weighed up whether pulling the bodies out might reveal some useful intelligence or not. It would take a great deal of physical effort for an uncertain result plus they would only then be returning them back into their bog-like grave. Far better they back trace as to where these Russian agents crossed into Ukrainian Territory.

Just under 4 kilometres from the scene of their unexpected death, the giveaway footprints in the snow led to the gap in the rusted chain link fencing.

Voicing his thoughts Tomek Jureki blurted through their headsets 'We now know where the foxes are entering the hen house!'

Later that afternoon with the entire team safely back in the cottage, Bartek, Kacper, Filip and Radek began to talk and think about how to capture whoever came through that breach in the border fencing.

Sipping their mugs of tea with honey, they reflected that Radek had made the right call in that traversing this particularly landscape at night was suicide in wintry conditions. Certainly after losing 3 agents in one go, daylight introduction of subversive elements would be Moscow's next step.

There was general consensus the reporting of their agents' deaths in the Pripiat-Stokhid wilderness would mean at least 24 hours before another encroachment into Ukrainian Territory. For once the elements were helpful. The weather forecast for the next 3 days was of increasing snowfall and high winds producing blizzard conditions. This meant neither Russians nor Polish Special Forces would be venturing anywhere. For once, they had the benefit of time to plan and the advantage of home turf.

Colonel Yedemsky placed the phone back in its cradle. How could 3 well-trained agents manage to throw their lives away for absolutely nothing in a water-filled bog? The buzzer went on his desk handset. Colonel-General Laskutin was ordering his immediate presence.

As he walked down the corridor, his mind was not only on replacements but also whether an escort might prove necessary. Boris Ivanov, the Colonel-General's aide-de-camp, waved that he should go straight into Ruslan Laskutin's office. Saluting, removing his military cap, and being motioned to take the vacant chair, Oleg Yedemsky sat down and waited.

'Colonel, matters are developing at a somewhat faster pace with regard to Ukraine. Are our sleeper cells being activated specifically for detailed targeting information on strategic logistical locations?'

'Yes Colonel-General – though we are continually asked by them for examples from rail junctions to oil dumps to Government buildings, making me seriously question the general intelligence of our sleepers.'

'Oleg, cut them some slack. They are volunteers who believe in Mother Russia and not paid mercenaries. If you have to provide an exhaustive list, then do so. Our Military have to have comprehensive information across the width and breadth of Ukraine in order to match targets for artillery and also maximise the impact of missiles as battle fronts evolve.'

'Colonel-General, we also continue to receive targeting coordinates for civilian buildings. Schools, hospitals, shelters, universities, kindergartens, shopping centres, recreational facilities, and residential blocks are seemingly legitimate targets.'

'They are Oleg – how can you even doubt that. Our military have demonstrated and practiced this strategy in Aleppo and

Grozny let alone the lessons from the Great Patriotic War. Whilst the expectation is the West will, like before, leave us to deal with Ukraine as we wish, a short war to remove Zelensky and his Government may ultimately prove necessary. However to ensure we not only bring the populace under control but also they exert maximum pressure on Zelensky to fold, our attack must strike fear and terror into their minds. Thus what might seem indiscriminate bombing or shelling will in fact be deliberate. In addition, if there is resistance bringing Ukraine to heel, the Russian Army will destroy brick by brick towns, villages, and even cities making them uninhabitable piles of rubble. This 'scorched earth' policy will be supplemented by a brutal occupation of any areas occupied. Ukrainian civilians caught up in hostilities, especially in the Donetsk and Luhansk regions, may well be transported to Siberia and our Far East whether they wish so or not. This has long been within our playbook to quell permanently any dissent in Russia since the days of Stalin. Surrendering Ukrainian Military will of course in many instances be summarily executed on the battlefield but that will be no surprise to you – this is war. You may be unaware of the specific indoctrination training that our Military has been carrying out. Many of our conscripts are from villages suffering from poverty and are virtually illiterate from non-existent education. Similarly, the parts of our reserves mobilised are in reality still just conscripts from previous years. They will form an 'ill-disciplined' army of occupation within the body of our professional Military politic; let off the leash occasionally to drink, loot, rape, torture and even kill indiscriminately. Barbarism only matched by destruction but together reinforcing fear and sheer terror across the Ukrainian population.'

'Do we have any concerns about the International response to such blatant breaches of the Geneva Conventions and the response of the United Nations Colonel-General?'

'Colonel – you cannot be serious! Importantly we hold a veto on the Security Council. Not respecting sovereign borders and territory is an issue but the West will see its response as 'democracy against autocracy'. That will be a major error as many countries would align more with the West if they were complaining about the sanctity of territorial borders being breached by force. As for war crimes, we have never signed up for the International Criminal Court and even if its investigators painstaking forensic investigation leads to hard evidence, do we care? No Russian will ever be held accountable or handed over for trial in The Hague.'

With the occasional light flurry of snow replacing the last two days of blizzard conditions, the cottage was a hive of activity as dawn began to break. Two 4 man patrols had already left on skis to take up positions to the left and right of the expected rendezvous point, the small wooden pier. The ribs were used to take and deliver 8 members of the team led by Filip Cuda across the lake to the pier. They disembarked to take up positions in cover to the north of the pier. One rib returned to collect Radek and Tomek Jureki who took up position amongst the water reeds.

Dawn broke some 20 minutes after Radek's arrival. It revealed a crystal clear light blue sky with no wind to speak of. In planning the entrapment, they had gambled that the illegal entrants onto Ukrainian Territory would stick to the same timetable. Thus it was with relief when the radio silence was broken by Master-Sergeant Stodola's voice –

'Helmsman 150 metres out'. A few minutes' later geese and ducks were briefly in flight as the wooden boat chugged into view. Again Radek's head set crackled, '8 hostiles 200 metres out – 5 armed GRU or FSB in arctic camo'. So his lucky guess that a Russian special forces unit would accompany the 3 agents to ensure both a safe cross-border infiltration and ultimately 'live' delivery to the in-country asset was correct. The GROM unit had surprise and firepower on its side but the plan was to take all 9 invaders prisoner. This was potentially more dangerous than simply killing them all in a firefight that would be over in a matter of seconds. Something that would no doubt have been absolutely fine with Colonel Nalyvaichenko even if checking their guns revealed full magazines.

Amongst the military gear in the cottage were 2 bull horns. These were now in the hands of the Master-Sergeants. As the agents and their protection unit came to halt in a single but spaced out file with the helmsman stood on the pier, puffs of snow erupted along the whole line from Filip's team. At that very moment, first Kacper and then Bartek gave the intruders a simple message 'You are surrounded – lay down your weapons immediately.' The helmsman turned for his boat to escape the trap but Tomek Jarocki's shot hitting his shoulder causing him to fall put an end to any thought of escape. They were surrounded and whilst dedicated Russians zealots, this was not their day to die. Another volley from Filip's group sending up puffs of snow had the 8 illegal and covert entrants dropping their rifles and handguns – resistance was pointless.

Radek could not criticise Tomek for hitting the helmsman. Shooting from the rib, while subjected to occasional swell, was inordinately difficult. At least whilst aiming for the section of side framing, the lake's movement had taken the bullet to his shoulder rather than leg. There was some schlepping to do.

The sequence in springing the trap was important. Filip's first volley throwing up puffs of snow along the entire line informed the intruders' marksmen were present. Running ahead to escape was immediately terminated by Kacper's announcement to be followed by Bartek's making it clear retracing their steps was not an option either. Filip's & his team's second volley ensured they remained motionless. When the helmsman collapsed, any thought of escape or resistance evaporated.

Nevertheless, Filip & his team held their position just in case any intruder suddenly, recovering from their capture, attempted to make a mad dash for freedom. Radek's order was clear if that occurred 'shoot to kill'. The weapons, knives, phones, and IDs were all collected and dumped in a large duffel. The 9 prisoners were roped together with their right arm tied tightly with cable ties in two places over their winter anorak sleeve. Another rope was looped and tied tightly round their waists leaving their left hand through snow gloves to hold the rope if necessary. At this point, Filip and the others emerged from cover looking somewhat frightening in all their over snow camouflage and sniper rifles. Radek and Tomek plus the other 2 soldiers vacated their ribs so Filip and his team could briefly return to the cottage. The prisoners had a 16 kilometre walk through drifted snow in parts so Radek expected, even with cajoling, this could take 4 to 5 hours. One of the ribs returned with Radek's and the others skis that had been left by the boathouse before heading back across the lake. Piotr Vrubel had in the meantime staunched the helmsman's wound and injected some painkiller. Clearly there was some similarity to being a chef and a surgeon.

Before this unlikely column left, Radek reminded them that they had been arrested for having made illegal entry into Ukraine and in view of their weapons probably not with the best of intentions for the Country's Government. Importantly, he added any attempt to escape would likely result in a fatal shooting with any survivors having to carry such dead weight.

Anyone laying on snow for even for a short period, and even on top of a thermal snow blanket, will become extremely cold quickly through lack of movement. Hence whoever was placed in the north end like Filip and some of the team needed to be warmed up. In addition, the humvees were to be driven to a pre-arranged rendezvous with the Ukrainian Border Guard who would then become responsible for the captives. However, Radek did not wish to disclose inadvertently the location of the cottage and for it to seem as if the Ukrainian Military had frequent patrols across the entire area. Should any of the captives speak to Embassy or other officials, their capture will be presented as bad luck as the 3 corpses were still where they had died and had presumably alerted the authorities. A day later they may well have escaped capture.

It was dusk as the column of escorted prisoners arrived. In what was normally a visitor car park in Spring and Summer, there was a 3 ton military truck with Border Guard markings. The Border Guards released the prisoners one by one from their rope bindings before apply handcuffs and shackles to their ankles. GRU or FSB special forces were dangerous people let alone the 3 undercover agents so extra precautions were wisely being taken. Filip had skied into the parking area with the duffel and began to brief the Head Border Guard, particularly as to the relevance of phone call logs and other information the phones should reveal for Ukrainian Intelligence. The wounded man should, after medical attention, be interrogated fully as he was clearly a spy and had to be guarded closely. As for the individual agents, including the wounded man, they should, in his view, be kept away from each other preferably in solitary and definitely away from the special forces unit if Ukraine's Interrogators were going to have any success in breaking them.

As the truck pulled away into the night with two Land Rovers bringing up the rear, Filip led the way through the woodland to the waiting humvees. What a relief they all felt unbuckling those skis and loosening the bindings. It had been an arduous, long, and tough day shepherding their captives but clearly rewarding in that it gave focus to the importance of their mission.

For once, Filip on behalf of the unit had something more positive to report into Colonel Nalyvaichenko's office rather than nothing. Though he wondered what the blowback might be of seemingly disobeying his orders.

Chapter 12

Colonel-Laskutin's raised voice could be heard along the entire corridor as he berated Colonel Yedemsky over a Ukrainian Border Patrol's capture of one highly important embedded spy within Ukraine's Ministry of Defence.

'If that is not damaging enough, we lose for the 2nd time in less than 72 hours not one but another three agents. What am I supposed to tell Generals Kirill Vasilyev and Vladimir Bogdanov *(senior directors of Special Programmes for our President within the Federal Security Service - FSB)* ?'

'Colonel-General our connection to this mess was solely Aleksey Makshakov – codename *'Kursk'* embedded with the Defence Ministry. We were asked to assist extracting 3 agents out of the Pripiat-Stokhid wilderness. We were not provided with a choice of meeting point but only one location. *'Kursk'* was selected from our personnel files because he had an intimate knowledge of the Prypyat and Stokhid river headwaters and their flow into the Dneiper. His hobbies were bird-watching and fishing. We were not told of their mission, or even separate missions, but simply asked to assist delivery as far as the Dneiper.'

'How on earth does that help Colonel?'

'*Kursk* sent an encrypted email to us. It warned that the wilderness was part swamp and wetlands where entry at night in winter could have other dangers than a random Ukrainian Border Patrol.'

'So do tell me how 20-20 vision in hindsight helps the GRU?'

'Colonel-General this is not being wise after the event, this email from *Kursk* was sent to the FSB Officer dealing with the planned infiltration.'

At this point, Ruslan Laskutin stopped pacing up and down his office waving his arms wildly whilst shouting angrily at Colonel Yedemsky. Walking back to his desk and sitting once in his chair, he spoke for the first time in the last 12 minutes in a calm and unemotional voice.

'Who provided the protection detail?'

'Belarussian Special Forces Colonel-General.'

'Do you think there is more to this arrest by a random Ukrainian Border Guard Patrol?'

'Frankly Colonel-General I do though not in terms of a security leak. Belarus Special Forces are selected on the same basis as our own elite teams. They submit to the same arduous training together at our main Spetsnaz base in Murmansk and elsewhere. They are used to shooting first and rather than asking questions. Hence, as we understand a normal Border Patrol may only comprise of 3 or 4 guards at the most, their training is not even on the same page let alone book as our Spetsnaz units, how could the Belarussian escort, if our information is correct, have been captured without any of them being injured or killed?'

'Fair question - the Ukrainian Authorities will ensure we have no access to any of our citizens for some months no matter what enquiries or protestations our Embassy or the Belarussians' might raise in Kyiv. How exposed are we in respect of *Kursk*?'

'His contact in the Embassy, Major Gennady Sidorov, has been recalled to Moscow awaiting reassignment. *Kursk's* family and children are presently under house arrest and guarded by units of the Ukrainian Anti-Terrorism Police.'
'*Kursk* will inevitably talk in order to protect and free his Ukrainian family.'

'Probably Colonel-General - yet given our Military's Plans and expectations it will be too late to influence events.'

A few days after the handing over of the agents and Belarussian soldiers, a unit of the local Ukrainian Border Guard on snowmobiles went to extract the three corpses from their mud and water tomb. Arriving at the spot, a murder of crows reluctantly flew away from their lunch to reveal heads that no longer had eyes, ears, and indeed cheeks containing no flesh. It was a ghoulish scene worthy of any Hitchcock horror or suspense film.

After gingerly wrapping ropes under each corpse's armpit and then tying tightly on the torso, each body was pulled from the swamp using a snowmobile. The corpse was then placed in a body bag and secured on a rescue sled; sleds that had become extremely helpful in traverse the swamp to place those ropes! It was noticeable that each body extracted was without footwear, socks, and trousers. This merely confirmed, rather like an animal cornering its prey, there was no escape for these men from the inanimate suction power of the mud. Death exacerbated by the more they struggled in sub-zero temperatures.

Colonel Nalyvaichenko's orders were specific that the body bags were to be delivered to the Government morgue in Rivne. Autopsies would be carried out there. The contents of their jackets and backpacks were to be left for collection and analysis by Ukrainian Intelligence officers dealing with, amongst other things, the interrogations of the prisoners now held in separate military prisons in Lutsk and Rivne.

The Polish Special Forces Unit continued their ski patrols within the forests and wilderness of the Pripiat-Stokhid National Park. However, there were no further incidents as a result of illegal entry from Belarus. The weather pattern was seemingly stuck in a groove of moderate snowfall at night with minus temperatures in the teens and snow flurries during the day under overcast brooding skies. In this half-light the day started just before nine and was over shortly after three in the afternoon. Radek was nevertheless pleased as the ski patrols were keeping everyone physical fit. In addition, the barn became a hive of activity as darkness fell. Sharpening and waxing skis for the following day plus oiling and cleaning weapons meant no time for idle hands and the curse of boredom impacting morale. Piotr Vrubel was always allowed along with Tomek Jureki priority in terms of dealing with their skis and weapons. It was a rather self-serving of the team as the chef and assistant had to prepare a hot supper and as the mission had progressed, Piotr and Tomek only cleaned their weapons.

With the plates cleared away and washing up underway on a rota basis excluding of course Piotr and Tomek, Pawel would tune into Poland's nightly newscast on TVN's radio channel. The reception was still very good in spite of Belarus's negative cyber activity. As the unit settled down to listen in a relaxed manner, suddenly the mood changed as the Newscaster announced startling 'Breaking News'. It was December 17th.

This afternoon shortly after 15:00 hours Moscow time, the Russian deputy Foreign Minister, Sergei Ryabkov, released the texts of two proposed treaties. The released documents were apparently provided to the United States and NATO earlier in the week. Although there was no deadline for talks, Russia wanted according to the Deputy Foreign Minister to begin negotiations without delays and without stalling, adding we can go any place and any time, even tomorrow. When asked whether the requests were unreasonable, his response was 'No', stating this is not about us giving some kind of ultimatum, there is none. Yet the seriousness of our warning should not be underestimated.

The newscaster asked Professor Krzysztof Michalski, Head of Geopolitical Studies at the Jagiellonian University for his thoughts-

The public release of the proposed treaties suggests that the Kremlin considers their acceptance by either party of its highly contentious list as highly unlikely. Hence Russia will have to determine its security alone and single-handedly.

With the steady massing of battlegroups over recent weeks all along Ukraine's border and within Belarus, it will undoubtedly be through the use of force and military might. The Kremlin's demands include a demand that NATO remove any troops or weapons deployed to countries that entered the alliance after 1997. This would mean much of Eastern Europe, including Poland, the former Soviet countries of Estonia, Lithuania, Latvia, and the Balkan countries of Romania and Bulgaria. Russia has also demanded that NATO rule out further expansion, including the accession of Ukraine into the alliance. Furthermore, NATO is to no longer to hold drills without Russia's previous agreement in Ukraine, Eastern Europe, or in Caucasus countries such as Georgia or in Central Asia. Clearly, such proposals will be viewed extremely negatively within the Alliance, particularly by Poland and the Baltic States. These latter countries have been warning for some time about Russia's wish to re-establish a sphere of influence over the region and the document is clear proof.

NATO's head, Jens Stoltenberg, has already ruled out any agreements denying Ukraine the right to enter the military alliance, saying it is up to Ukraine and the 30 NATO countries.

Whilst Russia implies the West's agreement would lower tensions in Europe and defuse the crisis in Ukraine, it has already stated ignoring its legitimate interests will provoke a military response. President Putin has demanded that the West provide Russia with legal guarantees of its security which is somewhat ironic from a nuclear power with more warheads than the United States, France, and United Kingdom combined. We can be certain the Kremlin's aggressive proposals will be rejected in Western Capitals as an attempt to formalise a new Russian sphere of influence over Eastern Europe. The proposed treaty with the United States also calls for the two countries to pull back any short- or medium-range missile systems replacing the previous intermediate-range nuclear forces (INF) treaty that the U.S left in 2018. This does of course overlook the reason for the U.S withdrawal that related to Russia's deployment of Iskander and other systems capable of carrying a nuclear payload.

The U.S State Department has already issued a statement that there will be no talks on European Security or response to the proposed treaties without our European Allies and partners being heavily involved. Western Intelligence agencies, especially those in the U.S and UK, have warned Russia is preparing for an all-out invasion of Ukraine in the first few months of the New Year. Russian tanks, artillery, missiles, and troops have already massed along Ukraine's borders and are being added to daily by yet more equipment and battle groups.

That the Ukrainian President, Volodymyr Zelensky, has called on the West for additional aid in case Russia decides to launch a broader offensive is indicative of the winds of war blowing into Eastern Europe. The threat is now very real.

Thank you Professor – I would like to ask our station's and TVN's International Affairs commentator, Douglas Staunton, for his reaction to these latest developments-

Russia demanded today publicly the U.S and NATO halt all military activity in Eastern Europe and Central Asia in a sweeping proposal. It would establish a Cold War-like security arrangement. Given many of the terms have already been dismissed as unacceptable, except possibly in terms of a fresh negotiation on intermediate nuclear arms, it poses a direct challenge to any diplomatic efforts in my view being successful in defusing Russia's growing military threat to Ukraine.

The proposals or rather demands have been floated in various forms in recent weeks by various Russian officials, including, we are told also to the White House, being voiced specifically by President Putin in a very recent video call with President Biden. Russia has seen increasingly Ukraine is drifting irretrievably into the West's Orbit and thereby, real or imagined, posing a grave threat to Russian security. We are also told President Biden made it clear that should Russia attack Ukraine the response will bring about sanctions that the like of which cannot even be imagined.

These school yard bully boy and blackmail tactics underline the notion that President Putin is willing to take ever-greater risks. He wants to force the West to take Russian security concerns seriously and to address from his perception historical grievances largely ignored for decades. Yet the Russian demands go far beyond the current conflict between Ukrainian government forces and Russian-backed separatists in eastern Ukraine. Most are directed not at Ukraine threatened by the troop build-up but at the U.S, NATO, and Ukraine's other Western allies.

Thank you Douglas – finally I would like to introduce Poland's Ambassador to NATO, Grzegorz Jodorowsky, and Mr Ambassador please your response to today's events-

It is hard to disagree with your earlier commentators regarding President Putin's direct involvement in events to achieve political ends through force. Something that is in direct conflict with the United Nations Charter that Russia, as a permanent member of the Security Council is pledged to uphold. Nevertheless, Ukraine's territorial integrity has already been compromised by Russia's illegal annexation of the Crimean peninsula in 2014. In addition, its further actions in fermenting and supporting militarily dissent in the Donetsk and Luhansk Regions have merely emphasized that self-serving contradiction.

This Russian proposal in the form of a draft treaty suggested NATO should offer written guarantees that it would not expand further east toward Russia. In demanding the written guarantee from NATO, President Putin and other Russian officials have reached into early post-Cold War history describing what they see as a betrayal by the West in 1990; asserting amongst other historical grievances, real or imagined, that NATO expanded to the east despite a spoken assurance from James Baker, then the US Secretary of State to the Soviet leader, President Mikhail Gorbachev – in spite of for example this latter inference having been confirmed by former President Gorbachev related solely to discussions about East Germany. Additionally, NATO is to halt all military activities in the former Soviet republics – now of course independent states extending from Eastern Europe to Central Asia. Russia has demanded NATO withdraws all its military infrastructure placed in Eastern European states after 1997 as a starting point for a new security treaty. NATO has already dismissed these suggestions as totally unrealistic. Within this proposal, Russia included a request for a NATO commitment it would not offer membership to Ukraine specifically. The Alliance's response was unequivocal that NATO countries will not rule out future membership for any Eastern European countries, including Ukraine. Furthermore, NATO officials have rebutted as completely unacceptable Russian demands for a veto power over now-independent countries to join NATO. As a defensive Alliance, we, NATO, have emphasized our openness to a diplomatic dialogue on Russia's security concerns. However, any discussion would also have to include NATO's security concerns about Russian missile deployments, satellite tests, disinformation efforts, and CYBER. Quite why Russia ludicrously suggests the West has, amongst other things, been instilling anti-russian sentiment in Ukraine beggars belief. Possibly the seizure of Crimea and the outright sham of support for the Separatists in Donetsk and Luhansk – smell the coffee. The actions of Russia's Army has more relevance to Ukrainians' attitudes and perceptions about Russia and Russians! 13000 Ukrainians have already died as a result of Russia's unprovoked aggression.

NATO has already confirmed if Russia does make a major new military incursion into Ukraine, as it seems to be planning, NATO will move more troops, in addition to the other defensive steps already initiated to bolster its Eastern Flank's defensive posture.

In closing, putting forward unrealistic demands is a deliberate policy by the Kremlin to ensure the de-escalation of the Russian Military build-up is impossible through diplomatic means. The Russians are well aware their demands are untenable and unachievable. They have a list of security concerns but so do we in NATO. In conjunction with the United States and our other European allies, we are willing to negotiate on a fully transparent basis. Nevertheless, as Russia continues this escalatory cycle it is difficult to believe such an agreement could be negotiated or consummated in good faith. Let's not forget Russia invaded Ukraine in 2014 and declared war. Sadly, but realistically, these Kremlin demands doom any talks between Russia and the West. An expansionist and revanchist Kremlin is paving the way for a full blown war in Ukraine.

Thank you Mr Ambassador – now to other news items

The Ambassador's last words were somehow left hanging and echoing in the air around the entire cottage – *'war in Ukraine'*.

Radek was looking at the flames of the log fire wondering what this would mean for Poland, Alexandra, little Maja, his parents, his men, their families, and Europe. The atmosphere was joyless and quiet – deathly quiet. To an outsider, such a response might appear initially rather strange. Surely professional soldiers, especially elite units like the GROM, would welcome the thought of battles to fight and wars to win as the unseen and silent 'Heroes and Warriors' that they are. However, the GROM and other special forces are not selected purely on physical strength and military aptitude. Other character traits are given equal importance; emotional stability, adaptability, teamwork abilities, physical stamina and fitness, sound judgment and decision-making and intrinsic motivation. The first three of these attributes point to a high degree of emotional stability and also speak to the relevance of the interpersonal traits of attitude and consideration for others. Intrinsic motivation can perhaps best be described as to an individual's personal conscientiousness and commitment. Perhaps it was no surprise there was no harmless banter filling the cottage after the newscast rather a measured apprehension about what the New Year might bring. No bottles of Belvedere were circulating amongst them – Life had taken a more serious turn. It was again snowing outside.

The following few days had the unit following its daily pattern of criss-crossing patrols across the National Park looking for any signs of human activity within their domain. Each patrol was skiing between 50 to 60 kilometres in the shortened hours of daylight which given the dangers within the terrain was no mean feat. Again Radek was grateful for the comfort for the routine in terms of morale as his units' thoughts began to turn towards the importance of being with their families and loved ones on Christmas Eve.

Filip received a message from Colonel Nalyvaichenko's office that he would be coming to the cottage shortly after dusk. It was December 22nd. Radek had anticipated a visit within hours of handing over the captured Russian agents and its Belarussian GRU escort to the Ukrainian Border Guard. Disobeying orders did not endear you with Higher Command.

Another stew was beginning to fill the ground floor living area with its delightful aroma. His men were recovering from the day's exercise after showers and generally lounging around reading, playing cards, chess, or discussing the chances of being home for Christmas Eve.

An ebullient and clearly very happy Colonel Nalyvaichenko entered the cottage carrying a crate of Hlibny Dar vodka that he placed on the dining table. Turning towards Radek, who had quickly realised far from a military bollocking something else was afoot.

'Major Król, you can always disobey a superior officer order but you have to be right and have God on your side! You are deservedly a lucky bastard. I am delivering Ukraine's best vodka – a present from Ukrainian Intelligence and a grateful Nation. I also have more good news in that tomorrow morning you are to be relieved and ordered to return home for Christmas Eve with your loved ones. Colonel Palamarchuk has organised a military transport for tomorrow evening to fly most of you to Gdansk from where you can make your individual arrangements to reach home. Major Król, you and this unit are to be reassigned to my colleagues in the Kyiv Military Defence District from December 29th.'

There were broad smiles all round particularly about being home for Christmas Eve!

'Colonel, thank you for all this news and our new orders but why have Ukrainian Intelligence on behalf of your Nation sent us the vodka?'

'Major Król, if Ukraine is to survive as a democracy it cannot sink to the methods of those Russian barbarians and fortunately you had the good sense to ignore my un-soldiery orders. In doing so, our Intelligence Service was able to identify the 3 live agents and also eventually the 3 dead ones. They were all officers from the FSB's designated department titled 'Special Programmes for the President'. This is a top secret department as you will all know within the Russian Federal Security Service specifically dealing with the assassination of political opponents like Navalny and foreign based enemies of the State like Skripal – to which now our President has been added as a target. The other Agent, who was wounded in the shoulder during your ambush, was a mid-ranking civil servant within our Ministry of Defence with access to details of the President's diary and also to classified information as to what equipment is being supplied by our U.S and NATO friends. Your unit's action has clearly prevented an assassination attempt and also identified a mole that would have seriously compromised our evolving defence strategy. As for the protection team, they might prove a useful 'make-weight' in some future prisoner exchange but for now they are kicking their heels in a Military Prison.'

'Did the autopsies on the dead agents Colonel provide any explanation as to why they fell into that swamp hole and froze to death?'

'Yes Major their blood alcohol levels were all excessive with even more vodka in their stomachs yet to be absorbed. Frankly, our clinical pathologists were surprised any of them could stand let alone walk through freshly fallen snow. Their best guess was that they were holding each other up and when the path took a turn to avoid the swamp hole, they just kept staggering straight ahead into that mud and water death-trap. Their backpacks did reveal a tightly protected and wrapped package containing the highly dangerous and toxic nerve agent, Novichok. This discovery understandably spooked the pathologists at the time but our Chemical Weapons people took the item away for destruction. It did prove useful though in forcing the replacement agents to be a lot more forthcoming when being interrogated. My intelligence colleagues dressed in himath chemical protection suits and wearing the rather forbidding breathing masks shook the three surviving agents' determination to say nothing. It certainly petrified those agents for them to confess their mission was to assassinate our President via a well-placed car bomb. What these arrests have highlighted is that this Russian State sponsored Presidential assassination will be an increasing threat Major. Now, how about a round of shots of Hlibny Dar for me to wish you all a great Christmas with your loved ones and equally great success on your forthcoming mission before I leave – you have undoubtedly a great deal of packing up to organise after supper?'

It was a seven hour drive to Mielec. After supper, the humvees were loaded with all their gear and shortly after 07:00 hours the convoy left as a Ukrainian Special Forces team relieved them at post. One benefit of being a military convoy was they were able to cross the border without even having to drop into second gear.

Most of the unit boarded the Hercules C130 that evening. Those others needing to travel to south west of Poland or elsewhere found rides with various base personnel heading to their relevant home-town or city. Mielec had become a temporary base for GROM Team 6 so they had all managed to shower and change into fresh combat uniforms before leaving. Radek was the last to leave exemplifying again true leadership – the safety and well-being of his men was paramount – his boots would be the first on the battlefield and the last to leave. He had been assigned a military limousine and driver to take him to Niepolomice. This meant last minute Christmas shopping in Tarnow prior to falling asleep in the comfort of the rear seat of the extended

Mercedes. As the vehicle stopped, he woke. It was 22:00 hours and it was beginning to snow. With present bags and duffel either side, it was time to surprise Alexandra or was it? The house lights on the covered terrace suddenly came on as did the external lights on his parents' home. Through the snow flurries and darkness shapes were moving towards him. He guessed Alexandra, Elsa, & Tomek accounted for three but who were the other four? There were shrieks of joy and laughter as the happy throng moved towards him. Radek recognised Matt Elliott's laugh who had been his best man at his wedding to Alexandra but who were the others. He recognised two of the other voices but could not place them immediately then it came to him – Gabriella Russo so the other shape must be Stefan Zysk! Then out of the flurries came 4 bounding St Bernards that he sensibly crouched to greet as suddenly there was his princess and goddess - Alexandra with tears in her eyes flung her arms round his neck. This happy throng were then hugging him and moving him slowly back towards the house with Alexandra's parents, alongside Christina (Matt's fiancée) and of course Gabriella who were in particular about to experience their first Polish Christmas Eve Wigilia supper tomorrow.

Inside at last, the open fire was crackling as spurts of flame enveloped the dry logs as champagne flutes were filled to rising chorus of the first toast – 'Welcome Home Radek Merry Christmas'.

His curiosity could stand it no longer 'Alexandra, how did you know I would be home tonight?' 'I have friends in high places husband!'

Radek smiled and raised his flute announcing the second of many toast still yet to come 'Lieutenant-General Grzegorz Politczek'.

Chapter 13

New Year came and went as Radek and the GROM unit found themselves implementing the Ukrainian Army's High Command's defensive strategy. However, this Polish Special Forces unit found itself not Kyiv or its hinterland but in the forests outside Sumy only 45 kilometres from the Russian Border. As the inexorable drumbeat of war edged ever closer in spite of various diplomatic overtures by various Western Heads of State, the GROM's role was to play their part in defeating the now expected invasion.

For all the Poles it was strange to realise that Sumy was in 1944 the base of the 1st Polish Army established by Stalin. What was somewhat more astonishing, Oskar Hansen, a Pole, had his entire art collection of some 300 works of Polish 19th Century Artists seized in 1919 by the Russian Communists for the proletariat ie the people of Sumy. As Radek walked round the Art Museum 103 years later looking at these paintings by Wilhelm Kotarbiński, Jan Stanisławski, Aleksander Orłowski, Juliusz Kossak, Franciszek Kostrzewski, Michał Płoński, and Michał Andriolli designated the Polish Art Collection, it was a strange feeling that by dint of politics and war these works were not in a Warsaw Gallery and remained unseen if not unknown to most of Poland.

Since 2014, the Ukrainian Army's High Command had concluded a Russian Invasion would be massive and on many fronts. Its objective would be to sweep through Ukraine crushing any opposition. Such a military strategy relies on the principle of momentum where the offensive force continually pushes forward at a rapid pace not allowing the defenders any time to regroup. The High Command considered the Russian Invading Army's key objective would be to move in from the north and northeast through Belarus and Russia with the intention of capturing Kyiv in a matter of days. If that were to happen and the Government was to be captured or killed, there was then the expectation the country would capitulate.

Therefore, the Russian Military had to be stopped from ever achieving and sustaining that momentum. The Ukrainians had to hamper and hinder every movement forward by the Russians so their military thrusts became bogged down and stuck. Notwithstanding the much-vaunted modernisation of the Russian Forces by the Kremlin, the reality was very different in a large part due to an over-reliance on outdated equipment and technology. Nevertheless, even with advanced planning and preparation, the Ukrainian military had significantly less firepower than the invading Russian Forces from tanks to artillery to air support. This meant the Ukrainians strategy had to combine halting or limiting Russian advances on the battlefields whilst also conserving their limited military resources.

Implementing this strategy meant the lead elements of any Russian assault had to be met with fierce resistance as bridges and other infrastructure is destroyed. Additionally, mobile Ukrainian units would have to use javelins and other anti-tank weapons to destroy tanks and other mechanised infantry vehicles. This would further disrupt any assault and importantly stop an advance gaining momentum while the Ukrainians establish strong defensive postures and positioning.

Having stalled such Russian Advances, the Ukrainian Army would have to carefully select its targets and conserve resources. Whilst the U.S, UK, and NATO had in particular assisted in professionalising and training its Army, the equipment supplied to date had been more defensive than offensive. In the absence of lethal aid such as artillery, heavy armour, and planes, the Ukrainian military would be in a potentially vulnerable position when engaging the Russian enemy. Modern day counter-battery systems allow for the detection of incoming rounds and enable the location of the firer with pinpoint accuracy. Any equipment loss is more significant for the Ukrainians smaller military in comparison to Russia's.

This basic requirement to use the Army's limited hardware to maximum effect enabled Ukrainian's Military Planners to focus on what were critical to the Russian Army's command and control capabilities. This meant destruction of the Russian air-defence systems was a critical objective and also its artillery with drone strikes. Destroying such systems would deny the Russians from achieving control of the Ukrainian air-space, hence allowing for more drone and air strikes. The Ukrainians had to also identify the locations of the Russian electronic warfare equipment and targeted those systems as they would be used to disrupt both Ukrainian communication and its drone operations.

Rather like in guerrilla warfare where officers lead patrols, the Military Planners would identify the Russian command nodes with the assistance of Intelligence and destroy such command posts. This would inevitably put the Russian forces into somewhat of a disarray, especially if in the process high ranking Russian officers were killed. However, the key point is that without command posts, the Russian military cannot synchronize its efforts and a further stalling of any offensive would be the result. It was akin to chopping off the head of a snake – its body was immobile without instructions from the Command Post!

The Ukrainian High Command had to ensure disruption and remove temptation from the table. The Military Planners believed that with the Russian Military objective of seizing Kyiv in a matter of days would provide tempting Russian tank columns on the highways. However, destroying the diesel resupply trucks made better sense than wasting resources on stationary Russian armoured columns. Tanks have a constant need for diesel fuel. Better to opt for targets that will have the largest effect and not to risk or waste Bayraktar TB2 drones on stationary columns that provide no threat.

These resupply vehicles or fuel trains, which are typically not armoured, are softer targets and require less sophisticated weaponry to destroy. Without resupply, the Russian advance cannot move forward and the inability to resupply is crushing to soldier morale.

In drafting this Strategy, the Ukrainian High Command and Military Planners understood if successful, the Russian Army will have suffered heavy losses in equipment and troops. The Russians would then likely switch to moving away from fighting on multiple fronts to concentrating their efforts on the Donbass. This would consolidate their forces and concentrate their attack on a single region and along the Black Sea Coast. Such a change will result in some of the current implementation strategies of the response to the invasion still being employed against the Russians. However, a more offensive nature as to pushing out these invaders from Ukraine's territory will, as U.S and NATO ramp up armament delivery, require the kit to be lethal from heavy armour to mobile artillery to sophisticated long range missile systems.

President Zelensky was well-aware of the need for more of everything and indeed of his High Command's concern not just for the start of hostilities but rather the end game. His Military could not have done more in planning, preparing, and executing plans for Ukraine's defence against any such further Russian Aggression. When fighting begins though, the Ukrainian Army will need a constant resupply of weapons and ammunition, much of which will start to flow from outside the country through overly lengthy supply lines; possibly with also the added issues of bureaucratic hurdles to overcome. Whilst the Government and Military were confident in the battle-planning and the Ukrainian Army's together with the populace's will to resist, resupply would be vital. After Russia is forced to regroup in the East and South, its resupply lines will be shorter. Maintaining a functioning Ukrainian rail and road system will be critical to survival. The Russians will increasingly target Ukraine's infrastructure with cruise and other long range missiles to disrupt or halt such resupply. Hence effective distribution of armaments and munitions to wherever needed on the battlefield has to be coordinated effectively.

In the forests of Sumy, the GROM team's role was to identify and destroy any vehicle that bore any resemblance to a resupply truck or vehicle carrying food and water, munitions, or diesel or indeed anything else. Whilst they would be on Ukrainian Territory, the Polish soldiers would be in combat behind the advancing Russian columns. They spent much of January familiarising themselves with the forest and trails, stashing munitions, and locating places to evade capture, apart from providing shelter from the weather. Every day it was minus 2 degrees with a mixture of rain snow and fog. It was completely unpleasant. The snowfall was insufficient to create in effect igloos to escape the elements . Hence the extreme cold weather tents for 4 soldiers in arctic white taken from the Mielec stores would come into their own with camouflage netting to deal with eventual warmer temperatures. Radek had resisted the Master-Sergeants urging to establish some permanent encampments now before hostilities began for two reasons. Primarily, the unit's effectiveness, and indeed its survival would depend on being highly mobile. This mission was completely different to being in Pripiat-Stokhid National Park where their operational base was both hidden and protected. Establishing a permanent site either prior to or immediately after war broke would be a tactical mistake – Radek was determined they would never spend more than one night in the same spot within the forest. He was also concerned that there would undoubtedly be a few misguided sympathisers if not spies. He was not going to allow anyone to know their tactical or other positions. Each day as January flowed into February, munitions and rations were carefully buried across the forest in waterproof bags with electronic locators for GROM's expected campaign behind enemy lines with no other external support for at least 6 to 8 weeks.

On Monday February 21st, the GROM team were relaxing after fulsome dinner in the Mess Hall and a day spent adding further stocks of hand-held projectiles of USSR vintage to the growing stockpile of hidden munitions from rocket held grenades to simple bazookas. Pawel was playing with the TV remote in their barracks when the programme was interrupted by the sight of President Putin speaking to the Russian Nation. It was a pre-recorded video and it was 21:30 in Moscow, 20:30 in Sumy.

The banter stopped in the barracks. Phonecalls home were suddenly ended and Russia's President now had all 20 of Poland's finest listening closely to every word.

Putin was repeating to them all his longstanding argument that Ukraine's borders were an artificial creation of Soviet planners. Russian land had been 'unjustly' placed within the Ukrainian Soviet Socialist Republic. It was no surprise but the truth was somewhat different. Internal Soviet borders reflected centuries-old cultural and political divides, as well as what the then Kremlin's own census found to be an ethnic Ukrainian majority throughout that territory, including in what is now eastern Ukraine. Putin's comments attempted to build on yet again his justification for annexing Crimea in 2014 - an implied mandate to assert Russian sovereignty over part or all of eastern Ukraine. This was his justification for the Kremlin's backing of separatists who, only with Russian Military support, still controlled parts of eastern Ukraine.

When Putin pointedly suggested Ukrainians should have thanked Vladimir Lenin, the founding Soviet leader, for Ukraine's current borders, it drew wry smiles of disbelief from the GROM. Smiles turned quickly to guffaws of laughter as Putin simultaneously presented himself as championing Russian nationalism through blood-and-soil territorial claims and fighting the 'disease of Ukrainian nationalism'. His continuing obsession with the breakup of the Soviet Union was not lost on his Polish listeners.

Maintaining Ukraine and other former Soviet republics were manipulated into declaring independence from the Kremlin by self-interested opportunists posed suggestions amongst the GROM audience that freedom from oppression and a better a life might be relevant! In reality, an overwhelming majority of Ukrainians *(including those in the eastern Ukrainian regions)* voted to establish an independent state.

When apparently the Ukrainian state was an act of theft from Russia and Ukrainians should still be under the Kremlin's rule, the GROM exchanged glances of scepticism that changed immediately to defiance as Putin suggested this applied to all former Soviet republics and Warsaw Pact countries.

This waffling monologue was making the explicit case for war - to seize parts of eastern Ukraine and by implication for all of Ukraine.

In Putin's and his regime's world, the modern Ukrainian state was divided by anti-Russian extremism. This made the GROM burst into laughter at the stupidity of the statement when it was self-evident Ukraine's ethnic and linguistic groups coexisted peacefully. Politics were not determined by language. Ties with the Kremlin over those with the West or vice a versa reflected democratic choices. Russia had seemingly forgotten its actions in seizing the Crimean Peninsula in 2014 and then fermenting insurrection in the Donbass might have more to do with a large majority of all Ukrainians becoming sharply distrustful of Russia.

Putin's indictment of modern Ukraine was a real stretch beyond reality. Suggesting a democratically elected government is not a real government but a clan of thieves and thus a threat to Russian security. By implying the illegitimacy of the Ukrainian State itself, Putin was making it abundantly clear no policy change or diplomatic concession could or would alter such a parody of illogical thinking. This was a simple declaration indicating there is no point in negotiation. The Kremlin was determined to remove Kyiv's leaders by force. The faces of the GROM were grim and sombre as the realisation came the dark clouds of war had become ever closer.

Russian officials and state media have sought to portray Ukraine's steps to raise the status of the Ukrainian language as part of a campaign to marginalize or even outright exterminate Ukraine's Russian-speaking populations. It was no shock to hear Putin once again raising such fictitious claims. Lies to justify a Russian military intervention to protect Ukraine's russian speaking populations? This rather smacked of 1938 and a page straight from the NAZI playbook. Similar disinformation by the Kremlin in 2014 of accusations, supported by grisly false stories of anti-Russian atrocities and genocides in Ukraine, provoked widespread anti-Ukrainian sentiment in Russia through the propaganda message being repeated again and again by its state controlled media. Leading the West from last November to call out almost daily the risk of Kremlin engineered 'false flag' operations to justify a widening of the conflict. Quite how the Kremlin can assert the right to dominate what Putin has called the 'Russian World' defies belief. For the GROM it was a downright and shameless effrontery to common sense.

Putin has long striven to prevent more of Russia's neighbours from joining NATO. Throughout the current crisis, the Kremlin has insisted that NATO revoke the Bucharest 2008 declaration regarding being open to membership for Ukraine and Georgia. The Poles exchanged glances of disbelief wondering did Putin really believe a purely defensive alliance was plotting to attack Russia or was this yet another extreme exaggeration for political effect rather than any sincere belief.

Whilst Putin went on to tell Russians that there is no point in constraining Russian foreign policy to avoid sanctions and suffering further economic isolation, was the Kremlin was also flagging to the West that their sacrifices will be futile?

As the broadcast degenerated into making false claims of Ukrainian military assaults on the separatist-held east, the Poles shook their heads in disbelief. Western governments had repeatedly claimed that their intelligence showed the Kremlin is planning to stage a supposed attack on Russia-backed forces. The intention was of course to substantiate the rhetoric of a fictitious Ukrainian campaign of terror abetted by hostile Western governments bent on attacking Russia. Whilst more akin to a fairy tale, it was more disinformation lapped up by a populace governed by the Kremlin's grip on its media and hence underlined the relevance of the West's warnings of 'false flag' activities as the excuse for a wider conflict.

Before the Poles could debate what they had just listened to for almost an hour (including comments being passed between them during the speech such as 'what on earth is Putin smoking' to which the reply was 'it must be horse shit' up to and including are his psychiatrists' regretting letting him out of therapy, Radek stood up.

'Gentlemen, these outlandish accusations of Ukrainian and Western plots to attack Russia are intended for the Russian public. This is to portray a further invasion of Ukraine as necessary to defend Russian families rather than a pursuit of the Kremlin's regional ambitions. Master-Sergeant Nowak please locate a 3 or 5 tonner, we leave tonight. Master-Sergeant Stodola please have everyone ready to leave with all our gear in 60 minutes. We are going to war.'

After that hour long and heated address spinning a narrative where the implications went well beyond recognizing the independence of two Ukrainian territories, Radek was not prepared to wait for a Russian targeted cruise missile to do more than disturb a night's sleep in a warm barracks. The speech had been awash with hard-line Russian nationalism, angry paranoia toward the West, baseless claims of Ukrainian aggression, a sense of lost imperial pride on the verge of reclamation and, most of all, invocations of history, much of it distorted or fabricated. It was a calculated series of justifications for a further invasion of Ukraine aimed primarily at the Russian public. Putin and his regime will need to maintain and sustain the reasons for such a war. In Radek's mind, apart from their allotted role to concentrate on removing resupply from the battlefield, the mounting body bag count returning to Ekaterinburg or elsewhere in Mother Russia would also become a major factor in the Kremlin eventually coming to the negotiating table.

There was a cleared grass area of about 10 to 12 metres deep running along the chain link and razor wire border between Russia and Ukraine before the Sumy forest began. Radek and Filip had placed their teams either side of 5 metre track that zigged and zagged through the forest. It ran for 100 metres in a straight line before making a left turn. On the Russian side of the border they watched as a crossing point was being created up to the border fence ready to be breached no doubt by a suitable Russian tank. Radek had assessed that any invasion would commence 2 or 3 hours before dawn guessing President Putin would make a live TV broadcast at 06:00 hours Moscow Time, meaning 05:00 hours in Sumy. By 10:00 hours that Tuesday morning, the GROM unit pulled back and headed for a fresh campsite for the night. Again at 04:00 hours the teams were in position but once more there was no movement from the Russian side of the border. Radek was beginning to doubt his judgement. Had he overreacted to Putin's Monday night taped broadcast as he was finishing his self-heating combat food pack? At this point, Filip was reading the label of what was allegedly purporting to be goulash. Motioning to Radek, he dipped his spoon into Radek's chicken curry. 'Do you know Radek I cannot tell the difference.' 'It proves do not read the label – it all tastes the same Filip.' 'What you are really saying is we had the luxury of fresh food in Pripiat-Stokhid National Park and now we have to pay the tallyman!'

Laying in his artic camouflage gear in the darkness, Radek could see the track clearly through his night vision googles, it was Thursday morning and just coming up to 05:00 hours. His headset intercom crackled 'advancing tank about to breach'. It seemed a matter of seconds before a column of T72s was passing their camouflaged positions. 'What was the count?' asked Radek. The consensus was 50. Pawel passed on the information to Ukrainian Army Sector waiting to ambush the column close to the end of the forest track some 15 kilometres later. There was a momentary lull before another and similar column of tanks thundered by at speed. An hour or so later a long column of mechanised infantry vehicles crawled by in comparison to the speed of the tank columns. Again this Polish Special Forces team were silent waiting for its preferred prey. Explosions in the far distance began to heard, coming closer, but still some considerable way from their position. The first oil tanker drove by disappearing round that first zig zag turn left followed by trucks with a battlefield cyber and communications vehicle coming to a halt at what was now a static queue of military vehicles. Nothing else could move across from the Russian side. The smell of diesel from idling engines began to fill the forest air.

The 15 kilometre ambush was all set to take place. The Ukrainian Army destroyed the first three tanks using just three well-placed hand held *'javelin'* anti-tank missiles. Taking out the first tank with no ability to manoeuvre would have made by-passing the stricken vehicle impossible with dense forest on either side. However, whilst adding to the degree of difficulty, destroying the 2nd & 3rd tank meant the columns command structure had also been eliminated. The Russian Army tank movement doctrine was, as the

Ukrainians knew, unchanged from the Soviet era. The U.S and UK had also highlighted in training what had been discovered in the Iraq War – Russian Tank design had perpetuated a basic fault in the T72 and thereafter. The problem relates to how the tanks' ammunition is stored. Unlike modern Western tanks, Russian ones carry multiple shells within their turrets. This makes them highly vulnerable. Even an indirect hit can start a chain reaction that explodes their entire ammunition store of up to 40 shells. The resulting shockwave can be enough to blast the tank's turret as high as a two-story building. This result had been achieved on those first three tanks. The driver of the 4th tank looked on in sheer terror, as did the two in the turret, as they watched their commander's tank explode and burn. The Ukrainians proceeded to repeat the process on each subsequent tank column leading to a number of crews just abandoning their tank where it stood. Filip's team was in place to start firing rocket held grenades and bazooka shells into the diesel tankers. Plumes of smoke and flame rose skywards alerting the Russian Military to Helmuth von Moltke's famous comment 'No battle plan survives contact with the enemy'! Transport Marshalls began to try to bring a tank column forward after reversing back various trucks in what was a resupply column. As Master-Sergeant Nowak's *'javelin'* hit the mechanised cyber communications vehicle with a deafening explosion, Piotr Vrubel's bazooka hit the truck straddling the break through access into Ukraine. It was a full munitions truck which then provided a fireworks display as the Marshalls and every other Russian in the immediate vicinity took cover. Filip's team and Radek's team were working mercilessly towards each other destroying every single vehicle from the oil tankers to the communications vehicle. The air was filled with burning metal, diesel, and human bodies.

Quite how the conscripts and other members of the Russian Army squared up to not being welcomed with flowers and smiles they had been told to expect was an open question.

Being forced to go a100 metres left and right from the new crossing made onto Ukrainian Territory by that now destroyed first tank, the Ukrainian army had mined the entire area in January in anticipation. Again the intention was to for the first explosion to be some 500 metres either way from the crossing that then armed those mines running back towards the entry made by Russians. The hope being that any ensuing column would be severely damaged by being caught in a web of detonations. Nevertheless, that was not the end of the 'kill zone' with less than 2 metres into the forest curtilage, a deadly matrix of claymores were waiting for any unsuspecting Russian trying to escape and shelter from the mayhem of vehicles being blown skywards.

The Polish Special Forces melted into the early morning fog and deep into the protective darkness of the forest leaving the smell of death behind. Eight kilometres away was another track running more directly towards Sumy. The Ukrainian Army was embroiled in a fierce fight with a mixed column of tanks and mechanised infantry fighting vehicles. Whilst the first three tanks had similarly been turned into burning metal, the following eight mechanised vehicles had not watched in horror but had either shown initiative or been ordered out. This result in a fierce battle as the Russians attempted to find the Ukrainians in the forest who were, apart from small arms fire, started to turn more vehicles into mechanised coffins. However, the Russian Advance was halted at least for now.

Radek advised through his headset to the Ukrainians that they were close and coming up behind the Russian infantry. Something planned in their military positioning on the battlefield as the defenders. The Ukrainians confirmed the priority was still the resupply convoy following on behind still more tanks and troops. For the GROM unit this meant swinging slightly north to access replacement munitions previously hidden during February. Restocked, the next 25 minutes were for the GROM unit rather like 'shooting rats in a barrel'. The element of surprise was still with the Ukrainians with the ferocity of the response against the invaders adding to Russian dismay. A number of the canvas covered resupply trucks were filled with troops which burst into flame when hit by bazooka shells. Whether they were conscripts or regulars, the end result was the same – incineration and the stench of burnt bodies.

Melting back into the forest, the GROM were once more silent and unseen. With no phones, radios, or other links to the outside world, apart from their comms link to the Ukrainian Command, in order to avoid requesting a Russian missile being zeroed in on their location, they all knew war had been declared but we unaware of Putin's formal announcement earlier in the day. It would be early April before a full copy of the text was circulated amongst them all when the siege of Sumy was finally lifted.

[President Putin had recognised the Donetsk People's Republic and Luhansk People's Republic signing mutual cooperation agreements between Russia and these two

'breakaway' regions on February 21st. 'Breakaway' does of course highlight the artificiality given the Kremlin had encouraged and supported insurrection with its Army since 2014. The following speech to the Russian Nation came on the heels of his earlier address to the Russian Nation on the evening of the 21st. At 06:00 hours Moscow Time, President Putin announced a 'special military operation' against Ukraine – another example to add to long list of disinformation and denial from today's Kremlin echoing a well-trodden path from Soviet times.

Respected citizens of Russia! Dear friends!

Today, I again consider it necessary to come back to the tragic events taking place in the Donbass and the key issue of ensuring Russian security. Let me start with what I said in my address of February 21st. I am referring to what causes us particular concern and anxiety – those fundamental threats against our country that year after year, step by step, are offensively and unceremoniously created by irresponsible politicians in the West.

I am referring to the expansion of the NATO to the east, moving its military infrastructure closer to Russian borders. It is well known that for 30 years we have persistently and patiently tried to reach an agreement with the leading NATO countries on the principles of equal and inviolable security in Europe. In response to our proposals, we constantly faced either cynical deception and lies, or attempts to pressure and blackmail, while NATO, despite all our protests and concerns, continued to steadily expand. The war machine is moving and, I repeat, it is coming close to our borders.

After the collapse of the USSR, the realignment of the world began, and the norms of international law that had been developed – the key, basic ones being adopted in the aftermath of World War II and largely consolidating its outcome – began to get

in the way of the self-proclaimed winner of the Cold War. Of course, in practical life, in international relations and the rules that regulated them, it was necessary to take into account changes in the state of affairs in the world and the balance of power. This should have been done professionally, smoothly, patiently, taking into account and respecting the interests of all countries and understanding one's own responsibility. But no, the euphoria from having absolute superiority, a kind of modern-day absolutism, and the low level of general culture and arrogance of decision-makers resulted in decisions being prepared, adopted and pushed through that were beneficial only for themselves. The situation began to develop according to a different scenario.

You don't have to look far for examples. First, without any approval from the UN Security Council, they carried out a bloody military operation against Belgrade, using aircraft and missiles right in the very centre of Europe - several weeks of continuous bombing of cities and critical infrastructure. We have reminded these facts to Western colleagues. However, they do not like to remember those events and when we talk about it, they prefer to point not to the norms of international law, but to the circumstances that they interpret as they see fit.

Then came the turn of Iraq, Libya, and Syria. The illegitimate use of military force against Libya, the twisting of all decisions taken by the UN Security Council on the Libyan issue led to the complete destruction of the state, to the emergence of a major hotbed of international terrorism, to a humanitarian catastrophe and a civil war that has not ended to this day. The tragedy, to which they doomed hundreds of thousands, millions of people not only in Libya, but throughout this region, gave rise to a massive migration wave from North Africa and the Middle East to Europe.
They ensured a similar fate for Syria. The Western coalition's military activities on the territory of this country without the consent of the Syrian government or the approval of the UN

Security Council are nothing but aggression and blatant intervention.

However, there is a special place for the invasion of Iraq, which was carried out also without any legal grounds. As a pretext, they put forward supposedly reliable information from the United States about the presence of weapons of mass destruction in Iraq. As proof of this, publicly, in front of the eyes of the whole world, the US secretary of state shook some kind of a test tube with white powder, assuring everyone that this is a chemical weapon being developed in Iraq. And then it turned out that all this was a hoax, a bluff: there were no chemical weapons in Iraq.

In this context, there were promises to our country not to expand NATO even one inch to the east. I repeat – they deceived us, in other words, they simply conned us. Yes, you can often hear that politics is a dirty business. Perhaps, that is so, but not to this extent. After all, such cheating behaviour contradicts not only the principles of international relations, but above all the generally recognised norms of morality. Where is justice and truth here? They were just total lies and hypocrisy.

By the way, American politicians, political scientists and journalists themselves write and say that in recent years, an actual 'empire of lies' has been created inside the United States. It's hard to disagree with that, as it's true. But let us not understate: the United States is a great country, a system-forming power. All her satellites not only dutifully agree, sing along to its music, but also copy its behaviour, and enthusiastically accept the rules they are offered. Therefore, with good reason, we can confidently say that the entire so-called Western bloc, formed by the United States in its own image and likeness, all of it is an 'empire of lies.'"

Despite all of this, in December 2021 we once again made an attempt to agree with the United States and its allies on the principles of ensuring security in Europe and on the non-expansion of NATO. Everything was in vain. The US position did not change. They did not consider it necessary to negotiate with Russia on this important issue for us, continuing to pursue their own goals and disregarding our interests. As for the military sphere, today, modern Russia, even after the collapse of the USSR and the loss of a significant part of its capacity, is one of the most powerful nuclear powers in the world and possesses certain advantages in some of the newest types of weaponry. In this regard, no one should have any doubts that a direct attack on our country will lead to defeat and horrible consequences for any potential aggressor.

As NATO expands to the east, with every passing year, the situation for our country is getting worse and more dangerous. Moreover, in recent days the leadership of NATO has been openly talking about the need to speed up, force the advancement of the alliance's infrastructure to the borders of Russia. In other words, they are doubling down on their position. We can no longer just watch what is happening. It would be absolutely irresponsible on our part.

Further expansion of the NATO infrastructure and the beginning of military development in Ukraine's territories are unacceptable for us. The problem, of course, is not NATO itself – it is only an instrument of US foreign policy. The problem is that in the territories adjacent to us – territories that were historically ours, I emphasise – 'anti-Russian' hostility to us is being created, placed under full external control; integrated within the armed forces of NATO countries and supplied with the most modern weapons.

For the United States and its allies, this is the so-called policy of containment of Russia with obvious geopolitical benefits. And for our country, this is ultimately a matter of life and death, a matter of our historical future as a people. And this is not an exaggeration – it is true. This is a real threat not just to our interests, but to the very existence of our state, its sovereignty. This is the very red line that has been talked about many times. They crossed it.

About the situation in the Donbass, we see forces that carried out a coup in Ukraine in 2014, seized power and are holding it through sham electoral procedures, and have given up on the peaceful settlement of the conflict. For eight years, for eight long years, we have done everything possible to resolve the situation by peaceful, political means. All was in vain.

As I said in my previous address, one cannot look at what is happening there without compassion. It is simply not possible to stand all this any longer. It is necessary to immediately stop this nightmare – the genocide against the millions of people living there, who rely only on Russia, only on us. These aspirations, feelings, and pain of people are the main motivation for us to take the decision to recognise them as Russian territories. The course of events and the incoming information show that Russia's clash with these forces is inevitable. It is only a matter of time: they are getting ready, they are waiting for the right time. Now they also claim to acquire nuclear weapons. We will not allow this to happen.

We have been left no other option to protect Russia and our people, but for the one that we will be forced to use today. The situation requires us to take decisive and immediate action. The people's republics of Donbass turned to Russia with a request for help.

In this regard, in accordance with Article 51 of Part 7 of the UN Charter, with the approval of the Federation Council of Russia and in pursuance of the treaties of friendship and mutual assistance ratified by the Duma on February 22nd with the Donetsk People's Republic and the Luhansk People's Republic, I decided to launch a special military operation.

Its goal is to protect people who have been subjected to abuse and genocide by the regime in Kyiv for eight years. And for this we will pursue the demilitarisation and denazification of Ukraine, as well as bringing to justice those who committed numerous bloody crimes against civilians, including citizens of the Russian Federation.

Our plans do not include the occupation of Ukrainian territories. We are not going to impose anything on anyone by force. At the same time, we hear that recently in the West there is talk that the documents signed by the Soviet totalitarian regime, securing the outcome of World War II, should no longer be upheld. Well, what is the answer to this?
The outcome of World War II, as well as the sacrifices made by our people on the altar of victory over Nazism, are sacred - they do not contradict the high values of human rights and freedoms, based on the realities that have developed today in the decades following war. It also does not cancel the right of nations to self-determination, enshrined in Article 1 of the UN Charter.

In this regard, I appeal to the citizens of Ukraine. In 2014, Russia was obliged to protect the residents of Crimea and Sevastopol from those whom you, yourself call 'Nazis'. Crimea and Sevastopol residents made their choice to be with their historical homeland, with Russia, and we supported this. I repeat, we simply could not do otherwise.

What is happening today does not come out of a desire to infringe on the interests of Ukraine and the Ukrainian people. It is related to the protection of Russia itself from those who took Ukraine hostage and are trying to use it against our country and its people."

I also need to address the military personnel of the Ukrainian armed forces.

Dear comrades! Your fathers, grandfathers, great-grandfathers did not fight the Nazis and defend our common Motherland, so that today's Neo-Nazis can seize power in Ukraine. You took an oath of allegiance to the Ukrainian people, and not to the anti-national junta that plunders Ukraine and abuses its people. Don't follow its criminal orders. I urge you to lay down your weapons immediately and go home. I want to make clear that all servicemen of the Ukrainian army who do so will be able to freely leave the combat zone and return to their families. Once again, I emphasise, all responsibility for possible bloodshed will lay on the conscience of the ruling regime in Ukraine.
Now a few important, very important words for those who may be tempted to intervene in the ongoing events - whoever tries to hinder us, or threaten our country or our people, should know that Russia's response will be immediate and will lead you to consequences that you have never faced in your history. We are ready for any turn of events. All necessary decisions in this regard have been made. I hope that I will be heard.

Compatriots, I am confident that the soldiers and officers of the Russian Armed Forces devoted to their country will professionally and courageously fulfil their duty. I have no doubt that all levels of government, the experts responsible for the stability of our economy, financial system and social sphere, the heads of our companies and all Russian business will act in a coordinated and efficient manner. I count on a patriotic consensus position of all parliamentary parties and public forces.

As it has always been the case in our history, the fate of Russia is in the reliable hands of our multinational people. And this means that the decisions made will be implemented, the goals set will be achieved, the security of our Motherland will be reliably guaranteed. I believe in your support, in that invincible strength that our love for the Fatherland gives us.]

Chapter 14

Breaking camp every morning was becoming a tedious but very necessary chore for the GROM. The dense forests of Sumy provided a certain safety but it was nevertheless increasingly dangerous. The Russian Military Command was proceeding to shell Sumy from its mechanised 'Malka' heavy artillery batteries on Russian soil. There was a steady sound of one or two artillery rounds being fired every three minutes followed by a gap of ten to fifteen minutes as the mechanised artillery piece moved its new firing position. This shoot-and-scoot capability allowed the Russians to avoid counter-battery fire even before the first shell hits its target located up to forty seven kilometres away. The impact on Sumy was of course devastating as the 'Malka' batteries and other artillery was brought to bear on the City. This artillery barrage, that included multi-launch missile systems like the GRAD, continued day and night. It became clear in a matter of days that along with Ukrainian military positions, firing on residential areas was not indiscriminate but by design. The increasing destruction across the entire City was not random but a deliberate strategy to terrorise the population into submission by the Russian High Command.

Across the Northern battlefront, the Russian advances were meeting fierce resistance and had as a result broadly stalled.

Feeding the demands of their forward troops had become a problem exacerbated by mechanical breakdowns and guerrilla like attacks on extended supply lines. The Russian High Command was reluctant to swamp the Sumy forest with infantry to hunt down and kill whoever was inflicting such damage. There were insufficient troops to carry out such an operation and its infantry was highly mechanised. It would mean utilising more elite forces like its airborne regiments. However, with losses of equipment, munitions, food, and diesel tankers plus cyber and control vehicles let alone troops being killed and wounded, something had to be done as battle lines were hardening and repeated thrusts into the outskirts of Sumy were being repelled. Increasingly long range cruise missiles fired from its Navy in the Black Sea and from within the Russian heartland of Rostov-on-Don were targeting hospitals, schools, and shopping centres in addition to specific targets that were supporting the Ukrainian war effort. Whilst the involvement of Ramzan Kadyrov's Chechens by the Kremlin was mainly for propaganda to spread fear across Ukraine, a battalion of 900 fighters was temporarily stationed in Kursk. The Russian High Command decided that deploying these battle hardened soldiers to root out and destroy whoever the Ukrainians were operating behind their forward lines in the forests of Sumy made sense – animals to hunt animals.

Radek sensed the GROM were not alone in the Forest. Whilst he had wondered at what point the 'Russian Bear' would find their mosquito bites too much to ignore, he soon had the answer. Loknya is a small village off the highway running between Sudzha in Russia and Sumy. The GROM were positioned on higher ground within the forest overlooking this tiny hamlet when a convoy of trucks arrived emptying a few hundred soldiers. A cold whisper came through his headset – 'Chechens'.

The Poles did not have long to wait for the barbaric acts of cruelty and malice, for which Chechens were infamously known before and after Grozny, to begin. These unprotected villagers faced a barbarian horde - people devoid of any humanity and undeniably evil. Their intentions were abundantly clear as they poured into the various villagers' houses to the sound of female screams and gunshots. Filip took off his helmet and beckoned Radek to do the same.

'We cannot sit up here and watch this looting, rape, and murder before our very eyes Radek?'

'On that you are correct!'

Radek put his helmet back on and gave the order to withdraw. Silently the GROM pulled back into the darkness of the forest and a few kilometres later congregated in one of the few small clearings within the entire woodland. Filip and a few of the other team members were questioning why they had done nothing to help the villagers.

'Gentlemen, our rather successful activities over recent weeks of destroying resupply convoys behind Russian lines has seemingly led to a violent 'pushback' from our Russian friends. Today the arrival of a few hundred Chechens, and there will undoubtedly be more being placed at other strategic points around the forest, is to hunt us down like vermin and kill us. The Chechens will, I expect, conduct counter insurgency sweeps criss-crossing the forest until we are found, cornered, and exterminated. We will receive no quarter. That said, I realise we all feel the Chechens are nothing worse than rabid dogs. Importantly, their activities whether in Chechnya, Georgia or even Syria have been alongside the full force of the Russian Military including its air force – they have not faced serious well-armed opposition. Some of you understandably wanted us to try and save those villagers from the indiscriminate abuse and torture they would suffer. However, we have a mission to fulfil that will save many more villages and hamlets from the war crimes'.

'So that's it Radek – we walk away and carry on 'ducking and diving' for more weeks?'

Radek noticed some unease and loss of eye contact as Filip Cuda said what many of them felt as Polish elite soldiers – atrocities were not to be ignored on the battlefield by the GROM.

'No I did not say that.' Heads rose to listen. 'You all volunteered for this mission but attacking the Chechens without a plan would have resulted in us losing people unnecessarily. Our advantages are surprise and knowledge of the terrain. Tonight we have darkness on our side and no moon. We are going to send a message to wherever the Chechens are camped around this forest that to enter this part of Ukraine means certain death. We are going to give them a war from which their survival will only be achieved through taking a ride back to Chechnya. We need to find the other Chechen encampments but that will be for tomorrow. Now we will plan our attack. Master-Sergeants let us go back to where we were and observe. Filip remember that book you were reading on booby traps start thinking about we can adapt in this environment. Set a perimeter until we return.'

The days were becoming longer but it was still pitch dark at 18:00. Six eyes were focused on the layout of the village first in daylight then through their night vision googles. The Chechens were living up to their infamous reputation as barbarians. By the late afternoon, many were completely drunk on looted vodka or other stolen alcohol as they foraged for food. The man in charge appear to be a Colonel but as he was carried, unable to stand, into one of the houses they waited. Were sentries going to be posted or were these Chechens so arrogant as to believe they were entirely safe on Ukrainian soil within the Russian Army's protective shield? It seemed so. Had any villagers survived? From the littered bodies in the street and those unceremoniously thrown like garbage outside the doors to their homes, the answer was an unequivocal 'No'.

After midnight, the first step was the disablement of the Chechens transport – there was to be no escape. Incendiary explosives were placed on every diesel tank and the timers set for 60 minutes. There was a slight concern that all the carousing and drinking might have led to a Chechen suddenly appearing to piss outside a door rather than using the facilities in the house or for a smoke but there was complete silence. Since the Russians had bombed a series of sub-stations there was no electricity in the village and that aided the GROM's deadly plans. Semtex bombs were camouflaged and placed on timers above the threshold of each front door to what were predominantly wooden structures. Similarly incendiary explosives were placed on each rear door or rear elevation – fire was going to be their helper in driving any survivors into the street. Between each building, claymores were placed for remote detonation. With night vision and telescopic sites, smell of death would soon be in the air. As Radek waited alongside Tomek Jarocki, he smelt death not just of the villagers but also of animals - not even dogs had escaped the random killing of goats and chickens.

When the trucks exploded into balls of flame, bleary eyed Chechens still drunk staggered into the street in varying stages of undress only to rush back in a house to grab their weapons to a man. However leaving became somewhat difficult as the semtex bombs sent shards of wood into each home just before the incendiary bombs exploded setting the house completely engulfed in flame. None of the GROM wasted a bullet on those Chechens who were running in the street alight and burning to death. Their sights were focussed on those attempting to run between the burning houses and escape. Detonating claymores halted such efforts with the survivors at the rear either meeting deadly fire from the GROM or from Radek and Tomek. After 10 minutes, GROM moved in methodically ensuring no Chechen survived continuing to speak Russian over their comms out of habit protecting their true identity. They found the Commanding Officer dead in a pool of his vomit but clutching a thin document case. This proved to be a great find as it provided the campsite locations of the other Chechens sent to kill them.

Tomek Jarocki, as the best marksman amongst many, and Piotr Vrubel, as his spotter were left at the observation point. The rest of the GROM melted back into the forest.

General Bolat Abubakarov of the Chechen 1st Regiment could not raise any response from Loknya the following morning. Having checked with Russia's Battlefield Command, Major – General Timur Morozov, it was agreed Abubakarov should travel with one of his Colonels who was heading towards the presently stalled front line for an eyes on assessment why there had been any delay in a response from drunkenness to anything else for the High Command and him. The drive on the highway was littered with burnt out shells of tanks and mechanised infantry vehicles evidencing the ferociousness of the Ukrainian Army's resistance to the Russians being very much uninvited guests on their land. What also stood out was the number of abandoned vehicles being comparatively high by comparison. Whether or not the abandonment was caused by mechanical breakdown or simply no diesel, where were the Maintenance crews? As the Colonel would discover later, Western sanctions were also depleting the resupply of parts forcing cannibalisation of similar vehicles presently mothballed Kursk and Rostov-on-Don military warehouses. Similarly, post-COVID global supply issues were not helping. For example, containers with manufactured military vehicle parts were stuck on Shanghai's dockside because of a City wide COVID lockdown under China's zero-tolerance policy. It was of course doubtful whether the parts would ever leave given China's wish to avoid secondary sanctions but that was irrelevant for now.

The Tigr armoured vehicle turned into the short single track road leading to Loknya. Coming to a halt at the beginning of the hamlet, the officers stepped out of the vehicle accompanied by two soldiers from 106th Airborne Division. They started to walk down the village's only street taking in the devastation and trying to understand what had taken place. Ukrainian villagers' bodies, mainly older men past 60, grandmothers', teenage boys and girls were visible amongst the many dead Chechens as the seeming funeral pyres of the burnt out wooden houses continued to smoulder. What had happened here? As they walked further down the street, the Colonel noticed each Chechen had been shot in the head – there were going to be no survivors. At that moment, a single shot rang out from somewhere along the forest edge. They all instinctively went to ground whilst looking for immediate cover. The Colonel turned to where the Chechen General had been standing. A single hole in his forehead was one thing but half his skull was seemingly smashed to smithereens inside what was left of his helmet. This was a deliberate kill shot with extreme malice – a hollow point bullet. 'Back to the Tigr' shouted the Colonel as the three survivors ran for the safety of their armoured vehicle.

Major-General Morozov listened to his Colonel's rather alarming report about what had probably taken place in Loknya. None of Chechens weapons or munitions had been collected, the execution styled 'tap' to the head of every Chechen, and the patience to wait for the Chechen Commander with a 'hollow point' to complete the slaughter – what did it mean? Whoever was operating in the forests of Sumy had no liking for the Chechen military that was an absolute certainty. The abuse and massacre of the Loknya villagers had provoked a very violent reaction yet it was painstaking in its planning and implementation. Morozov ordered the Chechen commanders at the other campsites to immediately each lead a detachment to Loknya. There needed to be burials of all the villagers in a communal grave to hide the war crimes committed against innocent Ukrainian civilians. The Chechens also needed to attend to their own dead including recovering the body of General Abubakarov. However, an intended consequence of these orders was to make the Chechens declare *'chir'* on the unseen enemy in the forest ie a Caucuses' blood feud meaning - *'we will find you, punish you, and then kill you'*.

Radek had scouted with Filip and the Master-Sergeants the two remaining Chechen encampments. There were certainly nearly 500 or more soldiers. There was no doubt that the GROM had stirred a wasps' nest. The loss of their Loknya colleagues and General Abubakarov, their leader from deployment in Syria, made them a very dangerous and relentless enemy. Radek and his unit were outnumbered more than 20 to one and were about to be hunted down – no different to vermin!

The Chechens were a larger force but still mobile unlike traditional Russian military. The GROM's tactics would have to be adapted to face an even more brutal enemy than the Russian Army. In particular, hit-and-run tactics and then luring the Chechens into ambushes would become the GROM's stock in trade. For the Poles, the Forest had been a relatively safe sanctuary since the start of the invasion but with winter ending and the Chechens, it could end up being their final resting place. Hence, the Chechens had to be made to fear the natural darkness of the forest and their unseen foe if the GROM were to win.

With this in mind, whilst Tomek and Piotr were waiting patiently to remove Abubakarov from the planet permanently, the GROM were setting booby traps along the immediate access paths into the forest from the Chechen encampments. Suitable positions were found for them to lob mortar rounds at night causing death and fire with incendiary rounds but also depriving the Chechens of needed sleep. The booby traps in many ways took a page from the Vietcong military manual. In the forest of Sumy pointed willow sticks, mines, grenades, and claymores plus improvised devices were created. Many were designed to maim or incapacitate rather than immediately kill a Chechen soldier. Firstly other soldiers were required to remove their wounded and dead colleagues thereby delaying and hampering their 'search and destroy' patrols. Secondly, it would also mean the traps were a psychological weapon. Word about the traps would spread amongst the Chechens as wounded and the dead were returned to the encampments. Thirdly, a daily ritual of burying, preferably with 24 hours of death in accordance with the Islamic Faith, their Muslim brothers could only reinforce those increasing fears of the forest and that an unseen enemy.

The willow sticks of varying lengths and width had a simple sharpened spike on one end to impale its victim. The sticks were smeared with faeces to also cause infection. Any Chechen stepping into such a pit would be unable to remove their leg without causing further damage as some of the sticks would also point downwards at an angle. The GROM depending whatever else was waiting on a forest trail dug pits beside each other. When a Chechen soldier fell in and needed help, his colleagues would then get trapped in the pit next door. This was usually where rocket propelled grenades and machine gun fire would then decimate an entire patrol.

Grenades had a trip wire attached to the safety pin so when a Chechen tripped the wire, the grenade would detonate.

The GROM also placed grenades inside used food tins with the pins removed. These were fastened low to the ground or tied to trees on either side of a path and connected by a wire. When the tripwire was triggered by a soldier's foot, the grenades were pulled from the cans, releasing the safety levers and igniting the grenades with devastating effect.
As the mines were placed including tripwires to claymores, there precise positioning, including all the other booby traps, were being marked on a detailed map of the GROM's forest kingdom. When hostilities ceased, these would all have to be decommissioned so it was once more safe for everyone to enjoy.

The next 2 weeks were a game of 'cat and mouse' as the Chechens chased an elusive enemy who attacked and then retreated luring their patrols into deadly ambushes. The frequent nightly raids on the Chechen encampments where a combination of indiscriminate and incendiary mortar shells amongst their tents ensured both chaos and interrupted sleep. Even doubling the night security patrols to protect the campsites did not lessen the debilitating regularity of such assaults. The GROM aided by their night vision kit and suppressors on their Hecklar & Koch MP5 meant a night patrol for Chechens was a one way ticket to hell. During daylight hours, chasing a seemingly retreating enemy for the Chechens turned into a different type of nightmare. Tired and exhausted Chechen soldiers were chasing mindlessly an unseen enemy headlong up and down forest tracks only for more death to be inflicted on their number. Exhausted from such exacting patrols, the Chechens made easy targets when returning to their base camps from selective sniper fire.

Major-General Morozov reviewed the Chechen Colonels' joint written report with consternation. A complement of 581 fighters had been whittled down in the 2 weeks since Loknya to just 301 being still fit to take to the forest battlefield. 109 had been killed outright, 67 wounded had died from septicaemia, and 104 had been transported across the border for urgent medical attention. It was clear to him that whether Ukrainian Special Forces or similar were operating in the forests of Sumy, the Chechens were not hunting them - they, the Chechens, were the hunted.

Looking at a map of the extended forest, the latest engagements with the enemy were slowly but surely occurring far deeper into the forest. Thrusts from the East with peripheral support from the northern and southern forest boundary made an attack from the West ie from the direction of Loknya, with simultaneously deeper advances from the East could well eventually encircle this troubling group of Ukrainian forces. He issued the appropriate orders. Whilst attacks on resupply vehicles had lessened over the last few weeks, the Ukrainian Army was increasingly pushing his forces back village by village. The Russian High Command had indicated that a strategy overview was underway. This might lead to a tactical withdrawal of the forces that had originally breached the northern Ukrainian border whereby the stalled Eastern Advance could be reinvigorated. This early warning enabled the Major-General to begin thinking about and then planning for a tactical withdrawal or retreat depending on one's perspective. In the interim, the expendable Chechens, more suitable as a force in urban warfare settings, could be left to organise themselves to penetrate the forest from the West and hopefully exterminate these vile people.

The GROM were physically and mentally tired. The absence of a permanent and safe base similar to their time in the Białowieża forest was a strategic weakness in the war they were presently waging. Continuously moving camp, consuming combat field rations, and of course too many weeks under canvas were all contributing to their sheer exhaustion and deteriorating physical condition. Life was becoming extremely difficult. Perhaps declaring a very personal war on Kadyrov's Chechens was not the smartest military decision Radek had ever taken with his unit. This emotional response to the murderous assault on the innocent and vulnerable villagers of Loknya was no doubt fuelled by having heard the many stories of similar war crimes committed by Chechens in Aleppo whilst in Idlib. Nevertheless, the outcome would have most likely been little different.

The Ukrainian Army's ferocious defence of Kyiv, Chernihiv, Sumy, and Kharkiv had inflicted huge losses of equipment and troops. The Russians were now falling back from Bucha and Irpin – did this mean a similar withdrawal from Sumy? If so, then the GROM's escape from a potential tightening Chechen noose had to be south- westwards where they would meet and rejoin the advancing Ukrainian Forces.

As Radek had reached the conclusion, it was time to return to civilisation, shaving, and hot showers, Ukrainian Army Command for the Sumy Region ordered the GROM to make a tactical withdrawal. The changing battlefield meant pushing the retreating Russians back to their own territory was now a counter offensive priority. In addition, harrying retreating Russians was now the responsibility of the

Ukrainian Military – the GROM had successfully completed their mission.

It was the GROM's last night sleeping in tents. Radek took his turn on watch with thoughts of a shave and an unbroken night's sleep uppermost in his mind. The night's silence was broken by the sound of an exploding claymore swiftly followed by screams of wounded or dying Chechens. The enemy was close, too close. When a grenade tripwire triggered another explosion on the other side of their tented camp, Filip Cuda with Master-Sergeant Stodola with the entire team exited to the south-west so as to set themselves up as a retreating defensive field of fire. Radek and Master Sergeant Nowak set booby trapped the tents and then exited on the path taken by Filip. Their night vision googles were extremely helpful as the thermal imaging highlighted the Chechens had surrounded them whether by good military planning or just plain luck. The entire unit had fixed suppressors to their Hecklar & Koch 416s. As previously drilled, either Filip's or Radek's original teams under the command of the Master-Sergeants would provide over-watch and defensive fire alternatively as their rolling withdrawal took place. For now, the GROM were still silent and unseen.

In any withdrawal, the risk of being out-flanked and then being caught in a 'killing zone' was always militarily possible. When seemingly thermal imaging indicated many, if not all, of the surviving Chechens of 1st Regiment were almost on top of their hurriedly vacated camp, the sheer numbers could overwhelm the GROM. Each Master-Sergeant, accompanied by two of the unit, were moving in parallel to the main body of the rolling retreat but some 100 metres on either side but constantly 200 metres to the rear in order to prevent encirclement and allow for catching the threat in crossfire.

Explosions back in their former campsite indicated the Chechens were closing in. Speaking through his comms, Radek ordered that the GROM should quicken the pace of their withdrawal. Asking for a quickly for volunteer, Tomek Jarocki joined him. They were going to engage the advancing Chechen patrols and slow them down whilst the unit established a defensive position closer to the south-western edge of the forest. The previous evening, as part of a prepared escape route, a mortar with a supply of incendiary shells and grenade launchers had been stashed for use if a surprise attack occurred. A practice followed every night since they had been operating in the forest.

Taking cover behind some fallen trees, the first mortar shell landed and exploded on impact in the GROM's former camp. With the benefit of their night vision, a number of Chechen patrols had gradually congregated amongst what remained of the GROM's tents and equipment. Tending to the few survivors of the booby traps, they were awaiting orders from their senior officers. Similarly, the other advancing Chechen patrols halted. The incendiary round sent a wall of flame into the gathering Chechens as a number turned into phosphorescent fireballs. Before the initial screams of dying and burning men fell silent while the other Chechens were falling over each other, the second and more devastating explosive round blew up with its shrapnel exacting a heavy price. Simultaneously both Radek and Tomek fired in rapid succession rocket propelled grenades directly at those stationary Chechen patrols. Looking through once more night vision googles, they began to purposefully shoot as quickly as they could from cover the leading two Chechens of those patrols they could see. It was not long before Radek's and Tomek's mussel flashes brought an increasing level of returning fire. Bullets were soon pinging and zinging all around them. Crawling on their stomachs for 40 metres to evade the hail of bullets, they took temporary shelter behind some standing timber before looking for fresh targets. The next 25 minutes had Radek and Tomek repeating the process. As soon as the incoming bullets started to pepper the trees around where they were once again temporarily taking cover, they moved sometimes crawling again or running half-crouched to a new firing position. Nevertheless, the danger of drawing the Chechen fire suddenly became apparent. It only took one bullet to ricochet off a tree hitting Tomek in his right thigh for their apparent success to turn into impending disaster. Radek applied an alginate powdered wound dressing and then tightly a battlefield dressing to act as partial tourniquet in stopping the bleeding. Whilst Radek was attending to his wound, Tomek, through gritted teeth as the alginate did its job, continued to select oncoming targets with a vengeance. They were some 500 metres from Filip and the GROM's defensive line. Radek spoke to Filip advising that they would coming towards them in a hurry – as fast as Tomek and he could master a three legged race!

There was a brief argument as Radek was bandaging his wound that Tomek lost. His suggestion Radek should leave him behind was turned aside out of hand. Tomek realised that he either made an attempt to leave with him or Radek would stay alongside him to kill as many of the enemy as they could before being overwhelmed. Filip ordered four of the team to fan out towards the stumbling Radek and Tomek and provide covering fire. The Chechens were less than 300 metres away and the hail of firepower was increasing by the minute. The GROM's rolling withdrawal continued but under increasing pressure. The Chechens were attempting to out-flank their retreat but meeting resolute resistance from the Master-Sergeants and their companions. Rather like, if one throws enough mud at a wall some will stick, similarly the volume of bullets coming from many directions meant the GROM began to suffer. Bullets were hitting targets like limbs rather than torsos and necks that were protected by lightweight ultra-high molecular weight polyethylene vests with high collar protection let alone their heads defended by bulletproof light weight combat helmets.

Both Master-Sergeants were reporting being under heavy fire but they had run out of grenades for their launchers. Radek ordered Filip to fall back and form a new defensive position 500 metres further back. The Master sergeants were told to come in from the flanks but then to keep moving to the edge of the forest. It was April 4th. Piotr Vrubel and Radek then laid down covering fire to protect the unit's retreat. Using their night sights, with incoming bullets zinging and pinging all around them, to identify any Chechen within 50 metres or less and then to remove the threat. However, the risk was they would quickly be cut off. So after every 5 to 10 rounds they would scuttle back to a new position taking out any thermal image on their flanks before addressing those oncoming Chechens directly coming at them.

Ukrainian Battle Command was speaking to Radek during this fire fight not only establishing what was happening during the withdrawal but also to advise the Russians were in full retreat. Clearly, either as an oversight or deliberately, Major-General Morozov had seemingly not ordered the surviving members of the Chechen 1st Regiment to halt its mission.

Another hour of fierce fighting continued. However the rolling retreat had brought the GROM to the edge of the forest and winter wheat fields. This would be their last stand as the Chechens would just cut them down in open country. As dawn broke, the GROM were low on ammunition and as a combat force, they were more than walking wounded. In these what were seemingly final moments, Radek was badly injured from an exploding grenade and was floating 'in and out' consciousness.

Master-Sergeant Stodola was ensuring everyone who could still fire a weapon had ammunition or someone next to him with hands or fingers that still worked to load. The forest had suddenly fallen silent. Looking immediately to the rear, Kacper was expecting to see Chechens moving to encircle their position. Instead Ukrainian Infantry was moving towards them. At first blinking in surprise, were they Ukrainians or was it wishful thinking on his part, he pulled out his field binoculars. They were 'friendlies'. Turning back towards the enemy, the binoculars were met with silence – the Chechens had left.

Filip Cuda was already dead along with Bartek Nowak. In the heat of battle Filip's femoral artery was hit and he very quickly bled to death. As for Bartek, a series of high velocity machine gun rounds had chewed through his body armour ripping apart his chest. 3 other members were too badly injured to be moved and were close to death. The remainder were carrying wounds somewhere like Tomek Jarocki with that bullet in his thigh. Exhaustion now set in as relief the fight was over – they were unable to take another step. Six weeks behind enemy lines had taken their toll on the survivors both physically and mentally. They were all gaunt from living on combat rations. They looked more like 'down and outs' than an elite special forces unit. Unshaven for weeks, days and nights in the same clothing, covered in blood – sometimes theirs, and a haunting look in their eyes, the GROM had given everything and more for Ukraine and Freedom on the battlefield of the Sumy Forests.

For Major-General Morozov, regrouping his battle group outside Belgorod before moving to join the Russian Army's main thrust to take the entire Donetsk and Luhansk Regions, the Chechen losses were inexplicable. The surviving Colonel reported that of the remaining 301 fighters only 166 were still capable of active service. With regard to the other 135, there were only 51 wounded – the rest had died on the battlefield. These were horrendous losses for any regiment. For the Chechens, their ranks had been more than decimated by a guerrilla unit making the Major-General seriously question whether their willingness and will to fight had been broken.

Russia's missile and shelling campaign across the Sumy Region including the regional capital, Sumy, had destroyed the majority of its hospitals. Those remaining did not have the surgical capabilities necessary to treat either Radek or a few of the other surviving GROM carrying serious injuries.

The Ukrainian Army Field Hospital was their first stop and for one of them sadly his last.

The coming days were a blank for Radek. He remained unconscious. Master-Sergeant Stodola was in command. Having got the survivors showered, shaved, fed, treated for superficial non-life threatening injuries, and rested, they organised the body bags to take their friends home to Gdansk, and Poland. A Ukrainian Military Medical train had been organised to take those soldiers with severe injuries requiring specialist medical treatment. The journey was tortuous and lengthy timewise. Whilst there were a limited number of doctors and nurses to tend the patients, the GROM were not nicknamed 'the surgeons' for no reason.

They had undertaken extensive medical training as part of their combat training in Gdansk. Hence, Master-Sergeant Stodola had the entire unit on the train together with the body bags of their fallen comrades in the rear refrigerated wagon. Tomek Jarocki and Piotr Vrubel paid special attention to Radek. Whilst most if not all the shrapnel from the grenade blast had been removed, some pieces were still embedded in his head. The battlefield surgeons had decided with limited scanning equipment that attempting removal might be more life threatening. The likelihood of the shrapnel pieces being straight rather than jagged was slim. They were not prepared to operate on that assumption so Major Król had to be a priority evacuation on the next hospital train to Poland.

When the train pulled into Lviv Station some 37 hours after leaving Sumy via Kyiv and Zhytomyr because of missile strikes destroying parts of the track, Colonel Chmura was waiting with Polish Military ambulances and humvees plus a fleet of civilian hearses. Once loaded, the column moved swiftly to the Medyka crossing at speed with the assistance of Ukrainian military and police motorbike outriders. The amazing performance by the GROM was spreading by word of mouth throughout the Ukrainian Army. Whilst it was yet another example of heroism in the defence of Ukrainian territory, Poles, their neighbours, had made the ultimate sacrifice. People wanted to know who these men were and are, especially as the destruction of the Chechen 1st Regiment became apparent. The Ukrainian Army, sweeping carefully through the forest checking and removing any remaining booby traps in accordance with the Master-Sergeant Nowak's map, found so many dead Chechens. When Ukrainian Intelligence reported on the intercepted messages from the Chechen leadership on the ground to Major-General Morozov, the true extent of GROM's success on the battlefield was beyond doubt.

A Polish Medical Air Rescue helicopter was waiting on the Polish side of the Medyka crossing to airlift Radek and the other critically wounded GROM soldiers to the Jana Pawla II civilian hospital in Krakow. The remainder of the convoy was then escorted by Polish military police on motorbikes directly to the Mielec air base where a Hercules C130 was already on the tarmac waiting for their arrival.

The Hercules came to halt. No sooner had the loading bay lowered and touched the tarmac than the Special Forces pallbearers in dress uniforms entered. Each coffin draped in a Polish flag was carefully lifted on their shoulders and slowly carried out of the plane. Master-Sergeant Stodola and the other survivors, some on crutches, appeared and lined up behind the coffins. A cold light breeze from the north swirled gently back and forth across the Gdansk airfield. Lieutenant-General Politczek was joined by the Minister of Defence, the

Foreign Secretary, and the Minister for Special Forces to acknowledge the duty and service by the fallen and surviving members of GROM Team Six for Poland. There was no brass band rather sadness at the very high price paid for democracy with still another four of their number critically injured and fighting to survive.

The bereaved families were supported not only by the families of the survivors but also the entire GROM. Some 1200 soldiers were mustered on the tarmac in dress uniform to honour the ultimate sacrifice paid by their fallen brothers-in-arms. Amongst the GROM, there was immense gratitude and pride in what Team 6 had achieved in the forests of Sumy where they were massively outnumbered. As each coffin was temporarily rested on trestles, the Honour Guard stepped forward over each coffin. The parade was ordered to present arms as a rifle volley of 3 shots was fired by the six-man Honour Guard to each coffin. However, the lone bugler playing 'the Last Post' was very emotive for all those present. There was no embarrassment as the odd tear flowed down a warrior's cheek as they remembered the faces of those lost on the battlefields of Iraq, Afghanistan, Syria, and now Ukraine.

There was no press presence or indeed media coverage as these activities would always be 'silent and unseen'.

Chapter 15

Doctor Maria Wozniak, as the leading neuro-surgeon at Krakow's Jana Pawla II hospital, had spent over 4 hours in theatre removing the embedded shrapnel in Radek Król's skull. Fortuitously, none of the grenade fragments had penetrated the cranium bone and in spite of it almost being a week since the blast, there was no infection much to the credit of Ukraine's Field Hospital surgeons cleansing of the wounds. It was to some extent the poor shape the rest of his body was in that was giving rise to concern. The femur in his right leg had been shattered by bullet and he had taken another one in his left shoulder leaving untold damage. As she worked on his head, an orthopaedic surgeon was attempting to piece together with pins and bolts his right leg. When Doctor Wozniak finished, the surgeon started rebuilding his shoulder. Their combined medical opinion was that their patient could well have damage from the explosion to his inner ears let alone concussion. Nevertheless, keeping him sedated and in a prone position had probably saved his life together with the blood transfusions in the Field Hospital followed by saline drips on the Hospital Train.

Alexandra had been phoned by Colonel Pawlukowicz once he knew Radek was in the operating theatre. Since February 21st she had not understandably received any contact once

GROM Team 6 entered its battlefield position. There was no point in worrying the Lady unnecessarily. She was now at Radek's bedside anxiously waiting for him to recover consciousness. Alexandra was joined later by Elsa, her mother-in-law, leaving Tomek, Radek's father, to look after Maja and the St Bernards in Niepolomice. It had been four years since Alexandra had seen Doctor Wozniak. The women recognised each other instantly. This gave Alexandra a much needed confidence boost as she was now 3 ½ months pregnant with Radek's and her 2nd child.

It was late evening before Radek regained consciousness but only for a matter of minutes. His vision was hazy. He could hear indecipherable women's' voices through hurting ears. However, all he could remember was the grenade blast before once more relapsing into sleep wondering where he was.

Doctor Wozniak was called but by then Radek was once more lost to the world. His vital signs were though improving with blood pressure stabilising and his heart rate close to normal with the help of the painkillers being administered. Notwithstanding it was unlikely Radek would regain consciousness until mid-morning the following day neither woman would leave his side. Doctor Wozniak explained the extent of his injuries. This would mean that he would be in hospital for some weeks and in pain as he was weaned off painkillers. Physiotherapy and learning to walk on crutches would also be necessary she told them. There was one other aspect of good news from the women's perspective – Radek would no longer be eligible physically to undertake the demands placed on a GROM soldier.

Radek was relaxing on the porch with his right leg stuck on a stool and his crutches nearby. He had survived. However, the loss of Bartek Nowak let alone Filip plus four other brothers-in-arms weighed heavily on him. Alexandra had made him a light lunch to enjoy as spring sunshine flooded the entire garden. A black mercedes limousine came to a halt outside the gate to what was the Family Król compound. There was also a large black suburban behind the mercedes. Alexandra pressed the remote and the vehicles drive through coming to a halt by the front steps leading onto the veranda. It was mid-May.

ABW's personal protection officers, carrying Belgian Herstal FN-P90 sub-machine guns for close protection details, fanned out round the compound. The St Bernards, thanks to Tomek's patience and hours of training, did not move but watched. At that point, the rear door to the limousine was opened by one of the officers. Lieutenant-General Politczek began walking up the steps as Radek struggled to reach for his crutches. A combination of Alexandra giving him a withering look to stay seated and Grzegorz ordering him not to stand meant doing precisely that - staying put. Another salad miraculously appeared which told Radek that Alexandra knew Grzegorz would be calling around lunchtime.

A bottle of cold sauvignon blanc was produced and placed in a chiller with orders from Alexandra to them both that under no circumstances was Radek to have a glass – alcohol and his medication were not compatible.

Grzegorz began, between mouthfuls of prawns, avocado, melon and marie-rose sauce washed down with his rapidly emptying and refillable wine glass, to update Radek on events. Before their conversation began, Radek asked about GROM Team 6. Grzegorz told him of full military honours being accorded to Captain Filip Cuda, Master-Sergeant Bartek Nowak, and two other members of his unit at Gdansk. When Grzegorz told him that some 1200 serving soldiers mustered in addition to the military pallbearers and rifle details in dress uniform, he smiled in satisfaction for his fallen comrades.

'I hope the pallbearers and rifle detail were all Navy for Filip and Bartek General?'

'You may rest assured – all Navy - the pall bearers for Filip were all officers, captains and commodores, and as for Bartek all senior Ensigns. Radek, I have never seen that before for any fallen GROM soldier. The other two members of GROM Team 6 were also accorded similar high respect.'

'Are the bereaved families being taken care of?'

'Of course Radek as are all the survivors of Team 6'

'General I am trying to understand how, as I listen to daily news reports, just how President Putin could have miscalculated Ukrainian reactions to the invasion. U.S Intelligence has hardly been accurate until now if we remember no weapons of mass destruction in Iraq or the Afghanistan US/NATO withdrawal. So how did Russian Intelligence ignore or not recognise the growth of 'Ukrainian Nationalism' since 2014?'

'A firm and historic belief in independence from Russia was given further impetus by Russia's seizure of the Crimean peninsula. Russia's artificial creation of rebellion in the Donbass over a population with absolutely no wish to be subservient to Russia or forcibly rehoused elsewhere across Russia made a peaceful people become increasingly angry over the last 8 years. The truth behind the bloodless takeover of Crimea has become common knowledge in that it was orchestrated by a small group of Russian military intelligence agents. Similarly, the so-called separatists in Donetsk and Luhansk have been shown to be Russians with its army in support. Quite why the Kremlin believed that this would not strengthen Ukraine's civilian population's willingness to resist is surprising. However maybe Russian Intelligence knew the truth but was unprepared to tell it to their autocratic President?'

'With the many cross border generational family connections and friendships since Soviet times, even with the Kremlin's grip on propaganda, how could any invasion not undermine morale within its predominantly conscript Army?'

'Good question Radek that even with Witoria Hanko's help, I would find difficulty answering. I am certain Putin is asking those very questions! Nevertheless, the fallacy of the Kremlin proposition that just because in parts of Ukraine people spoke more Russian than Ukrainian made them Russians in Putin's mind has been shown for what it was – complete balderdash. No different than the Americans considering the English to be Americans. Hanko has flagged though an alternative strategy that might have some credence given the Russian Military's traditional tactics of war by attrition and annihilation by levelling cities like Mariupol and non-military targets like villages to uninhabitable piles of rubble plus just killing man, woman, and child – a 'scorched earth' strategy.

Her alternative theory though is interesting. In part, it revolves around initially the problem of a severe shortage of water in Crimea since its seizure in 2014. The North Crimean Canal, constructed in Soviet times, had taken water from the Dnieper and fed a number of irrigation canals within Crimea sustaining in particular its agricultural land and production. When the Ukrainians built a dam south of Kalanchak (some 16 kilometres north of the Crimean border) across the canal, the entire 2014 harvest was lost. Subsequently, the land has, in the absence of irrigation, accumulated soluble salts in the soil that hinder the growth of crops by limiting their ability to take up water simply because of those excess salts. Hence on the first day of the invasion, Russian troops advancing from Crimea established control over the North Crimean Canal. Two days later, explosives destroyed the dam that had been blocking flow since 2014. Water supply was resumed to the Crimean peninsula. Secondly, in 2010, the 'Yuzivska' natural gas field in the Donbass was discovered with total proven reserves of around 70.8 trillion cubic feet. Shell, the UK & Dutch, oil major had been expected to begin production in 2017. However, the development was immediately halted in 2014 because of the wider hostilities in the Donbass between Ukraine and Russia. Did this mean the Kremlin saw the development of such a strategic Ukrainian asset as a direct threat to Russia being the major provider of gas to Europe or more simply its strategic position in its control of gas supply to over-reliant Europeans? Thirdly, in these times of Climate Change and thus Food Security becomes more relevant, if Russia was to acquire Ukraine, it would move to being the 2nd largest producer of global wheat. If taken with China's production, these states would control more than 32% of world supply. These are clearly more rational arguments for Kremlin's use of force in that water food production and energy resources have long been reasons for war in human history.

Nevertheless, in my view, restoring water to Crimean farmland, controlling the global wheat market, and securing a major gas field might be added benefits from a successful invasion. Nevertheless, the primary objective was always to seize Kyiv and to remove President Zelensky from power. In the light of inaccurate or withheld intelligence, the expectation, and no doubt in their pre-invasion briefings, had been the Russian Army would be broadly welcomed so it was extremely ill-prepared for both the military and civilian responses. I also do not believe Europe's deep decarbonisation goals by 2050 that, do of course directly challenge Russia's energy based economic model, were wrapped up in either Putin's or the Kremlin's pre-invasion decision making. '

'General, if it is not an imposition, it has been hard for me, with all my postings and missions in Ukraine over the last six months, to gauge Ukraine's success or otherwise. With the Russian Army now regrouping to the East, seemingly intent on securing the Ukrainian coastline to make the Black Sea and Sea of Azoz purely Russian controlled lakes, and the previous territorial stalemate in the Donbass, what is your take on the War?

'How long have we got Radek?' He emptied the last of wine from the bottle and lit a cigarette with his precious zippo. Before Radek could answer, Alexandra appeared to clear the plates and establish whether they were ready for homemade cheesecake and coffee.

'My take - well quite why the performance of the Ukrainian Military came as such a surprise to Western commentators and so-called experts rather dumbfounded me. Since 2014, the United Kingdom and Eastern members of NATO, in particular, have trained, equipped, and armed the Ukrainian Army to a good operational standard and fighting effectiveness. A professional army somewhat battle hardened from facing the Russians in the Donbass and with a structure like NATO's military of senior non-commissioned officers within the ranks, a far better battle readiness. Hence Ukrainian units enjoyed autonomy. Its army is encouraged to exploit opportunities on the battlefield even in the absence of clear direction or orders plus they are motivated to fight. On the other hand, the Russian command chain is rigid and its culture does not encourage enterprise. Thus what challenge did a conscripted Russian adversary with no expectation of resistance and an arrogance of invincibility within the Russian High Command present? Lest we forget, the Ukrainian Military have been planning for 8 years on how best to defend against a wider invasion by Russia. The Ukrainian way of war is a coherent, intelligent, and a well-conceived strategy calibrated to take advantage of specific Russian weaknesses. Mobility by the Ukrainians contributed to forcing the Russian Army into static positions for long periods by attacking their logistic resupply. Actions you indeed also followed in the Forest of Sumy with Team 6. As a result, the Russians suffered high losses from such attrition both in equipment and indeed troops led to a victory in the battle for Kyiv. This has of course completely recast the political endgame of Russia's invasion. Putin's attempt to seize all of Ukraine has, as we can see, been dramatically scaled back. Today it is a far more limited effort to seize territory in the east and south of Ukraine.

Similarly, denying the Russian Military total air superiority is also a factor in Ukrainian success. Contesting control of the skies has allowed Ukrainian forces to manoeuvre. It made Russia's air force also nervous that they could be subject to Ukrainian air to air attack apart from ground to air missiles. The Ukrainians were never going to gain air supremacy. Simply the Russian air force is too large and Russian Army is of course well provided with anti-ground to air systems. Nevertheless, the Ukrainians made it difficult for Russian airpower to patrol over areas of battlefield. Thus Ukrainian forces prevented Russia from winning control of Ukraine's airspace by combining a range of systems, including its small number of highly effective MiG fixed-wing aircraft, advanced anti-air systems, and a plethora of handheld ground to air weapons such as Stinger and now longer range Starstreak missiles. Russian aircraft have and do bomb Ukrainian positions. However, these missions do seem to be very much to be of the in-and-out variety whilst in Ukrainian air space. More recently Russian fighter bombers have launched cruise and similar missiles from Russian airspace so, despite the numerical superiority there has been only a limited attempt to exercise of airpower.

Russian logistics and communications were made difficult as Ukrainians cities became fortresses making access complicated from roadblocks to demolition of road bridges. Nevertheless, Kyiv was in many ways also saved from Russian occupation by the fierce and resolute defence by the Ukrainian Army in Chernihiv and Sumy. These two cities sit astride the main road systems running from the northeast into Kyiv, and both cities withstood daily Russian attempts to take them. By holding these cities, and almost all others close to the borders of Russia and Belarus, the Ukrainians have not only forced Russian troops to contemplate street-by-street fighting but also made it impossible for Russia to move troops by rail into the Ukrainian heartland. By forcing the Russian Military to route its invading battlegroups and troops to take longer and trickier routes as cities were by-passed, they were open to attack from behind their lines as GROM Team 6 showed. The Ukrainians then allowed the Russian forces that had maneuvered around their city fortresses to become strung out along roads as they advanced. The Russian Army had made their situation worse by invading during the muddy season when Ukraine's famous black earth turned into treacle. This confined its heavy armour and mechanised infantry to narrow roadways further limiting their ability to move, especially when vehicles from tanks to trucks to mechanised vehicles needed fuel or maintenance. With the Russians in such a vulnerable position, the Ukrainians then launched attacks on those long Russian columns. These attacks included air-power famously delivered Turkish-made Bayraktar drones, special forces, long-range artillery, and even more conventional formations. The Ukrainians stretched Russian personnel so thinly that they sometimes failed even to defend such columns.

Increasing casualties caused by these harassing attacks and the fierceness of the defence hampered Russian attempts to build up sufficient forces to surround or even assault Kyiv. Their advances on the highways and roads from Sumy, Chernihiv, and the northwest to Kyiv met such dogged resistance that the Russians lost, in my opinion, all appetite for the fight. The Ukrainians used light and manoeuvrable forces to take advantage of Russian vulnerabilities and achieved victory. Using handheld weapons, like Javelin anti-tank missiles, operated by small groups attacking columns from all sides, the Ukrainians regularly disabled Russian tanks and trucks often blocking roads and the ability to resupply. Their logistics lines became stretched in terms of fuel and ammunition required to maintain the constant momentum of an advance. This was evidenced by the number of Russian vehicles abandoned completely intact but without fuel.'

'General, Ukraine has not yet won the war. The Russians' strategic aims are now totally concentrated on the east and south of Ukraine. Can the Ukrainian Army adapt to an offensive rather than defensive stance in order to regain lost territory?'

'In my view the Ukrainians, having witnessed the Russian failures in heavy assault, will decide to avoid making the same mistakes. If the Ukrainian Military continue its light and attritional warfare, it will not result in a swift end to the war. A drawn out conflict suits an autocracy like Russia where Putin's control is vice-like and any dissent removed to a siberian gulag. For democracies, sustaining the political will over a prolonged period of time becomes a far tougher hurdle.

At present, after a very timid response from the West to Russia's military build-up last year, the performance of the Ukrainian Army, the resoluteness of the populace exemplified by President Zelensky, and the atrocities so far revealed in Bucha, Borodyanka, and Makariv have belatedly united the West. Major commitments have been made to supply weapons, including those with more offensive capabilities, and of course money to enable its Government to prosecute the war.

As Western electorates attempt to grapple with the seemingly wonton destruction of cities like Mariupol and villages of no apparent strategic value, the fundamental issue relates to Russia's traditional military doctrine being defensive in nature. It relies heavily on artillery and cannon fire to destroy an enemy. Such tactics do not necessarily work well for offensive operations, especially when going against a modern army that has its own artillery, drones, and counter-artillery systems. Moreover, as these operations push into cities, these tactics will likely only result in a large amount of damage to civilian infrastructure. While the Russian military has shown little, if any, concern about firing on civilian targets, even if there is no military benefit. Now U.S mobile howitzers have finally reached Ukraine's Eastern front, Russia's artillery will be vulnerable to counter-artillery attacks. However, reducing cities like Mariupol to a barren wasteland of rubble and TV screens showing nightly the aftermath of missile strikes from hospitals to kindergartens has energised electorates, and thus politicians. Putin, his regime, and even its wider population have become pariahs in a modern world. Whenever hostilities end, there will be no business as usual for decades or longer whosoever is President of Russia.

Our country made an appalling blunder in not just re-badging its fleet of MiG 29s months back and simply not advertising the matter to the whole world. This was a poor call by our President and Government, especially when the US had agreed to backfill our air force with state of the art F35s. That said for Poland and the Baltic States plus our Slovak and

Romanian friends know the only trustworthy Russian is a dead one. Ukraine has to win on the battlefield as any ceasefire or peace will be broken when it suits Putin and his regime. This means, apart from our MiGs, the West must now supply land to sea cruise missiles capable of sending the Russian Black Sea fleet to join the Moskva. The Ukrainians need to make similar strikes to the one on that Belgorod military oil dump and on any munitions or resupply columns within Russia. I am not advocating destroying the Rostov-on-Don military headquarters. Nevertheless, a fighter bomber launching a cruise missile over Russian airspace targeted on a rail hub in Western Ukraine or similarly such a weapon from its Black Sea fleet has to be fair game. The best analogy is that of retired U.S four star general Philip Breedlove, a former Supreme Allied Commander Europe of NATO Allied Command Operations. He likened the discussions in Washington to supply limited range missiles as no different to an International Tennis Player only being allowed to enter any competition on the basis of never being allowed to serve ie receive only.

The reticence in the West about not provoking Russia into a wider conflict and then telegraphing what armaments are under consideration is wrong conceptually. This is compounded by the U.S then being an apologist for what it is then going to ship - somehow overlooking who has invaded who and the destruction and death Russia has inflicted. Personally, I cannot see why Kharkiv or Sumy or elsewhere can be shelled from inside Russia yet the Ukrainians are not meting out similar medicine to Russians on solely military targets – what or who is holding them back?

The core logistic functions have to be fulfilled whereby supplies of armaments, equipment, tactical mobile air defence systems, and munitions are transported to where they are needed in a timely fashion. This will also include diesel, engineering capability, maintenance, and medical crews. Russia now has the advantage of shorter lines of resupply where Ukraine faces the opposite. I know Mielec and our Army are doing a great job moving all this kit across the border but this war will be won or lost on who manages resupply best. President Zelensky was absolutely right to quote Winston Churchill's famous wartime response to President Roosevelt of '... Give us the tools and we will finish the job ...'

'General, what does our military intelligence service know about the Russian soldier's morale?'

'Radek if I was a surviving member of the 1st Chechen Regiment my wish would be to return to the Caucuses as soon as possible.'

Both men laughed.

'The Russian Army's major problem with the morale of its soldiers is the fundamental culture of indifference to such military personnel. Whilst there are unproven stories of desertions and also a failure by conscripts to report for military duty, there is broad agreement that more than 25,000 Russians have been killed since February 24th with doubled that number wounded and unfit for combat. The High Command's unwillingness to retrieve the dead, dying, or wounded from the battlefield merely highlights its disdain and that their lives are totally expendable. Similarly the refusal to liaise with the Ukrainians to identify the dead has undermined any ability to match the patriotic energy of the Ukrainians. The lack of any support for the families of the fallen soldiers merely adds to the distrust and doubts about the war they are waging. Morale issues will only be intensified by military occupation of seized regions or territories where patriotic civilian Ukrainians have already shown Russians they are neither welcome nor rescuing anyone from oppression. If the present eastern offensive by the Russian Army loses momentum, the impact within its ranks will become increasingly toxic. Changing road signs into russian, replacing Ukrainian Mayors, making the rouble legal tender, and providing or insisting on Russian passports will not win the hearts and minds of Ukrainians with the memories of looting and other atrocities. A deadly insurgency will begin.'

'As of now, the rouble has regained or bettered its pre-invasion value, do you see sanctions being a credible weapon in helping to stop this war?'

'Our Prime Minister and Government have repeatedly warned the European Union about its reliance of Russian energy in recent years, particularly Germany's involvement in Nord Stream II. Until both gas and oil are no longer Russian, the European Union is subsidising Putin's war of choice. However, spare parts for vehicles and microchips for missiles are increasingly becoming in short supply, most Western companies have closed permanently their businesses, airlines no longer fly to Russia, its populace can no longer holiday or visit the West, and its economy is tanking. Putin's savings with the Oligarchs are being methodically found and tediously unearthed, including the closure of the open sewer of the City of London. It has been, as a leading Western financial centre for well over a decade, a disgrace. A laundry for illicit russian money and subsequent asset acquisition assisted by the City's equally greedy 'professionals' from lawyers to bankers to tax accountants. Sanctions will work but clearly they need time. Weaning Europe off Russian Energy in particular is the key economic pressure point on Putin's ability to fund his war.'

'One of the lessons learnt so far from the COVID pandemic and now reinforced by Putin's war of choice is global supply lines will be shortened and also made secure. General opinion seems to be a combination of on-shoring and sourcing only from friendly like-minded states will become the new normal.'

'Agreed'

'General, history has shown politics and religion do not make easy bedfellows. Yet Vladimir Gundyayev, better known as Kirill, the Patriarch of Moscow and all Rus' and Primate of the Russian Orthodox Church, continues to support Putin's war even as the bodies of mutilated men, women, and children are discovered in Ukrainian towns recently occupied by Russian troops. It seems the invasion of Ukraine has become a 'Holy War' for Russia. Putin has woven nationalism, faith, conservative values, and the restoration of the Russky mir *(Russian world)* as that mantra. His constant message has been to reiterate Putin's disinformation from the pulpit no different to Russian television. The West has, according to Kirill, been engaging in the suppression and extermination of people in the Donbass for years because of the refusal to hold gay pride parades.

With media coverage of Orthodox priests blessing missiles, planes, and troops seemingly endorsing the destruction of people's homes and lives, I can only think of Loknya where the Chechens' looted, pillaged, and murdered innocent civilians.'

'Are you angry or surprised?'

'Neither, when Soviet archives confirm Kirill was a KGB agent and an active officer of within its organization how can anyone be shocked by any of this Patriarch's statements. Yet describing Putin's rule as 'a miracle of God' does seem being more than economical with the truth. Kirill may well have brought the Russian Orthodox Church far closer to the Russian State but he has provided spiritual cover for Putin's regime's autocracy. So not angry, more disgusted General that the spiritual leader of probably 100 million orthodox faithful attempts to give moral credence to Russia's invasion. When Christian religions are supposed to embody 'peace and love', preaching such positions destroy and undermine any credibility that they may be accorded by believers or non-believers.'

'The current war in Ukraine is not the first time Kirill, as Patriarch, has condoned bloodshed Radek. He saw Putin's destruction of Syrian cities such as Aleppo in Crusader terms as a fight against infidels and terrorism – a Holy War. Nevertheless, Kirill's support of Putin is less an ideology of the Russian Orthodox Church and more an ideology of Putin's Revanchist State. Kirill is no different to the Oligarchs dancing to the Regime's tune but in his case it is payback for the Church operating tax free – cynical, but true in my opinion.

Looking big picture, it must be Finland's and Sweden's recent applications to join NATO as a real game changer strategically for the northern flank of the Alliance. The Baltic States in particular are both delighted and relieved. As for Putin's ranting about NATO's expansion, Finland's and Sweden's decision to do so has been voiced publicly by their Governments and electorates as entirely due to Russia's unprovoked invasion of a neighbour. This must be yet another unexpected consequence and own goal for Putin's and his regime's ill-considered invasion.

So Radek you have had me hopefully filling in some of those blanks for you in respect of the war but how do you see your future?'

'General I have to face facts that a man with a rebuilt femur cannot justifiably lead either Team 6 or another GROM unit on active service. My days of being behind enemy lines are also I believe over in a battlefield setting.'

'So you are seeking retirement in Niepolomice and a quieter time with your beautiful wife, young Maja, your unborn child, and not forgetting your parents next door after recent events?'

'Well it is hard to argue against such a life General.'

'This autumn, Colonel Kuba Pawlukowicz will retire after some 30 years of active service. I want you to take his position in ABW. By then you will be walking without crutches and broadly fully recovered physically. I do not want your answer today. However I would like you to think about the role and of course discuss matters with Alexandra before making any decision.'

Lieutenant-General Politczek stood up and continued '... stay seated Radek, I am expected in Mielec. I will take advantage of your facilities and then find Alexandra to thank her for your kind hospitality.'

'General' was Radek's nodded acknowledgement.
A few minutes later Alexandra appeared – 'Darling I am just going to walk the General to the gate.' Before he could even nod a response, they were soon in animated conversation out of Radek's hearing ambling towards the General's waiting limousine. With his driver stood to attention holding the open rear door of the extended mercedes, Alexandra gave him a hug and kiss. Closing the gate she gave Radek a wave and began to walk back towards him. Radek smiled - what a cunning old fox Grzegorz is.

THE END

Many thanks for reading 'Russian Stratagem'. If you enjoyed the story, and have a moment to spare, then I would really appreciate a short review on your purchasing store or favourite stores' sites. Your help in spreading the word is gratefully received

NOVELS BY JOE DANIEL

CONDUCT BECOMING as an ebook in January 2020-
link if UK www.amazon.co.uk/dp/B083P5KW9C
link if Poland or worldwide
www.amazon.com/dp/B083P5KW9C

CONDUCT BECOMING* as a paperback in July 2020-
link if UK www.amazon.co.uk/dp/B08D54RGCW
link if Poland or worldwide
www.amazon.com/dp/B08D54RGCW

SOFIA'S LAW as an ebook in June 2020-
link if UK www.amazon.co.uk/dp/B08B44P89G
link if Poland or worldwide
www.amazon.com/dp/B08B44P89G

SOFIA'S LAW* as a paperback in July 2020-
link if UK www.amazon.co.uk/dp/B08BWHQ9D4
link if Poland or worldwide
www.amazon.com/dp/B08BWHQ9D4

BRAMSTON GREEN as an ebook in November 2020-
link if UK www.amazon.co.uk/dp/B08MCB33JT
link if Poland or worldwide
www.amazon.com/dp/B08MCB33JT

BRAMSTON GREEN* as a paperback in November 2020-
link if UK www.amazon.co.uk/dp/B08M8CRLT6
link if Poland or worldwide
www.amazon.com/dp/B08M8CRLT6

THAT'S LIFE as an ebook in August 2021-
link if UK www.amazon.co.uk/dp/B09DX36VN5
link if Poland or worldwide
www.amazon.com/dp/B09DX36VN5

THAT'S LIFE* as a paperback in August 2021-
link if UK www.amazon.co.uk/dp/B09DMTVKR3
link if Poland or worldwide
www.amazon.com/dp/B09DMTVKR3

RUSSIAN STRATAGEM as an ebook in June 2022-
link if UK www.amazon.co.uk/dp/B0B4Y6WGG6
link if Poland or worldwide
www.amazon.com/dp/B0B4Y6WGG6

RUSSIAN STRATAGEM* as a paperback in June 2022-
link if UK www.amazon.co.uk/dp/B0B4K1BWNX
link if Poland or worldwide
www.amazon.com/dp/B0B4K1BWNX

*[*all the titles are planned for conversion into Audio Books utilising the services of ACX by Audible.com, an Amazon.com subsidiary, and a leading provider of audio content and entertainment. Release had been planned for 2022. However, a combination of COVID in California and technical issues have temporarily delayed this positive intention]*

Printed in Great Britain
by Amazon